Sunset in Kentucky

Sunset in Kentucky

Carol Walls Howell

John & Doris —
Enjoy another journey
Carol Walls Howell

abbott press®
A DIVISION OF WRITER'S DIGEST

Sunset in Kentucky

Abbott Press books may be ordered through booksellers or by contacting:

Abbott Press
1663 Liberty Drive
Bloomington, IN 47403
www.abbottpress.com
Phone: 1-866-697-5310

ISBN: 978-1-4582-0322-9 (sc)
ISBN; 978-1-4582-0324-3 (hc)
ISBN: 978-1-4582-0323-6 (e)

Library of Congress Control Number: 2012906424

Printed in the United States of America

Abbott Press rev. date: 07/26/2012

ACKNOWLEDGEMENTS

Thanks to my friends who have read, laughed, listened, and encouraged me during the writing process. I give special thanks to my friend, Diane Baker, for reading and offering her editing ideas from the beginning of my writing adventure to the final end. Breanna Chapman, thank you for your computer expertise.

I give love and thanks to my husband, Carl, and the rest of my family who stand with me and encourages me, no matter what project I attempt.

God bless all my friends and family who have helped me become who I am today.

CHAPTER 1

BRADY AND ANNA MARIE

It was a cloudy Sunday morning—dreary actually—and a light rain was coming down. Anna Marie had made sausage and gravy to eat with yesterday's leftover biscuits for breakfast. She and her husband were wearing their Sunday clothes and were almost ready to head out the door. Brady held his green-eyed, lovely wife close and kissed her on her cheek. He was aware by the size of her fully rounded midsection that her time was nearing. Soon she would deliver their first child. Brady and Anna Marie were married in Reeds Crossing, Kentucky on Christmas Eve, December 1833.

"My sweet Anna, I'm so lucky to have you for my wife. You are all that I will ever need. Now here we are about to become a father and a mother. We have so much to be thankful for. No man could want more than this."

Brady kissed his wife passionately and caressed her hair. She kept her head tilted up toward him and gazed into the gentleness he showed her with his eyes. "I felt a connection with you from the time we met at the barn warming dance over at Sara and Peter's place," Brady said. "You were standing by yourself watching Carter Riley as he played the fiddle. He was smiling and tapping his toes, truly enjoying himself, and you were smiling and tapping your toes, both of you lost in the music."

"I wasn't really watching Carter," said Anna. "I was watching him play that instrument … the connection that was there between the player and the fiddle. He was lost in the sounds he created, and so was I. Music is just in a person. I can't imagine what this world would be like without music. Thank goodness God created songbirds. Their music can fill your soul with peace and happiness."

"I don't know anyone who can sing as lovely as you," he said softly.

1

"Music is in your soul. You are by far the best singer in the church choir."

"Such sweet talk," she said flirtatiously. "Thanks for the compliment. Speaking of the church choir, don't you think maybe we should start for church soon?"

Brady walked with his wife to the cabin door and helped her step out into the misty day. In the distance there was a little rumbling of thunder, a promise of more to come. He had already hitched the horse to the buggy and had tied it up close to the front of the cabin. She struggled getting into the buggy. Even with Brady's strong grip on her arm, the added weight of the baby made it difficult. The buggy was covered, so they would be somewhat protected from the rain today. Brady placed a blanket over Anna Marie's lap to insure her warmth. "That should help," he said. He walked over to the driver's side of the buggy and climbed up with ease. Gathering the reins, he clicked his tongue, and they were on their way as the horse fell into an easy trot down the path to the road. They wound around a grove of trees, most of which were either in full bloom or had already dropped their blooms and were covered now with leaves that were nearly full sized.

Now on the road they started up the first small hill. As the horse trotted along, they saw a doe and her fawn off to the side. The deer stopped their grazing for a short while, checked for danger as they watched the horse and buggy pass by, and then continued their morning fare. Over the hill and down along the meadow, the buggy made its way to the river. Muddy River it was called. The nearby farmers had been busy keeping the beaver population under control. Big Al would go down to the creek and fish often. If he saw those pesky beavers working on a dam upstream, he would take a trap up to where they were working and set it nearby. He would continue to trap the beavers until he had enough pelts to take to town with hopes of selling them for a tidy sum. The pelt money filled a need for Al and his family. Brady slowed the horse down and forded the river with ease. He made a mental note to get back to that crossing soon and add some stones where the riverbed had washed so the crossing would remain safe to travel over. As soon as they made the crossing he urged the horse back up to speed. They passed Big Al and Lucy's place. They were only two miles—about twenty-five minutes—from town and just another short ride to the church. They should arrive in good time.

Anna Marie said, "Look over there. I saw lightning." Right away the thunder rolled overhead and rain sprinkles started falling. "We may get to the church just in time before it rains harder."

"Do you think you would be all right if we trotted along a little faster?" Brady asked.

"Go ahead; I think I'll be okay." Anna Marie gripped the seat a little tighter as their speed increased.

The lightning came quicker now, and the thunder was almost a continuous roll above their heads. The rain had picked up to a steady pace. They pulled up to the church along with some of the townspeople. Brady jumped down off of the buggy and quickly tied the horse to the hitching post. He rushed around to Anna's side and helped her down. She clung to his strong arms, and they were soon inside where it was dry. They felt much calmer and safer than they had only a few moments ago.

Several of the women were at Anna's side. "Are you all right?" "Do you feel okay?" "Can I help you?" "Do you need a towel to dry yourself?"

"I'll be just fine," Anna Marie answered. "We had to hurry Mandy along a little faster. She did a good job bringing us here safe and sound."

"You must be especially careful now considering your condition," the minister's wife said. "No one here wants you to have any problems."

The lightning and thunder continued roaring along during the entire church service. It wasn't good weather for anyone to be out and about. Some of the little children were crying and clinging to their mothers. It was difficult for the older members to keep their attention on the message the preacher was bringing that morning as the lightning, rolling thunder, rattling doors and windows, crying babies, gusts of wind. Everyone watched the flashes of lightning, what else could they do? At last, the final hymn was sung. "Amen" murmured the congregation.

One woman's comment echoed the sentiments of all those present: "Now what can we do? It's too stormy to go outside."

The women and children huddled together and the men looked outside. Everyone decided that they all must stay in the church until the storm played out its fury. Full acceptance of the circumstances that held them hostage replaced the anxious moments of just a short time ago. Rain had blown in over the windowsills and under the main church door. The children naturally were drawn to the minipuddles. They flipped water drops at each other with their hands, and giggles soon replaced tears. The mamas and papas talked about the weather and what they were planning to do in the week ahead. After what seemed like a long stretch of time—actually only an hour or so—the storm had passed through on its way to other farms, hills, and valleys. The men pushed the door open, and the families began to make their way out. Tree branches, leaves, stray weeds, and bits and pieces of wood covered the walkway as well as the buggies. The horses were soaked, and drops of water fell from tree leaves and buggy coverings.

Big Al and Lucy gathered their five children as the families headed to their buggies. "Follow us home. We should stick together—no telling what the road will be like," Al hollered to Brady and Anna Marie.

"Sure thing," Brady replied. "Lead on." He turned to Anna Marie and asked, "Are you feeling all right?"

Anna smiled and nodded. "Except for this baby kicking like thunder inside me, I am just fine," she said.

Brady clicked his tongue and snapped the reins lightly, and they were on their way. They didn't know what this stormy Sunday held in store for them.

The trip to Al and Lucy's home went well. They had to drive around a few tree limbs and washes on the road. The wind was now just a breeze, and a few brave birds were flying about checking for bugs and worms. Some of the birds were perched on tree limbs nearby whistling their own special tunes. A doe and her bunnies were hopping around bushes and tree trunks nibbling on the freshly washed grass, oblivious to the two horses and buggies passing by.

Al and Lucy reached their farm and waved good-bye. "Come visit us," yelled Lucy.

"Don't you worry. We'll be back soon. We want to hear some more of Big Al's stories," said Brady. "Have the popcorn ready."

They all waved good-bye. Brady urged the horse on down the road. It wasn't long before the horse and buggy were approaching the river. The water had risen after the hard rain, and now it boiled across the rocks and tree roots. Limbs and leaves coursed past. There wasn't any way the buggy would make it across. Anna Marie let out a short scream as she felt the spear of pain. Brady stopped the buggy. He turned and held her arm.

"Brady, I think the baby is coming. What will we do?" Anna said.

"Let's head back to Al and Lucy's place. I'll turn the buggy around right now."

Brady hastily headed the buggy back down the road they had just covered. He snapped the reins a little harder this time. No time to tarry.

The labor pains increased a lot faster than Anna thought they should. She doubled over and groaned with each one. As Mandy trotted over the big hill, Brady noticed that a tree had fallen right across the road. There were stones and stumps alongside, and there was no way to pass. He jumped out of the buggy and began tugging at the tree. It was of no use. He remembered that he had left a rope in the back of the buggy. He quickly grabbed the rope and wrapped it around the base of the tree. He then had to unhitch the horse from the buggy and tie the loose end of the rope to the harness. In a short time, he and the horse had cleared the tree off of the road. Having accomplished the task, Brady hitched Mandy back up to the buggy. Anna remained bent over with labor pains.

"Brady, do you think we'll make it to Lucy in time?"

"All I know is that I am going to do my best to get you there. It's only a short way now. Try to hang on." Anna was excited and yet scared ... very scared. *Here I am,* she thought, *a grown, married woman expecting to give birth to her first child, this little creature I have carried and loved. But I certainly don't feel very sure of myself. What if we don't make it to Lucy's in time? I may well have to have this baby out here in the open, woodsy countryside! And there's nothing here in the buggy for comfort or warmth or protection. I know Brady will do all he can, but how will he know what to do? He'll hold my hand, but I need more than that. I don't even know what to do myself! I've never been with any other woman who was giving birth. I know only bits and pieces of overheard conversations, interspersed with jokes and laughter.*

"Oh, God, please let us get to Al and Lucy's home in time," Anna prayed.

Brady had his hands full, pressing the horse and buggy as fast down the road as he could and trying to be cautious enough so as to not harm his beautiful wife and the unborn baby. On they raced against the elements of nature and the ticking of time. *We're almost there,* Brady thought, *just around the next bend is Big Al's.* He saw the cluster of trees along the side of the home of the Bannings' place. Brady pulled the buggy up close to the cabin and hitched the horse. He ran to his wife's side and, as quickly as possible, helped her to the ground and guided her toward the front door. Lucy, having seen them come to the house from the road, was already at the door to greet them.

"My Lord, what is goin' on?"

"It's my Anna. She's having the baby. Anna began labor just as we got down to Muddy River. The river was running over the bank with all the rain water that had come down, and we had to turn around and start this way and ..."

"Never you mind telling the whole story right now. We have to get the little missus to bed so she can go about her business. Understand?" Lucy led Anna to the bedroom at the back of the cabin.

★ ★ ★ ★ ★ ★ ★ ★ ★ ★ ★ ★ ★ ★ ★ ★ ★ ★ ★

Big Al had sent his children to the loft to play quietly. Now he took Brady by the arm and guided him toward the kitchen table. He knew his job was to keep Brady as calm as possible, especially as Anna's labor became more intense. Al took a small box from the shelf above the fireplace and brought it to the table. It was a rough-hewn box that he had put together several years ago during a snowstorm. The snow had been so deep neither man nor animal dared to be outside. With just the knife that he carried with him every day, he had worked several evenings beside the oil lamp scraping and carving the irregular chunk of wood until the shape suited his purpose. The box now held his collection of Indian arrowheads, and a fine collection it was.

Al took the lid off of the box and proceeded to dump the contents onto the table. "Look at this, would you? Did you ever see such a collection?"

Brady looked at the arrowheads and moved his hands over them. He picked up a few and examined them. "I've never seen arrow heads like these. Where did you find so many?"

"Most were along Muddy River," answered Al. "You know, I've spent many, many hours on the banks of that river. When the fishing is slow, I prop my fishing pole up on a forked branch and just start looking along the bank. Indians liked to camp along a waterway, you know. Sometimes they would stay a short time, and other times they would stay a month or more if the food was plentiful. When they moved on to another place, they would almost always leave something behind like tent poles, pieces of pottery or, as in this case, arrowheads.

Suddenly, from the bedroom, Anna Marie let out a scream that made the men jump. Brady jumped up and started to go to her, but Big Al caught his arm once again and shook his head no. "You can't help this time, Brady. Nature will have its own way. Neither you nor I can do anything. Lucy has had her own children, and she's helped others birth their babies. Your child will come in its own time. Let's hope that she won't have a long, hard labor. Come, look at the arrowheads here, and maybe we can figure out what some of them were used for."

Time crept by. The old clock on the mantle seemed to tick louder than usual. The rain outside was beginning to slow down, interspersed with a few rumbles of thunder and the scratching sounds of limbs and sticks blowing around. Every time Anna shrieked Brady would stiffen his body, deeply regretting that his beloved Anna was going through such suffering. Suddenly they heard a small, muffled cry. Then they heard a smack, and a full-blown baby's cry filled the air. The two men quickly rose from their chairs, and both grinned widely at each other.

Al shook Brady's hand, "Seems you got your baby, young man."

At about that, time Lucy opened the bedroom door. She smiled and said, "You got yourself a baby boy. Come, see for yourself. Anna did a fine job bringing your baby into this world."

"Thank you, thank you, Lucy." Brady peered into the bedroom and hesitated at the sight of both his wife and his son before he went to their side. He kissed both their cheeks. His heart was filled with a joy that he had never felt before. *My own son*, he thought.

The storm had blown its last flurry of wind and rain, and now the clouds parted as a bright, golden stream of the setting sun broke through. It glowed through the tree limbs and came all the way to the west window of the bedroom where the three huddled together. A new beginning was upon them.

Brady and Anna Marie and the baby stayed with Big Al and Lucy for several days until Anna was strong enough to travel home. They decided to name the baby Patrick James. Brady rode back and forth from his farm to the Bennings' home every day, as he cared for his livestock . He had quite a responsibility, but nothing a strapping young man couldn't handle. At the evening of each day, he was tired but quite happy. Then the day arrived when he could take his family to their home.

CHAPTER TWO

THE FOX

It was autumn in Kentucky. The trees, bushes, and vines were all displaying various colors of red, yellow, brown, and orange. The hot summer temperatures had ended, and the days were growing noticeably shorter once more. The wheat fields and cornfields had been harvested, and the grain was stored away to be used through the cold, blustery weather that lay ahead. Brady and Anna Marie would grind wheat and corn into meal for themselves, and the rest would feed the horses, the two sow pigs, and the cow and her calf while they were sheltered inside the barn. One whole side of the barn, except for the pig stalls, was filled with grasses that had been cut during the summer. These would also be fed to the animals. The barn was located about fifty, Brady-size steps from the kitchen door north of the cabin. Against the far side of the barn, Brady had built a lean-to that enclosed a chicken roost. No farm was complete without its own flock of laying hens and a couple roosters. He had also built a fence that encircled the barn and the barn lot. This provided twofold insurance—it kept the animals near if they somehow got out of the barn, and it provided a barrier between the farm animals and any wild animals.

Brady entered the kitchen door with a bucket of fresh milk and set it on the worktable next to the wash stand. A cold rush of air entered the room with him. Anna Marie set a plate of fresh biscuits on the kitchen table along with scrambled eggs, butter, and jam. Baby Patrick, lying in his little bed close by, was now almost four months old. He smiled at his mama and papa and cooed as he happily examined his fingers. He flung his arms around and kicked his legs.

Brady went over to his boy and said, "Good morning, Pat." Patrick kicked and waved with a flurry. Brady picked him up and carried him to the table. He sat down with Patrick on his lap and took a sip of his coffee. A man couldn't be any prouder of a son than he was. Patrick had inherited his daddy's hair and eyes, true to the Patterson lineage. Patrick's eyes followed his mother's movements around the kitchen and reached for his daddy's coffee cup each time he took a sip.

"You are a little too young to have coffee for your breakfast," Brady told him. Little Pat smiled and stuck his fist into his mouth and sucked on it. Brady put Pat back in his bed. Anna had now sat down and joined hands with Brady. They offered a prayer for the day and its blessings and had their breakfast.

"I plan to go out and cut some more firewood this morning. We don't know how hard the winter will be, and I want to be sure you and Pat stay warm. Big Al and I will be cutting dead trees down in the draw west of his house."

"I'd better pack you some food. You'll get hungry after two or three hours of such hard work."

"Not a bad idea. We plan to quit at noon. We can haul only so much at a time. I'll hitch Mandy to the wagon and take it over there. She needs to be exercised too, you know."

They finished their meal. Brady put on his work coat, hat, and boots. Anna handed him a small sack in which she had packed molasses cookies and dried apples. He kissed Anna and Patrick good-bye and went out to the barnyard to continue his day. He hitched Mandy to the wagon. After having loaded his axe, maul, splitting wedges, and anything else he might need, he climbed aboard and signaled Mandy, who obliged by trotting down the road. He whistled a little tune as he went along. When he came to Muddy River he saw a couple beavers working on a dam upstream. He slowed down as the horse carefully pulled the wagon across, then picked up the pace once again. *I must remember to tell Big Al about the beavers,* he thought. With the beavers still in his mind, he looked up in time to see a fox dash through a thicket of bushes. The fox disappeared into the brush before Brady could grab his rifle and take a shot. *Fox pelts should bring a very good price,* Brady thought, *and that would give me extra money to get Anna a gift for Christmas.*

Brady arrived at the Bennings' home and saw Big Al outside, sharpening his axes in preparation for the work that lay ahead.

"Hey, neighbor," hollered Big Al. "'Bout time you got here." Al laughed heartily.

"You got a problem with me?" Brady yelled back. "You know if we could get a bridge over that river down there I could make better time."

"Yeah, well when are you going to cut the planks for the bridge?" Al retorted.

Brady jumped down off the wagon and grabbed Al's arm and acted as if he was going to wrestle him down. They struggled like schoolboys and laughed. Big Al was just like an older brother to Brady. Each man felt a special connection with the other.

"Are you ready to head for the trees?" asked Brady.

"Yep, guess I am."

Al put his axes into his wagon and climbed aboard. They both snapped the reins on their horses and started on their way. The morning proved to be productive, and both men got a good-sized load of wood to take home. Brady had shared his cookies and apples mid-morning when they took a little breather from the hard work. As they rested up, he remembered to tell Big Al about the beavers and the fox. Al told Brady to be sure the chicken coop was shut tight or else that fox would be having chicken for dinner that night. Brady agreed. The wind had kicked up, and the cooler air sent a chill down their backs as they traveled home.

Brady added the new wood to the stack that he had already started, unhitched Mandy, put her in the barn, and headed for the house.

★ ★ ★ ★ ★ ★ ★ ★ ★ ★ ★ ★ ★ ★ ★ ★ ★ ★ ★

The fall days had cooled until now the colder weather, typical of the winters of the Kentucky hills, was upon them. There had been a hard frost a few weeks ago, and ice had formed in the water tank a few times already. Anna had begun sitting of an evening, after Patrick had been fed, and she had taken up knitting.

She had learned to knit as a young girl, having been taught by her

Aunt Ella who lived with her family. Aunt Ella was older than Anna's mother. She had been married to a horse trader and harness maker named Amos Goddard. They had not been blessed with any children, so Ella busied herself knitting shawls and bedcovers or almost anything she was asked to knit, and she sold the items at the village mercantile. When Amos was only thirty-five years old, he was killed when he was tending the horses he had stabled. He was walking and exercising a big, black stallion one evening at sundown. While he was checking the stallion's left horseshoe, the horse reared. Amos tried to steady the horse, and he almost succeeded, but suddenly the horse jerked and started throwing his head around. He rammed Amos hard into the log fence several times. Amos dropped down onto the ground and grabbed his chest. His heart beat only a few times before he was gone. The accident sent shock waves through the village as he and Ella were very well thought of by the townspeople. Ella tried living alone, but her grief was too great to bear. Anna's father and mother decided they should ask Ella to live with them. So it was.

★ ★ ★ ★ ★ ★ ★ ★ ★ ★ ★ ★ ★ ★ ★ ★ ★ ★ ★

It was now mid December, and it snowed often. The routine was set concerning the daily chores. First thing every morning, Brady would give grain to the horses and milk the cow, feed the pigs with scraps mixed with the extra milk that they couldn't use, fill a pan with dried corn for the chickens, check the nests for eggs, break the ice in the water trough, and put warm water in the chicken water pan. Then he had to do it all again in the evening. He also had to muck out the stalls, and every two or three days, he had to add fresh straw bedding.

Then one morning Brady saw something he didn't want to see—egg shells on the floor of the chicken coop and a dead laying hen. Something had gotten into the chicken coop. He found a hole where a board had been broken. He found small tufts of reddish hair caught in the ragged edge of the board. He could think of only one animal that could have done this—the fox he had seen early in the fall. He would have to figure out a way to get the scoundrel.

When you live on what you raise, be it fruits and vegetables or animals, nothing must go to waste. Brady saw that the invader had eaten only a leg and a wing off the hen. He knew the hen hadn't spoiled, because of the cold weather, so he picked it up and headed for the house. A hearty chicken dinner actually sounded pretty good. They hadn't had that for a good, long while.

"Anna," he called, as he walked up to the kitchen door. "We need to put on a pot of water to boil."

Anna Marie opened the door and saw Brady standing there holding the dead hen.

"What happened?" she asked.

"Something got into the chicken coop, killed this laying hen, and broke some of our eggs. I think it was probably the fox I saw alongside the road a while back. I guess I'll need to hide outside tonight and wait to see if he tries to come back for another free meal. I'll have my rifle loaded and ready. Let's get that water hot, and I'll scald the hen and pick the feathers off for you. You can finish the cleaning, if you know how," he teased. He knew that she had been dressing chickens for years.

Anna Marie flipped her dish towel at him and said, "Oh, my. I just don't think my delicate hands could possible do such a thing. Why, that is such a nasty thing to do that I may just have to have Lucy come and do it for me," she teased back. She curtsied, lifted one hand and curled up her pinky finger, prissy-like, and turned back inside. Brady laid the chicken down and followed her inside into the warm kitchen, grabbed her in a big bear hug, and kissed her.

"Well," he said, "I might just have to go to town and find me another woman who can cut up a chicken and make me a fine dinner!" Anna Marie giggled with him. He kissed her again. "I sure do love you, Mrs. Patterson," he whispered into her ear.

"And I love you, Mr. Patterson," Anna whispered back. Together they got the chicken cleaned and ready for the pot.

That night, after he had filled up on stewed chicken, biscuits, boiled potatoes, and cabbage, Brady wrapped up in his winter coat and hat, grabbed his loaded rifle, and went outside by the two pine trees close by the chicken coop to see if he could get the fox. It was only a short time, maybe thirty or forty minutes, before that wily critter crept through the fence and went toward the hole he had made in the chicken coop the night before. The fox paused and looked around, as if he might suspect something amiss, and in that brief moment, Brady aimed the rifle and fired. That fox would never get another chicken of his! Brady waited a few moments and watched the animal as he flinched and fought for his life, but Mr. Fox soon gave up. Brady got up, grabbed the dead fox and carried it into the barn. He would tend to the chore of skinning it come morning. Brady already knew what he would do with his prize. He would take the pelt to town as soon as he could, and he would buy a present for his Anna. Maybe he would find something to give Pat—a rattle or a peppermint stick.

A week later, that is exactly what Brady set out to do. He saddled Mandy, put the fox pelt in his saddlebag, checked the list of provisions Anna Marie had given him, mounted, and headed up the road toward Reeds Crossing. When he got to town he went directly to the mercantile. Brady knew John Bower, the owner of the mercantile. He was a fair man. He would buy good pelts, and when he got a pile, he would take them up the river and sell them for a nice profit. Brady had been extra careful when he skinned that fox. He was sure that he would get top dollar for it.

"Mornin', John," said Brady.

"Mornin' to you," answered John.

"Whatcha got new in the store here for ladies?"

"Why do you need to know that? Are you in trouble with the missus?"

"Nope. I got me a real fine fox fur here I would like to sell you so I can buy a special something for Anna Marie. It's nearly Christmas, you know, and she's at home alone a lot of time with the baby, cookin' and cleanin'. She hasn't complained or nothin'. She's the best woman I could've ever married."

"Yep, she sure is a fine young lady. I've known her and her family for many years. Let me see that fur you brought."

Brady produced the fur and laid it out on the counter. He smoothed the fur with his hand. John looked it over front and back and saw only a few tiny nicks where the skinning knife had slipped.

"Mighty fine fur you have there. I haven't seen a fur of this quality in some time. I'll give you three dollars for it."

Brady quickly replied, "Sold!" He never thought it would be worth that much. "Now, show me something for my special gal."

After looking at several different items, Brady settled for a china teapot with two cups and saucers. They were painted with bright blue-and-yellow wildflowers, and the pieces were already nestled nicely in a gift box. Remembering her love for wildflowers, Brady knew this would be the perfect Christmas gift.

"Would you happen to have a paper you could put around this box?" Brady asked John.

"I'll get Martha to come in here and wrap it for you. Martha, come here. I need your help. Brady here needs to have this wrapped up for the missus."

John handed Martha the tea set, and Brady handed John the list of provisions Anna Marie had sent with him. Both went right to work, and in no time Brady had his supplies and his gift. He was all ready to go.

"Wait a minute," he said, "Give me a couple peppermints to take to the baby."

"Take three, Brady," said Martha, "one for each of you. Consider it a Christmas gift from us, and you be careful going home, okay?"

"Thanks a lot, Martha. You and John are very kind to do that. See you next trip into town."

Having said his good-bye, Brady walked out of the mercantile. Across the street he saw his friends Jim and Frank. They waved and beckoned for Brady to come over. He put his treasures in his saddlebags, being extra careful with the gift box, and went across the road to visit with his friends, whom he hadn't seen for quite a while.

"Hello, boys," Brady said.

"Well, look who got off the farm and made it into town," said Frank jokingly.

"I had business to take care of for the wife."

"Like what? A powder puff?" asked Jim. "I bet she has you all wrapped around her little finger."

"You're probably right," Brady chuckled. "We needed some

15

supplies for the kitchen. What are you two whippersnappers doing with yourselves?"

They looked at each other and back at Brady. "We're thinking about leaving Reeds Crossing and heading out. There's going to be a search party go up the Kentucky River to look for new places to homestead. We'll probably go with them," said Jim.

"That right? Sounds risky. When will this take place?"

Frank answered, "I suspect not until after winter breaks. Not real sure. Want to go with us?"

"I don't see how I can, you know. Anna and I have our place started."

"We wouldn't be gone too long. It would be just like when we were much younger, just the three of us going out into the woods, exploring," said Jim.

"No, I just can't. I have Anna and little Pat now to care for. Sounds like a great adventure, though."

"Just think about it. Let us hear from you if you change your mind," Frank replied.

"I'd better start back home, boys. See you around."

Brady mounted Mandy and trotted back toward his farm. He had a warm glow of satisfaction inside for the way things had worked out for him. The fox, the dead chicken, the meal, the fox hide, the good sale price—all these things had worked together so he was able to get his wife a nice gift. Mandy made her way along the road while Brady was busy with his thoughts ... the tea set for Anna, the peppermint sticks, Jim and Frank. The next thing he knew, he was nearly to his home. Smoke was curling out of the chimney, and frost edged the window frames. He knew his cabin was as warm as his heart at this time. After stabling his horse and giving her some feed and water, Brady made his way toward the kitchen door with an arm full of supplies. He had stashed the tea set in a safe place in the barn, not wanting Anna to know about the gift just now.

Brady burst into the kitchen and quickly shut the door. Anna was sitting in the rocking chair feeding Pat. She cheerfully called out, "Hello. I was looking for you to return about now. Did you get everything?"

"Sure did," Brady said, smiling. "Is everything okay with you and Pat? I missed you both. Something sure smells good. I can't wait to eat supper."

"It so happens that I made an apple pie this afternoon."

"Yum. Is there some coffee left in the pot? I think I'd like a warm drink before heading back out into the cold."

"Yes, I saved it for you. Apple pie and coffee go real good together, don't they? Well, you'll get your pie for dessert later tonight, how does that sound?" Anna told him.

"Mighty good. I'd better get busy and get the rest of the chores finished. I'll carry more wood in for the stove first."

Brady drank his coffee and warmed his body, and then he bundled up and headed out. He brought back enough wood to last through the night, and then he went to the barn. In less than an hour he returned with the milk bucket.

After they ate supper, they topped the meal off with the pie, and then Anna cleaned the table and dishes. Pat hollered and fussed so Anna went to his bed, picked him up, and went to the rocking chair to nurse him.

Brady decided this might be a good time to tell Anna what he had been holding inside. "You know, Jim and Frank are telling me that there are groups of men scouting up the Kentucky River. Much of the land north hasn't been settled. Folks are looking for other places to take their families. Jim says that in other states, like Indiana and Illinois, the farmland is very good. There are stories of the deer and wildlife being plentiful. They said that most of the Indians have moved farther west, but there may be some small warring groups still around with the idea that they will fight to keep their land." He talked on for some time about exploring, and Anna wasn't quite sure what to make of the conversation. She put Pat to bed. Brady added oil to the lamps, except for the one left burning, and they went to bed. The only sounds of the night were a couple of hoot owls calling out and the crackling sound of

17

logs burning in the fireplace. So the day closed, quiet and warm. Brady cuddled Anna in bed, and sleep came upon them.

★ ★ ★ ★ ★ ★ ★ ★ ★ ★ ★ ★ ★ ★ ★ ★ ★ ★ ★

Christmas day dawned with sun shining on the snow, sparkling brightly. It made Brady's eyes squint tightly when he went out that morning to do his chores, even with his hat brim pulled down. He hurried more than usual this morning. He couldn't wait to see Anna's eyes when she saw the present he had for her. The picture of her face as she looked at the present dominated his every thought that morning. When he had the chores all finished, he went to where he had hidden the special gift there in the barn and picked it up. He was pleased with himself having found the perfect gift for Anna. He walked back toward the cabin, holding the present behind his back, hoping she wouldn't see it. When he entered the kitchen, she was nowhere in sight, so he laid the package down on a chair and proceeded to remove his coat, hat, and boots.

"Anna Marie," he called. "Where are you?"

"Just making up the bed and putting clean clothes on Pat," she answered.

Brady sat down and poured himself a hot cup of coffee, hoping it would help take the chill away from being out in the cold winter weather. Anna came into the kitchen carrying Pat, who was cooing to his mama as she nuzzled his neck. His hand grabbed a lock of her hair and tried to pull it to his mouth. "No, no," Anna said to him. "We don't eat hair," she said laughing.

"Give Pat to me," Brady said, "and I will give something to you."

"Really? And what could you possibly have to give me?"

"I guess you will have to wait to see."

Anna sat Pat on Brady's lap.

"You know, this is Christmas Day, and I think it is traditional to give gifts to those we love. Anna Marie, my love, I have something for you." Brady picked the present off of the chair and held it out to Anna. Her eyes were twinkling. She wasn't expecting anything, knowing how little money they had. She sat the gift on the kitchen table and began removing the string and wrapping. As soon as she saw the tea set, she gasped.

"Oh, it's beautiful. Blue and yellow wildflowers are my favorite. Now I can have Lucy over for a proper tea. Brady, how in the world did you manage this?"

"Give credit to that wily fox that got into the chicken house. I sold his hide for a mighty nice price."

"Thank you, it's a wonderful gift. But you know what? You aren't the only one with secrets. I have something for you." She twirled around and headed to the bedroom.

She reappeared only a minute later with something wrapped up in a tea towel. She placed it on the table. "Here, I'll take Pat while you look at your present," she said.

Brady slowly opened up the tea towel to reveal a new pair of wool socks and a scarf. She had knitted every spare moment she could when he was out working, which was a challenge while caring for the baby.

"This is perfect," Brady stated. Brady wrapped the scarf around his neck and felt its warmth. "You couldn't have given me anything better." Then he turned to the baby. "I have something for you, little fellow," Brady told his son. He handed him a candy cane and a stack of wooden blocks. He sat Pat on the floor so he could play.

Brady and Anna hugged each other. Happiness filled all of them in their warm little cabin, there on the farm in the wilderness of Kentucky. And so, the winter days continued until the winter eased, the cold air gave way to warmer days, birds began singing and nesting, and the promises of spring approached.

CHAPTER THREE

VISIT FROM FRANK AND JIM

Anna Marie sat in her rocking chair on the front porch, holding Pat. It was a mild, spring day, and the mid morning sun felt nice and warm. It was good to be able to go outside and smell the fresh air and sense the awakening of everything after the cold, dreary, dormant days of the winter. She spread a small quilt on the porch and put Pat down so he could move around on his own. He was nearly nine months old now, and was crawling some. He would pick up anything that he could get his hands on and, more likely than not, try to put it in his mouth. She had to watch him constantly. About a month ago she had been sewing buttons on a blouse and thought that he was at her feet playing with one of his little toys. Next thing she knew, he was choking. She didn't know why he was choking so she picked him up and hit him on the back, but that didn't help. She turned him upside down, shook him, and patted him on the back—and out popped a button! What a scare he had given her! She had unknowingly dropped a button onto the rug and, quick as a snap, he had picked it up and put it in his mouth.

Pat was sitting there on the blanket looking around. A rabbit hopped by a few feet away, stopped and looked around, twitched its ears, then nibbled on the fresh, new grass growing in front of the house. Pat pointed and waved his arms around and made baby sounds to the rabbit. That didn't seem to faze the rabbit as he ate his way toward the edge of the yard. Anna and Pat were both content to be there on the porch away from the confinement of the cabin, each one lost in private thoughts.

Anna didn't feel well this morning. Her stomach was queasy, and she didn't know why. She decided to make chicken soup for their lunch as that might make her stomach feel better. Brady would have to have an extra sandwich to fill him up for the rest of the day. *He should be coming along in a short while,* Anna thought to herself. She was content to sit there in the warm rays of the sun and wait.

There had been several warm days in a row. Anna had not felt well on any one of those mornings. She was thinking that just maybe there was more going on inside her than she realized. She hadn't mentioned this to Brady—or anybody else. Anna decided she would take the horse and buggy into town and pay a visit to the doctor. She would tell Brady about her decision when he got home.

An hour of so later, Brady returned to the house and Anna told him of her plan. Being concerned for his wife, he told her that he would drive the buggy and go with her into town.

On their way into town, they stopped at the Bennings' and asked Lucy to take care of Pat for a little while as they had business in town. Within the hour they trotted into the outskirts of Reeds Crossing and headed directly for Dr. Joseph Woodland's office. Brady waited in the front receiving room while Anna went into the doctor's office. It wasn't long until she and the doc came out to where Brady was waiting.

"Tell me, Doc, how is my wife?" asked Brady.

"Your wife will be just fine soon. She is going to have a baby this fall, probably late September or October. Congratulations!"

"Oh, my gosh! Why didn't you tell me?" Brady asked Anna, and he gave her a hug. He turned to the doctor and held out his hand to shake hands with him.

"Thanks, Doc," he said. "Come, Anna, let's go to the boarding house and eat lunch."

"Eat? I'll try. Just remember, my body does not like food very much these days," she told him as she smiled. He took Anna by the arm and gently helped her as they walked the short distance to the hotel.

When they entered the boarding house, Brady looked over and saw Jim and Frank sitting at a table eating. He waved a friendly hello to them.

"Who are they?" Anna asked.

"They are my friends from when I was young, Jim and Frank," Brady replied. "We went to grade school together, and we also got into some mischief together. Oh, yes, we had some fun times."

"Do I know them?"

"You probably don't. Those are the guys I told you about who are planning to explore up the Kentucky River to look for new homesteads. It sounds like a great adventure to me." Anna Marie looked at him questioningly. "Anna, I could never go off and leave you, especially now with the new baby coming."

"But you would like to, wouldn't you?"

"I can't lie to you. Yes, I would. There is so much to see in this country. A lot of people are leaving with the wagon trains, heading out for new places to live."

They ate in relative silence and engaged only in talk about children and the coming summer. They finished their lunch and headed back to the Bennings' to pick up Pat and tell them the good news.

A short time later they arrived at Big Al and Lucy's home to find them on the front porch, Lucy holding Pat. Their children were enjoying the outdoors, playing and romping.

Lucy had a concerned look on her face. "Tell us what you found out. What's wrong? Is it something serious?" asked Lucy.

Anna and Brady looked at each other and grinned. "Yes, it's serious. We're going to have a baby about late September," Brady told them.

"You're getting another baby? Well ain't that just somethin'," Big Al remarked. "You are two lucky people. Many children make good families. Let me shake your hand, friend." He extended his big hand out to Brady.

"I'm not sure about all this. We didn't plan to have another baby this soon."

Lucy handed Pat to Anna and hugged them both. The two women sat down in the rockers on the porch and fell into easy conversation about their children. Brady and Al discussed fences that needed repair and decided they should start soon as possible. Brady also told Big Al about Jim and Frank and what they were going to do. When Anna heard their names mentioned, she started listening to the men talk.

"Brady," Al said, "If you want to go away for a short while, Lucy and I could look after Anna. I would check on her every day. Why she could even come and stay here some of the time. What do you think about that?"

"I have to get my crops in the ground, and my milk cow is going to calve again this summer," Brady explained.

"I'll tell you what. We'll work together and get your crops in as early as possible. I'll move your milk cow over here. When she is ready to calve, I'll take care of her. We'll be sure that Anna and Pat have milk and butter. She'll be welcome to go with us to town any time she needs supplies."

"You know, I don't know about all this. I had better talk this over with the wife."

Anna felt a chill quiver through her body. She couldn't believe what she was hearing. *Would Brady really leave me to go exploring?* Her heart was beating so hard that she could hardly catch her breath. *This was not part of the plan when we got married. No, he won't go. He has always done the right thing. He needs us as much as we need him,* she convinced herself. On their way home, Anna stayed quiet. Her thoughts were occupied with "what ifs" concerning Brady and his adventurous friends.

★ ★ ★ ★ ★ ★ ★ ★ ★ ★ ★ ★ ★ ★ ★ ★ ★ ★ ★

As he drove the buggy, Brady talked to Anna and noticed her thoughts were far away. *Something's wrong,* he thought. *What did I do?* He simply didn't realize that the idea of him venturing out into the wild and leaving her alone was overpowering to her.

★ ★ ★ ★ ★ ★ ★ ★ ★ ★ ★ ★ ★ ★ ★ ★ ★ ★ ★

That evening, after they had eaten their meal, Anna cleaned Pat up and put him to bed. Brady sensed his wife's quiet mood. She went to the bedroom without saying anything and started undressing. Brady followed and gathered her into his arms. She felt, for a moment, that she was being held by a stranger. She thought, *Will my life be like this from now on?* He kissed her on her neck and shoulders and stroked her hair. "I love you so much," he told her.

"I love you," she said.

"Let me show you how much you mean to me." He removed his clothes and finished removing hers, kissing her shoulders and neck. He lay down on the bed beside her. He resumed kissing her and tenderly moved his hands over her body. She soon responded with caresses on his body. Their passion mounted. She kissed his chest, neck, and all over his face. She gasped as he caressed and kissed her body. Their lovemaking reached a fevered height. He couldn't wait any longer as he rolled over to her. She matched the rhythm of his pulsing body, and they joined together as one. He groaned, and she matched his with her own, higher-pitched sounds. When the lovemaking climaxed, he drew her as close as possible. The fears she had had were now erased as she lay entwined in his arms. A gentle peace filled her soul.

★ ★ ★ ★ ★ ★ ★ ★ ★ ★ ★ ★ ★ ★ ★ ★ ★ ★ ★

A few weeks passed. The spring weather continued getting warmer, and rain showers came and went. Brady and Big Al prepared the ground for crops and planted the fields with corn and wheat. They would start working on fixing fences next. Anna Marie had gotten past most of her morning sickness. The baby inside her was growing and was now plainly showing. Pat was beginning to learn to walk and trying to say some words. She would take him out in the yard and they would pick the wildflowers that were up and blooming. She showed him how to place the flowers in the small basket that she carried outside. They both would hold the basket handle and carry it into the kitchen. Pat would take a flower out of the basket with his tiny hand and say "petty," which meant *pretty*, or "fower" for *flower*, and then he would carefully put the flower into a tin filled with water.

On Saturday, June fifteenth, Brady was just finishing the morning chores. He came out of the barn from checking on his pregnant cow and saw two men on horses riding toward his place. As they approached closer he recognized who they were—Jim and Frank.

"Mornin', Brady," they both said.

"Mornin'. Just in time for a cup of coffee. Tie up your horses and join me."

The men rode up to the hitching post, dismounted, and wrapped the horse reins around the post. By this time Anna realized that someone had ridden to their place, and she peered out of the front window. Her heart started pumping hard as it had back at the Bennings' place a few weeks ago. She recognized who the men were.

"Anna," Brady called, "will you bring a couple cups of hot coffee out here? We have company."

Anna went to the kitchen and filled three tin cups with coffee, and took them outside where she set them on the porch railing.

"Jim. Frank. This is my beautiful wife, Anna Marie," said Brady.

"Pleased to meet you," they both said.

"You remember Jim and Frank don't you? They were at the boarding house when we ate there a while back."

"Yes, I do," Anna replied. As Anna stared at the two men, she felt as if her legs were too heavy to move.

Anna was brought back from her trance when Brady spoke to her. "Anna, are you all right?"

"What? Yes, I'm just fine. I need to go into the cabin and check on Pat."

"Thank you for bringing us the coffee," Jim said politely.

She couldn't think of anything more to say to them as fear gripped her on the inside. She turned and headed back toward the cabin to check on Pat. She stumbled as she went up the porch steps but recovered. She was thoroughly shaken by the appearance of the two men.

★ ★ ★ ★ ★ ★ ★ ★ ★ ★ ★ ★ ★ ★ ★ ★ ★ ★ ★

The three men sat down on the porch, first engaging in small conversation about the weather, horses, and crops. Then Jim spoke up, "Brady, Frank and I are going to go up the big river to do some scouting in a few days. We would like for you to go with us. We've already bought up some food supplies and other things that we might need, and we have two more men—good scouts—who are going with us.

"I'm not sure I can go. You know I have a family to care for now. How long will you be gone?"

"We figure three or four weeks," Frank said. "You still have a rifle, don't you? In case we see a bear or wolf?"

"Sure thing. I shot a fox last winter. Caught him getting my chickens. He had a real, nice hide."

"That so? What do you say? Are you in with us? We'd really like you to go," Frank insisted.

"Let me do some talkin'. My neighbor has already told me that he would look after things for me should I need to be gone any length of time. It'll have to be all right with the wife," Brady said.

He already knew it would be hard to convince Anna that he would be safe and she would be taken care of by Al and Lucy.

"Good enough. Can you get word to us by mid week ... say Wednesday? We'll meet you at Smity's stable that morning if it all works out," Jim asked.

"I can't give you a sure answer till I can get things worked out."

The men shook hands good-bye. Jim and Frank untied their horses, mounted, and rode back toward town. Brady felt a stir of wanderlust inside like a match being struck and a flame leaping forth. He could hardly contain his desire to seek out the rivers, forests, and prairies. He was torn between the love for his family and the chance to go out into the undiscovered, unsettled land. He would have to go to Anna and see if there was a chance that he might persuade her. *Am I behaving like a little boy who wants his own way? No, I'm not. I believe it's in a man's nature to want to seek out new opportunities. Yes, that's what I'll say to her. Other men have gone out exploring and found many great, new lands.* Having bolstered up his courage, he headed for the cabin.

Anna Marie was sitting in her rocking chair nursing Pat. Brady entered the cabin, treading softly. Anna looked at him then back down at her baby, not uttering a word. Brady put his hat on the clothes hook beside the door and sat on a chair next to Anna. His hand brushed her cheek. He could see tears forming in her eyes. He sensed the struggle going on between them. He knew that she knew what he wanted to do.

"How could you go away?" she asked.

"Sweetheart, I wouldn't stay away a long time. Just this once, let me see what I can find. There is a big, new world out there. We're young, and now's the time to do what's best for our family."

"Don't do this. I need you here." The look in her eyes pleaded.

"Big Al and Lucy will take care of you and Pat. They have assured me of that."

"I can't agree to let you do this. I need you. We need each other." The tears spilled down her cheeks and she closed her eyes.

Brady didn't say any more. He kissed her on the forehead and decided to let it rest for now. He went out to look in the barn where he kept his tools. He picked up his hatchet and proceeded to sharpen it, then his axe. He brushed Mandy and cleaned her hooves. He got the pitchfork and cleaned the old bedding out of the cattle stall, then he put fresh dried grass down for the cow and calf. He was beginning to have thoughts that maybe he should give up the idea of going away for a while. He was making Anna feel miserable, and now he was starting to regret the whole thing.

★ ★ ★ ★ ★ ★ ★ ★ ★ ★ ★ ★ ★ ★ ★ ★ ★ ★ ★

Sunday morning brought a calm sky. Brady got up a little earlier than usual and made the morning coffee before Anna rose from her sleep. He stepped out on the porch and inhaled the fresh morning air. He saw a variety of birds searching for worms and bugs in the grass, and others were flitting from limb to limb on the nearly fully leaved trees, singing their morning songs. He looked up into the heavens and thought, *God, be with Anna and me today and help us with all that we do.* Brady finished his coffee and went to the barn where he started the morning chores. It didn't take long, and he made his way back to the cabin. Anna and Pat were awake. Pat was standing in the kitchen, holding on to a chair and saw his daddy come inside. He looked toward the door and said, "Dada." Brady looked at Pat, went over to him and knelt on the floor.

"Good morning, son," he said. "How's my big boy this morning?"

Pat reached his arms out and Brady picked him up and gave him a big swing round and round. Pat giggled with joy. Brady held Pat and walked over to Anna. He gave her a peck on the cheek and said, "Mornin', sweetheart."

Anna smiled and said, "Good mornin'. You were up early today.

It's Sunday, you know. We need to eat and start getting ready to go to church."

They finished breakfast. Anna Marie gathered up diapers and other baby needs and the family Bible. Brady helped Anna get into the buggy and they were on their way to church. The usual gathering of friends were there, all filled with the talk of their farms and children. Preacher Martin preached his sermon with a quieter tone than usual. His focus was the love of Christ for everyone. Perhaps the sermon was a prelude pointing toward a young couple who planned to be married the next week. He stated that, when we accept people that come into our lives with understanding, forgiveness, and trust, we will then know the true meaning of Christ's love in each one of us. Actually, it applied to the entire congregation. He concluded with a verse from the bible, I John 4:18: "There is no fear in love: but perfect love casteth out fear: because fear has torment. He that feareth is not made perfect in love."

Anna reached for Brady's hand, looked directly into his eyes, and smiled. He squeezed her hand and smiled back at her. She knew deep in her soul that their love for each other was strong and secure. The whole service seemed to have instilled security and unbounded trust in Anna Marie toward her husband and had removed the fear she had held inside for weeks. When the service ended, Big Al and Lucy rounded up their children and left for home. As the wagonload of family lurched out of the yard, Lucy turned and called out, "Come by and see us if you have time. We have plenty of food for two more today."

"Maybe we will. Thanks," Brady answered.

Brady helped Anna Marie and the baby into the buggy, and they left for home. Anna once again reached over and held Brady's arm. He sensed a closeness with his wife that had been missing for some time.

"Should we stop by the Bennings' place today?" he asked.

"I suppose we could. It would be nice to visit with Lucy."

"Anna, I want to talk to you now before we go any farther." Brady guided the horse and buggy to the side of the road and stopped beneath a shade tree. He turned and looked at her face-to-face, holding her hand. Speaking softly he said, "Would you agree for me to go scouting with Jim and Frank just this one time? I promise I won't be away a long time.

28

This is something that I have wanted to do since I was about fifteen years old. All I have ever done is work on the farm. If you are dead set against me going, I will never mention it again. But—maybe …just maybe—you could say yes. It would mean so much if I could do this with your blessing."

Anna was still feeling the power of love that had been preached only a short time ago. She nodded her head and said, "If this urge to scout is that strong, I won't tell you no. I will miss you every day. I realize now that you need to go to see what is outside of our little world." He pulled her and Pat close and kissed her fully on the mouth with a renewed passion. "Let's go see Al and Lucy," he declared. At that he snapped the reins, and the buggy resumed its progress up the road at a new spirited pace. In only a short time they were going up the path to Big Al's house. Brady tied the horse to a post and they went up to the front door and knocked.

"Come on in, neighbor. You're just in time," invited Lucy. "Kids, make room for Brady and Anna Marie."

Al brought two more chairs up to the table and they all ate, visited, and told stories. Even Lucy and Al's children enjoyed laughing at all the funny tales they heard. Al told one story about Preacher Martin and his pumpkin patch: "You know Preacher Martin raises pumpkins each year so the women in the congregation can make pumpkin pie for the community Thanksgiving dinner. Me and my friend, Henry, both twelve years old, and two older boys went out one fall evening after sunset and raided the preacher's pumpkin patch. At first we meant to take only one pumpkin each, but we ended up taking twice that many. In the excitement of the evening, we managed to step on several pumpkins and mash them while we picked out the best pumpkins we could find. About that time, the preacher's hound started baying at us boys. Talk about scared! We ran to the woods as fast as our feet would carry us. After that, every time we went to church for several Sundays afterward the preacher talked about the Ten Commandments, mainly the sin of stealing. He had a scowl on his face and he would stare at all of the young boys, looking for one of us to look guilty. Henry and I would sit there and try not to giggle, especially when the preacher looked our way. We would bow our heads and hold our hands over our eyes. We never did tell anyone about the night in the pumpkin patch, and nobody ever figured out who did the dastardly deed."

Everyone laughed and laughed. One by one, the children left the table until the four adults were left sitting there. There was a short lull in the conversation so Brady spoke up and said, "I have something important to discuss with the two of you about this summer."

Big Al and Lucy looked at each other then back at Brady and Anna Marie. "Talk to us. Go ahead, tell us what's going on," Al said with urgency.

Brady took Anna's hand in his then spoke up. "Anna and I have talked this over and she has agreed that it would be all right for me to go scouting for a short time, maybe a month or so. I won't go until I know Anna and Pat will have someone to care for them. Could you do that for us? I know it's a lot to ask, but just maybe it could work out."

"Is that all?" asked Lucy, relief clear in her voice. "You almost scared us both to death. Of course we'll take care of them, and our two older boys can help do chores. When do you plan to leave?"

"Uh, I'll probably be leaving in the next few days."

Brady took a deep breath then stood up and shook Al's hand. "Thanks. You two are the best neighbors anyone could have. Big Al looked at his wife, who was smiling. They all talked a little more, then Brady and Anna said their good-byes and left for home. The question had been asked and answered. From now on, their lives would be different.

CHAPTER FOUR

THE SCOUTS

Jim Bates and Frank Justice arrived at the Patterson home Monday morning about an hour after sunrise. They had two other men with them, Charlie Nelson and Johnny "Joker" O'Riley. Joker O'Riley was a man of many trades. He was a general handyman, especially appreciated for his repair skills by the widows in the county. He was also a farm hand for hire. The men in the county who knew Johnny had nicknamed him Joker because he could always either tell a funny story or make a joke out of just about any incident that happened. There was never a dull moment when Joker was around. When planting season or harvest time rolled around, farmers called on Charlie to help out. Charlie Nelson harvested trees and cut logs and fence posts. The smaller tree limbs he cut up for firewood. He always had enough firewood for his family and some available for sale.

"Mornin', Brady," hollered Frank.

"Mornin', Frank. Mornin', boys," Brady replied back.

"It looks like a great day for us, don't you think?"

"Sure enough. I see you brought Charlie and Joker along. Welcome. Glad to have you along for our trip."

"Well, when Jim and Frank talked to us about what you two were doing—looking for new farmland—we decided it was a good idea," Charlie responded.

"Do we have all the supplies that we need, including a map?" Brady asked Frank.

"Don't worry. With the five of us taking supplies, we shouldn't be short of anything," Frank said.

Brady told the men, "Wait outside. I have to go inside to see my wife. I shouldn't be too long."

The men dismounted and walked their horses over to the watering trough. They visited among themselves about the upcoming trip north. They talked about stopping in Lexington. Frank and Jim had gone there a couple years ago when they needed to buy supplies that the mercantile in Reeds Crossing didn't have. They talked how big a city Lexington was getting to be and that you could buy anything you wanted there. Charlie and Joker decided that they needed to get bigger canteens to take along on the trip.

Brady went into the cabin to say good-bye to Anna Marie and Pat. Anna was sitting in the rocking chair, holding Pat. She looked up at Brady when he came through the door. She was not smiling. She knew why he had come in ... that he was ready to leave. He walked over to her and Pat and knelt down beside her. He wrapped his arms around them both and held them firmly. Tears streamed down Anna Marie's cheeks. She knew that going on this scouting trip was something that Brady had to do. He released his hold on her, took her hand in his, and looked into her eyes.

Brady spoke to Anna, "You know that I love you and our son more than anything in this whole world. You will be all right with Big Al and Lucy looking out for you. This trip means a lot to me. I'm doing this for all three of us. I'll find new, fertile land that we can live on and raise good crops for our family. The time will pass quickly, you'll see, and I'll be back home and we'll all be together again."

Anna Marie put Pat down to stand by the chair and wrapped her arms around Brady's neck and they embraced one another. He kissed her passionately. When he released her, she took a deep breath, wiped her tears, and smiled at Brady. "I love you," she said. "I really don't want to be left here alone, but I realize, deep in my heart, that this scouting trip is very important to you. Pat and I will miss you. Now, take the bag of food that I put together for you and go join your friends. Know that every evening when the sun goes down, you and I will be seeing the same sunset. I will be with you in spirit, and you will be with me."

Brady placed his hand on her face for a moment then stood and turned toward the door, grabbed his hat off of the peg and the bag of food from the table where Anna had left it for him, and he went out.

The four comrades stopped their small talk and watched Brady as he checked his saddle and tightened the cinch before mounting the quarter horse that Big Al had loaned him for the trip. Anna Marie, holding Pat, came outside and stood on the porch, watching as the men mounted their horses.

Frank, Jim, Charlie, and Joker all waved to Anna Marie and Pat, "Take care and stay well. We'll be back soon," Frank called out.

Brady and his group of friends waved hearty good-byes and trotted down the lane. Anna Marie took Pat by the hand and they walked out to the edge of the yard where wild flowers were blooming. She sat on the cool grass and turned Pat loose to pick all the flowers he wanted. He picked and picked and laid each one carefully on her lap. Anna felt peaceful in this moment. She had Pat, whom she loved, and she carried in her body another child.

★ ★ ★ ★ ★ ★ ★ ★ ★ ★ ★ ★ ★ ★ ★ ★ ★ ★ ★

Brady and his friends rode their horses along at a steady pace, putting several miles behind them before they decided to stop for a rest. They found a nice grove of trees next to a small rivulet. They let their horses drink and forage in the soft, green grasses. The men opened their food bags and ate as they rested. They didn't lack for conversation. Charlie and Joker kept the men entertained with some of their stories. The two men had been pals for years, since they were boys and Joker's family had moved to the farm next to Charlie's home. Joker had two brothers and so did Charlie. The boys would get together after the morning chores were done and spend the rest of the day together. What one couldn't think up another one would. They would have foot races or they would go to the creek and try to gig frogs. They would sneak one of their mom's sharp knives from the kitchen, find some straight tree branches, and sharpen them for spears. They would go to the pond and throw their spears at the frogs, and once in a while they would actually spear one. More times than not, one of the boys would fall into the pond. By the end of the day, the boys would jump into the pond, clothes and all, until the day that they got caught. They all got a good spanking and were forbidden to ever go frog gigging again. The men laughed uproariously.

Brady spoke up, "Men, we had better be back on our horses and head out. We need to try to make it to Lexington before dark, right?"

Frank told Charlie and Joker, "Your stories are mighty entertainin'. I'm looking forward to hearin' more."

The two men looked at each other and grinned. "We have enough stories to last this trip," said Charlie.

All the men mounted their horses and rode on. It was a hot, humid July day in Kentucky. The horses' hooves were kicking up the road dust, which settled onto the sweaty men. When they reached the edge of Lexington late in the afternoon, they were caked with the grime of the day. They came upon a church that seemed to be good place to spend the night. There were trees in the churchyard and a lean-to shelter, probably used to store firewood. There was a small house next to the church. They figured the pastor must live there. The five scouts dismounted and led their horses to the shade of a large oak tree.

Brady spoke, "Do you think we might stay here for the night if we get permission from the pastor? Frank and I could go ask him."

The other men nodded their heads in agreement. Brady looked at Frank and said, "Let's go."

When the two men approached the front of the parson's home, the door opened and a bewhiskered, elderly man stepped out of the house. His face had the look of a man who had dealt with many problems, sporting age wrinkles on his brow and cheeks. He had bushy, gray eyebrows and on his left hand were large burn scars that drew up the skin on his hand.

"Evenin', men," the parson said. "I'm Jason Cordman."

"Evenin'," Brady and Frank both replied.

The preacher observed the dust on the men's hats and clothes, then he looked across the yard at the lathered horses. "Looks like you men have had a hard day's ride."

"Yes, you could say that. We came over here to ask your permission to spend the night in your churchyard. We'll tie up our horses and I thought that, just maybe, we could bunk out there in the lean-to.

Tomorrow we'll ride into town for more provisions and be on our way," Brady stated.

"Where do you fellows come from?" asked the parson.

"We live on farms near Reeds Crossing," replied Frank. "We're on a scouting trip up the Kentucky River toward Indiana."

"That right?"

"We heard the farmland is mighty good up that way. We want to find ourselves a fine piece of ground and move our families up there."

"I heard the same thing. If I was young again, I might just do the same thing. Well, now, you look like a good bunch of honest fellows. Go ahead and camp out there. It should be a good sleeping night, although you might hear some barking dogs down the road."

Brady and Frank thanked the parson for his hospitality, shook hands with him, and bid him good night. The two men walked back to the other men waiting in the churchyard.

"Men, you can unsaddle your horses. The parson gave us his okay. We're goin' to spend the night here," Brady stated.

It wasn't long until the men had their horses tethered under the trees where they grazed on the fresh, green grass. They carried their saddles and placed them on the ground inside the lean-to. They pumped fresh, clean water from the well and filled their canteens. The men sat together and ate from their food bags. They talked about the day's travel and discussed what they might do on the morrow. Feeling weary from the long day's ride, one by one they settled down in their bedrolls. The evening air was cooling down, which would make for a good night's sleep.

Daybreak came with the chirping of the birds that had nested in the nearby trees and the faraway barking of a few dogs. The men carried water to their horses before they ate that morning. The parson came out of his house and walked over to the churchyard.

"Mornin', men. How was your night?" queried the pastor.

Jim, who had his horse over beside the well, answered, "We slept just fine. That there lean-to helped keep the night air off of us."

Joker quipped, "I stayed awake all night. Didn't sleep a wink. I was looking for the Holy Ghost to come and get me."

"Good one," said Charlie. All the men laughed.

"Say, the wife said to invite you men over for breakfast. She has made up a big batch of biscuits and gravy. She says you young men need a good hot breakfast to start your day."

The men looked at each other, smiled, and nodded their heads.

"That'd be real good. Thank you. We'll be right over," said Jim.

The men entered the parson's kitchen and were met with the smell of fresh coffee. They washed up, removed their hats, and sat at the table.

"Men, I would like for you to meet my wife, Angeline."

"It's a pleasure. Good to meet you," replied Brady, and the other men followed his example.

Angeline set out a breakfast fit for royalty. There were fresh-made biscuits, milk gravy, butter, honey, and jam.

The parson offered a prayer, "We thank thee, Lord, for this food you provided for this meal. Bless each one of us this day. Lord, I ask that you be with these men as they travel and keep them from harm. Amen."

The men ate heartily as they exchanged stories with the parson and his wife. Brady and the rest of the men thanked the two for their kind hospitality and rose to leave. They all shook hands and said their good-byes as they walked toward the door.

"God be with you today and the days ahead on your journey," the pastor called out.

"We thank you for all you have done for us," Brady replied.

The men saddled their horses, left the churchyard, and rode down the road to Lexington.

The main street in Lexington was cobblestoned and bustled with activity. People were coming into town with their wagons to get supplies, women were going in and out of the shops, children were playing, and the smithy was hammering away on his large anvil. Charlie and Joker were on the lookout for a mercantile where they could find the canteens they wanted. There were some women dressed in finery, but most were dressed in their ordinary clothes—long dresses that had been washed many times. As they rode on farther, they came upon a train station alongside the railroad tracks. Right there in front of them was a steam locomotive, the likes of which they had never seen. The men dismounted and tied their horses to the hitching post in front of the station, which also provided a watering trough for the animals. The sign on the front of the rail station said Lexington and Ohio Railroad.

"I'll be jiggered!" exclaimed Joker. "Look at that train. What do you think of that, Charlie?"

"Look at the size of it—and, look at the size of that smokestack," Charlie said as he gazed at the train.

All five of the men walked up close to the train, attempting to take in the whole concept of its size and its working parts. They looked at the train for several minutes.

"Are you here to buy tickets to Louisville?" the agent asked the men.

"Oh, no, we're just passing through and we stopped to see your locomotive," Frank replied. "Whoa, that's quite a machine."

"Yes, it is. Do you know that this train track is eighty-five miles long? It starts here, goes to Frankfort, and ends near Louisville. I believe that the railroads are going to change America," the agent told them.

Brady commented, "Yes, I think you're right." He looked at his fellow scouts and said, "Well, boys, we had better move along." With that being said, the men went to their horses, mounted, and continued on their way. Soon they arrived at a large mercantile where they bought additional food and supplies. They filled their knapsacks with their new purchases, mounted, and trotted on down the road. They rode westward toward Frankfort, which would take three to five hours of good travel time. The day was beastly hot, which was normal for mid summer. The heat made it difficult for the men to drink sparingly from the water they had in their canteen. They rode for a good two hours and stopped near a small farm where there was a pond that was shaded by the trees that grew along one side. They had been there a short time when the man who owned the farm came over to see them.

The farmer asked, "Are you men traveling somewhere?"

Frank answered, "Yes, we plan to follow the Kentucky River north to Indiana."

"That sounds like quite a trip. You aren't very far from the river, only an hour or so ride. What's in Indiana?"

"We hear that there is good farmland. If we find some, we can move our families up there."

"Is that so? I've heard the same, but you know it would be too much for me to try such a trip. If you men want some water, help yourself. Be careful as you ride up north, especially along the river. I've heard that there are small bands of Indians around that aren't very friendly," he warned.

"Thanks for the hospitality and the advice. We'll remember what you told us," said Charlie.

Once again that day, the men mounted their steeds and rode on toward their destination, the Kentucky River. The men were sweltering hot that afternoon. When they drank the warm water from their canteens, it didn't seem to help them much. Onward they pushed, following the road along the hilly terrain without much conversation. At last they saw ahead of them the trees and bluffs that indicated that they had arrived at the Kentucky River. It was a beautiful sight to see the clean, clear water rushing along, splashing over the tree roots and rocks. Brady pointed out a couple of good-sized fish jumping in the stream.

"Fellas, we've made it to the river," Frank said, "and now we can head north and travel right alongside on the river bank. We should ride until near sunset, if you all agree, before we make camp."

Brady spoke up and said, "We could stop an hour before sunset and maybe we could catch us a few fish to cook for our evening meal. What do you think?"

Charlie and Joker and the other two agreed that sounded like a good idea. Frank took the lead as the five men rode single file on the small path leading northward. They were now traveling at a slower pace than they had been on the road, but it was cooler because of the shade from the sycamore and shagbark trees growing along the bank. There were some bends and turns in the path of the river, and the banks were covered in greenery. They saw grey squirrels racing along the tree branches and an occasional cardinal, its red feathers flashing in the sunlight as he took flight. After a good hour of diligent riding, the men began to talk among themselves about where they should stop for the night. They rode around a river bend and came to a small, flat clearing carpeted with thick bluegrass that would lend itself as a good campsite.

"Let's stop here and call it a day," Frank said. "I think we all need some rest. We've covered a lot miles today."

Sore from the day's ride, the men slowly dismounted their horses and loosed the straps of their saddles. They led their horses down to the river's edge and let them drink their fill. While the horses drank, the men washed their arms and faces in an attempt to remove some of the road dirt.

"Ah, that cold water really felt good on my face," said Brady. "I think I'm ready to catch us some fish for supper. What do you say, Charlie?"

"I'll take my horse up to the shade and I'll join you. Joker, you comin'?"

"Sure thing," Joker replied. "I'll tell Frank and Jim that we'll catch the fish, and they can build the campfire. That should be a good deal, don't you think?"

"Yes, indeed. Makes my mouth water just thinkin' about fish roasting above a hot fire!"

The five scouts cared for their horses and placed their saddles and bags where they decided to sleep that night. Frank and Jim rounded up stones for the campfire site and agreed to gather the firewood as the rest of the men headed for the riverbank with great expectations of catching enough fish for a meal. The day had been hot, with no wind, and the humidity of the evening was hardly bearable. The men had a couple small shovels with them. They dug around an old, rotten tree stump that was lodged in the side of a small embankment and they located enough earthworms to bait their hooks. They threw their lines into the river, intent to succeed at their self-appointed mission.

Joker threw his fishing line out and jerked it back, over and over. He swatted mosquitoes and kept moving around, unable to sit quietly and fish.

Charlie said to him, "What is wrong with you? You are bouncing around like a kite on a string. You'll never catch fish moving around like that."

"I don't know. I guess I sat in the saddle too long today and I can't keep from moving."

About that time Joker got a hit on his fishing line that jerked his arm.

Brady shouted out, "He's got a big one! Hang on, Joker. Don't lose him!"

Joker gave a yank and then pulled on his line. The men worked and got the fish on the bank. It was a huge catfish.

"Whoopee!" hollered Joker. "Now *that's* a big fish! This big guy will feed all of us."

Brady and Charlie wrapped up their fishing lines and helped Joker dress his catfish. The campfire was blazing and ready to cook the catch. After the fish was cooked, the men sat around the campfire and ate their fill of fish and biscuits.

"I've got to hand it to you, Joker. You invented a new way to catch fish," quipped Frank.

"I figure if Samuel Morse can send signals on a wire, I can jerk a line and seduce a fish to bite my baited hook," said Joker laughingly. The five comrades continued to sit, visit, and rest, content after their meal. They watched the orange glow of the setting sun across the banks of the river. The heat and smoke emitted from the fire kept the insects from assaulting the men as night crept upon them. They soon abandoned their circle and went to their bedrolls for the night.

CHAPTER FIVE

ANNA MARIE

The farm and the cabin felt suddenly quiet. Anna Marie didn't know what she should do. Her purpose there at their cabin seemed unsure. There was no need to rush about cooking the noon meal; there was enough food already prepared for her and Pat. She heard the clock on the shelf ticking, and it seemed noticeably louder to her. Her vases of dried flowers sat undisturbed, just a remembrance of the time spent searching them out and enjoying their newly bright blooms. Pat was happily playing with his toys on the floor, making his baby sounds and kicking his feet. Nothing had changed, really, except Brady wasn't there. She had never experienced this "alone" feeling any time during her marriage. It would take more time for her to fully comprehend that Brady was away for more than just a few hours. She picked up her knitting and sat in her rocker, trying to remember just where she had left off with the knitting project.

The day passed minute by minute. Anna fed and cared for Pat in the usual manner. As it became late afternoon, she took him into the barn to fetch feed for the chickens, then she scattered the feed in the chicken coop and cleaned the water bowls. Big Al had the livestock at his farm, except for their horse, so there was no need to check on any other animals. She brought Pat out to the porch with her to enjoy the sunset and the cooler summer air. They stayed outside until the air chilled and persuaded them to move inside to the warmth of the cabin. She lit the lamp, which cast a warm glow within the room. She sat on the floor with Pat, and together they played. He was able to crawl and pull himself up onto his feet, holding onto the furniture. He would stand straight, letting go at times to stand alone.

Anna said to Pat, "Look at you. It won't be long until you'll start walking." Pat sat down abruptly and started clapping his hands. Anna and he clapped their hands and laughed together. He crawled over to her. She picked him up and hugged him lovingly. *I am so thankful to have you*, she thought as she kissed his cheeks. She took him into the bedroom and prepared him for bed. Loneliness overcame her again as she looked at her bed and realized that, for the first time ever here in their home, she would be sleeping without Brady beside her. She rubbed her hands over her ever-expanding midsection, which held her next child. She made up her mind that she must be strong. *Many women have endured being alone and have done well, and so shall I.* She went back to her rocker and her knitting. She worked until she became sleepy, put the project aside, and got ready for bed. So ended the first "alone" day.

★ ★ ★ ★ ★ ★ ★ ★ ★ ★ ★ ★ ★ ★ ★ ★ ★ ★ ★

Each day seemed to pass in a similar manner; the only variance was when she washed clothes, baked bread, scrubbed floors, or tackled other big chores. It had been two and a half weeks since Brady left. Big Al had checked on her regularly. The first week Brady was gone Anna Marie went to see Lucy twice. The first time was only for a friendly visit. Lucy gave Anna the encouragement she needed. She and Lucy talked and laughed together while Lucy's children played with Pat. Soon the afternoon passed and it was time to go home. Anna had relaxed. The second time, Anna went with Al and Lucy to town to purchase some supplies—dried beans, bacon, potatoes, and more yarn. For Anna, it was an outing that she needed. The confinement in her cabin, with no other adult to talk to, was starting to bother her. Each Sunday she had gone to the Bennings' home. They went to church together and she had then shared Sunday dinner with them and spent the afternoon. Big Al took her to the barn to see Brady's cow and her new calf. Both were doing well.

There had been about four days of cloudy and cool, rainy weather. The wind had started blowing early in the week and never subsided. She and Pat were held captive inside the cabin except for the daily trips to the chicken coop. She had three setting hens, which were setting on eggs to hatch. They had been setting for about a week now. The baby chicks weren't due to hatch out for another two weeks. She hadn't had any trouble with any varmints getting into the chickens since Brady shot the fox.

This particular morning she noticed that Pat had a runny nose and was coughing. She doctored him as she knew best, but it didn't seem to help. His cough became deeper as the day went along, and he was turning beet red by the end of each coughing spell. She began to worry about him. He cried and fussed, which was unusual to his nature. She felt his brow and it was feverish. By mid afternoon, she decided to hitch up Mandy to the buggy and go see Lucy. There was a light sprinkling of rain with some wind, but she made up her mind that she had to do this. Pioneer women had an inner core of strength upon which they could rely when they needed it. They got into the buggy. She had bundled her little boy to stay dry, and put on her jacket. In the buggy, she covered her legs with a quilt and headed down the road. She made the trip in good time with no problems, with the exception of a few gusts of wind that made the quilt flop around. She pulled in front of Al and Lucy's home, hitched the horse, and took Pat with her to the front porch. By this time Al had noticed she was there and opened the door.

"Come on inside where it's dry. What made you get out in this rainy weather?" asked Al.

"It's Pat. He woke up sick this morning and has gotten sicker all day long." Pat started a coughing spell. Lucy came into the room where the two were talking.

Lucy stated, "That's quite a cough. When did he start getting sick?"

Anna said, "Just today. He woke up with a runny nose and cough. It's gotten worse all day long. I've done everything that I know to do for him."

"Let me hold him," Lucy said. Anna placed him in her arms. "This little guy's burnin' up! We need to put a cold cloth on this head." Lucy went over to the washbasin and handed Anna a washcloth. Anna dipped the cloth into the cold water and handed it to Lucy. Lucy placed the cool cloth on Pat's forehead and carried him with her over to the rocking chair and sat down.

"Poor li'l fellow, he's not feelin' a bit good," Lucy murmured to Pat.

"What should I do with him?" Anna asked.

"You should leave him here with me. I'll take care of him and you go back home. With you bein' in the family way, you don't need to get sick."

"I can't do that!" Anna exclaimed. "He's my baby."

"Yes, he is, but you need to think about that little baby growing inside of you. You don't want to lose him, do you?'"

"Of course I don't. Please, let me stay with him." Anna said pleadingly.

Lucy spoke softly, "It's for your own good. I'll have our boy, Matthew, take you back home. Now don't you worry, it will all work out just fine."

Big Al called for Matthew to come and told him he was to take Anna Marie back home. Matthew went outside and tied his riding horse to the back of Anna's buggy. The rain had stopped, but it was still cloudy and breezy. Anna, in her haste to take Pat into the Bennings' home, had left the quilt on the buggy and it was soaked with rainwater. Matthew put the quilt behind the seat. Lucy continued to console Anna as she left her child behind. Anna climbed into the buggy, and she and Matthew started on their way back to the Patterson farm. There wasn't much conversation as they traveled down the rain soaked road. When they approached Muddy Creek, they could see that the largest volume of the rainwater had already passed downstream and they had no difficulty making the crossing. The horse trotted up Anna's lane to the cabin. Matthew halted the horse right at the cabin door and helped Anna off of the buggy and up the porch steps.

"I'll put your horse and buggy in the barn and curry her for you," Matthew told her.

"That would be very nice of you," Anna replied. "Would you like a warm cup of tea before heading back home?"

"Sure. That sounds good."

Anna walked into her home, went to the fireplace, and decided to build a small fire, just to take the chill and dampness out of the air.

There were some small kindling pieces in a bucket. She arranged in the center of the fireplace. As soon as the fire was lit and the flames were jumping up, she began to feel the warmth in the room. She put a couple dippers of water into the teakettle and hung it on the hook above the flames. She removed her jacket and placed it on the coat hook by the front door. After a short while, Matthew came back to the cabin. Anna had the tea ready for the two of them. They sat down at the kitchen table and sipped their hot tea, which warmed them.

Matthew spoke up, "Mandy is brushed and wiped down. I also gave her a couple handfuls of grain and scattered some fresh straw in her stall. She should be all right until morning."

"Thank you. You've been very helpful, Matthew. I may need to ask you for help with my garden. You know I can't bend over very well now. This rain we've had will make the weeds grow fast, but we won't be able to work until the ground dries out some."

Matthew replied, "I think I could arrange that. I could ask my brother, Jack, if he would help out. If you're like Ma, you'll want to put up some vegetables for the coming winter."

"That's my plan. Brady and I worked together on planting the garden, but with him gone and me in my condition, I don't think I can do it all by myself."

Anna put some bread and butter on the table to share with Matthew. They sipped their tea and talked together about gardening dos and don'ts. After Matthew made sure that there was enough wood in the cabin to last at least a day, he said his good-bye and left for home. Anna watched him ride up the lane and onto the road to his place. She turned and slowly looked around inside her home. Each thing she saw stirred a memory. She went into the bedroom, took off her shoes, and lay down. She pulled the top quilt over herself and hugged Brady's pillow. At first the tears slowly filled her eyes, and then she gave in and cried hard. She sobbed until she couldn't sob any more. The pillowcase was soaked with her tears. She lay there until darkness surrounded her. Anna was alone. She forced herself out of the bed and went to the kitchen and lit the lamp. She remembered Lucy's last words to her, "Everything will work out just fine." She sat at the table, folded her hands in prayer, and prayed, "God, heal my baby. Help Lucy to get rid of his fever and his cough. Be with my husband and keep him safe until he comes home to me, and please make it be soon. God, I ask you, please keep this little baby inside of me healthy. Amen." She felt soothed after having said her prayer. She decided to go to her rocker and knit a while. *When morning comes,* she thought, *I will go see how my boy is feeling.*

Morning came with clear skies and sunshine—a glorious morning that made the birds sing and her rooster crow. After Anna had something to eat, she put on her chore jacket, picked up her egg basket, and went out to care for the chickens. She gave them feed and water and opened the door so they could go outside and scratch around for bugs or whatever they could find. With a few exceptions, the water puddles had emptied themselves by flowing to the lower parts of the land. She had gathered half dozen fresh eggs and was on her way toward the house when Big Al rode up to the barn. He almost frightened her as he dismounted from his horse.

"Mornin', little lady," he greeted her. "How are you feelin' this fine day?"

"Good," she answered. "How's my boy doing? Is he better?"

"That's what I came to tell you. His fever broke in the night. I think he's over the worst part. Lucy gave him warm lemon tea last night and kept a cold cloth on his head for several hours. She plans to feed him some homemade chicken soup two or three times today. She'd like to keep him at least another day or two because she wants to be sure that he continues to get better. We don't want you to come down with whatever made him sick. Would you agree to that?"

Anna paused and then answered, "I guess I should. I had a hard time being alone last night, but I'm better now. I'm sure you will both take good care of Pat. I want him to be well and come back home. I miss that little guy."

"I know you do. The missus has had a lot of experience with sick children," he consoled, "and they made it just fine. She'll give him some warm cow's milk. It won't hurt him. Is there anything that I can do for you today?"

"No. Matthew brought wood into the house for me last night. I don't think I'll be using much now with the warm sun shining today. Give Pat a hug from his mama. Let me know if anything gets worse for him; otherwise, I will be fine."

Big Al remounted his horse, waved good-bye, and trotted off. Anna's spirits lifted higher now that she knew her boy was getting better. She walked up the steps to the porch and sat in the porch rocking chair, leaving the eggs by the door. Once more she placed her hands on her belly and rubbed it. She felt the baby inside moving around, and she knew that this little one was healthy and growing.

Anna's mind moved back in time to when she was a young girl and she was visiting her Aunt Ella and Uncle Amos, before he was killed. Anna was practicing how to knit. Knit and purl, knit and purl … she worked back and forth, trying to make a scarf to wear with her winter coat. She had the scarf about twenty rows long and was feeling quite proud of herself when decided to carry it across the room to a different chair. On the way, she slipped and dropped the knitting needles, scarf, and ball of wool on the floor. As she picked it all up, somehow the stitches came off the needle, and then she pulled on the yarn and unraveled some of the knitting. The kitten Aunt Ella had in the house raced over and started playing with the ball of yarn. The ball rolled across the floor. Anna grabbed at the loose yarn and the scarf unraveled even more. The kitten got its claws stuck in the ball of yarn. Aunt Ella grabbed the kitten and carefully pulled its claws loose just in time to keep the whole project from being destroyed. Anna Marie looked at the would-be scarf, looked at Aunt Ella, and the two of them laughed and laughed. Aunt Ella sat back down in her chair and wiped tears from her eyes. The two of them decided that whenever Anna was going to work on her knitting, the kitten would have to be shut in another room of the house.

Anna smiled as she recalled the memory and wondered what had become of that scarf. She thought, *Later I will go look in the box that I brought here from Mother and Dad's and see if it's in there.* Anna got up slowly, picked up her basket of eggs, and went inside. She busied herself working in the kitchen. She made a pan of vanilla pudding with the milk and eggs she had left from yesterday. She made herself a sandwich for her lunch and ate a bowl of fresh pudding. The rest of the day passed routinely for her. Knitting, chores, washing dishes, and resting filled her time. Late in the afternoon, Anna sat on the porch with her shawl around her shoulders and back to keep the evening chill away. She was awestruck at the beauty of the sunset. The rainbow of colors made by the setting sun showing through a few puffy clouds caused her to marvel at the creation. The changes in the horizon made her wish that she had the ability to paint the beauty that she was witnessing. Her thoughts turned toward Brady. She wondered if he was looking at the sunset at this moment. *Where could he be? Are the men taking risks as they ride the sparsely traveled roads of northern Kentucky? I know that there could be Indians still living in the wilderness areas.* The thought brought a chill to her body and she clung to the shawl wrapped about her. She scolded herself. *Don't think such things. You know Brady can take care of himself.* The sunlight faded in the sky revealing orange, purple, and red colors that created a whole new palette that had not been there earlier. A few birds fluttered from limb to limb in the trees nearby as they looked for their nests. She heard the hoots of owls as they called out into the night. She watched the evening stars twinkling high above, quietly absorbed in the sights and sounds which surrounded her. *The only way this evening could be more serene*, Anna thought, *would be if Pat and Brady were both there with me to share it all*. After sitting for an unmeasured passage of time, she got up from the rocker. She looked out one more time at her little world, turned, and went into the cabin.

CHAPTER SIX

ANNA MARIE—2

It had been three days now since she had taken Pat over to the Bennings' home. Anna arose from a good night's sleep and looked out the bedroom window to see a beautiful sunrise. The clouds parted, and there was a promise of a beautiful summer day. She brushed her hair and pulled it back with some side combs and hairpins. She proceeded to the fireplace and stirred the few remaining ashes, revealing some live coals, and then she placed a few wood chips onto the coals to encourage the fire to spring forth. She went into the kitchen and put water into the teakettle for her morning tea and placed the kettle on the hook that protruded from the side of the fireplace over the fire. She already knew what she was going to do today. As soon as she dressed, ate, and finished the morning chores, she was going to hitch Mandy to the buggy and go see her little boy. The reports from Al each day reassured her that Pat was much better, and she really didn't want to be alone any longer. She wanted her boy back home with her. So, that is exactly what Anna did.

The buggy ride proved to be rougher than usual as the road had been traveled during the rainy spell and mud had dried into hard ruts. Mandy trotted slowly, and yet it seemed the buggy wheels managed to find each bump and hole in the road. Anna felt herself being jostled about although she was sitting on a padded seat. The ride was especially rough when they crossed Muddy River. Many of the large, flat rocks that had been placed to make the crossing possible had been washed downstream, adding to the difficulty of making the crossing. That obstacle didn't lessen Anna's exuberant feelings ... feelings she had been experiencing all morning. She felt like shouting news headlines to the world, "Child recovers from illness. Mother and child happily

49

reunited." She knew this was premature thinking, but how could she think otherwise? Anna looked around at the countryside as she and Mandy traveled along. She enjoyed the look of the freshly blooming wildflowers that blanketed the roadside and continued deep into the woods. She made a mental note to bring Pat here. The two of them would pick a basket of flowers for her vases and tins that were sitting on the shelves back at the cabin.

Anna arrived at the Bennings' home mid morning with high spirits. Matthew Benning was standing with his brother, Jack, under the big maple tree by the front porch. Matthew and Jack waved hello to Anna and stepped up to help halt the horse.

"Mornin', Anna," they both said.

"You're away from your farm early today," said Matthew.

"Yes, I am. I had to come see my boy. He isn't sick today, is he?"

"No, ma'am. Ma was feeding him some breakfast this mornin' and he was eatin' just fine."

Lucy appeared at the front door at that moment, holding Pat and smiling.

"Look there, Pat," she said. "There's your mama."

Pat began wriggling feverishly, saying "Mama, Mama!" He reached out toward Anna. Anna fairly bounced up the steps of the porch and took her boy from Lucy and gave him a big squeeze. Pat's little arms were tight around his mother's neck.

Lucy said, "Come on inside and let's visit. I'll make us a fresh cup of tea."

The two women went inside to the kitchen table. Pat was still clinging to his mother. Anna felt quite at home, as Lucy was like a second mother to her.

"Pat seems to be so much better," Anna stated. "He doesn't have a fever or runny nose anymore. Lucy, you've nursed him back to health. How can I ever repay you?"

Lucy replied, "Heaven's sake, girl. You don't owe me anything. That little fella is just like one of my own."

Anna Marie held Pat on her lap while she sat drinking her cup of tea. Lucy was washing and cutting vegetables for the pot of soup she was making for the family's noon meal.

Lucy said, "Anna, you may as well stay and eat a bowl of soup with us today. I always make plenty of food. Say, did you remember that a week from Sunday the congregation is having a picnic dinner after church? I plan to take fried chicken and potato salad. What do you think you'll take?"

"I haven't given it much thought so far. I might bake a chocolate cake. That's Brady's favorite, you know. It sure would be great if he could be home by then."

"I don't suppose you've heard anything from him, have you?"

"No. He said he would be gone at least four weeks, maybe five. He has been gone more than three weeks now."

"That time will pass quickly," Lucy said knowingly. "Al had an urge to take off with his friends when we had been married a couple years. They were going to ride to the Mississippi River and go south to see what the countryside was like. After they were gone about fifteen days, they had mosquito bites, rashes, saddle sores, and all kinds of misery. They endured rainstorms and dust, sticky, hot weather and they were plumb worn out. They came back dirty and hungry. He hasn't mentioned taking off on another adventure since then," Lucy added, "And you know what? Jack was born nine months later."

The two women laughed and laughed. Anna said, "That won't happen to me, I'm already carrying another baby!" The women continued laughing until tears streamed down their cheeks.

Anna Marie stayed until mid afternoon and enjoyed the company of the Benning family. Anna Marie and Lucy decided to go to town on Monday, if the weather wasn't rainy, and shop together.

Anna then said her good-byes, took Pat, and left for her own home. She felt so much more complete now that she had her little boy with her. Thoughts of Brady were heavy on her mind after hearing Lucy's story about the trip Al had made many years before.

★ ★ ★ ★ ★ ★ ★ ★ ★ ★ ★ ★ ★ ★ ★ ★ ★ ★

Lucy and Anna Marie arrived in Reeds Crossing mid morning the next Monday. The weather had remained fair and sunny, so the roads were good to travel on. They stopped first at the mercantile. Lucy looked at the yard goods and bought material to make her three girls new dresses and plain, dark brown material to make the four boys and Al new pants. She planned for the girls to help her with the sewing, as they were old enough to produce half decent handwork. Anna decided that she could use some material to make some clothes for Pat as he was growing so fast. The women then bought kitchen supplies and loaded everything into Lucy's buckboard. Lucy drove the horse and wagon down the street to the front of the boarding house and hitched it there. The two women went inside to have a cup of tea before heading back toward home. Sitting at the table was the owner's sister-in-law, Pricilla, who had married his brother, Jeremiah. Anna had known about Pricilla, but had never spoken with her.

Lucy spoke. "Hello, Pricilla, so good to see you. How are you and your family?"

Pricilla replied, "We're all just fine. My two boys are growing like weeds. How is your family?"

"They couldn't be better. Pricilla, do you know Anna Marie Patterson? She married Brady Patterson."

"Hello, Anna Marie. It's a real pleasure to meet you. I think that my husband, Jeremiah, knows your husband."

"Could we join you? We want to have a cup of tea before heading back to our homes. We've been shopping at the mercantile. The men stayed back on the farm to cut hay. You know the saying, 'make hay while the sun shines.'"

"Of course you can join me. Anna Marie, you'll have to tell me all about Brady."

The ladies chatted for nearly an hour. Anna told Pricilla about Brady and his friends going away on a scouting expedition, and how she expected him to return in two or three weeks. The three women shared stories about their children, husbands, and their lives.

Lucy talked about the time that Al and Matthew, who was about seven years old at the time, found a bee tree in the grove of trees at the bottom of the hill past the barn. "Matthew said to his dad that he would sure like to have some honey. Al told Matthew that it was dangerous to bother bees during the daytime, and that it was better to try to get their honey after sundown when the bees would be quiet. When they came in for supper that evening, honey was all Matthew would talk about. 'Dad and me are going to get some honey tonight!' Al was a little nervous about bothering a beehive, but he didn't want Matthew to know. By this time, all the children were excited about going to get the fresh honey. After supper, we picked up couple lanterns and a small crock to take on the all-family march to the honey tree. Al picked up a small hatchet to chop on the tree's trunk, and we all made our way toward the now-famous bee tree. The wind was blowing and rustling the leaves on the bushes and trees along the way. We could hear bird and animal night noises, and the children were wide eyed with the adventure. We came to the bee tree and Al pointed at the hive, which was just above the first large limb. We didn't have a ladder to climb, so he was going to have to shinny up the tree trunk. He stuck the hatchet handle into his pants and started up the tree. He was about halfway up when Matthew saw a pair of glowing eyes looking down on his dad. 'Look out, Dad. I see big shiny eyes. There's somethin' up there!' Al's head quickly jerked and he looked up. A big ole raccoon jumped right down onto his shoulders. It startled Al so that he let go of the tree. The raccoon and Al fell right down onto the ground. That raccoon was stunned, and he tried to run, but all he could do was wobble around. Al lay there on the ground and looked around at the raccoon and started laughing. When we realized that Al wasn't hurt, we all laughed. After we all calmed down, Al decided that he could try to climb the tree one more time. This time he succeeded. With the hatchet, he cut a hole in the tree big enough so he could reach in and take chunks of the honeycomb out. We filled the crock with fresh honey that night. The children had an adventure that they have never forgotten—and a sweet treat as well."

"That was a wonderful story," Pricilla stated. "I hope one day my family will have adventures that I can tell my friends about."

Lucy said, "I know you will. As long as there are families, there will be stories."

Anna Marie smiled. *When Brady comes home,* she thought, *I'll have stories to tell him and he'll have stories to share with me.*

Pricilla asked, "Lucy, would you and Anna like to join a group of women who get together twice a month and work on their quilts?"

Lucy replied, "I could probably go once in a while. What about you, Anna Marie?"

"Yes, I would be quite interested. I want to meet more of the women my age who live around here. I could also use help with my quilting."

So it was decided. All three of the women would plan to attend the quilting bee, which was to be at Pricilla's home a week from Wednesday. Lucy, Anna Marie, and Pricilla said their good-byes and parted. Pricilla stayed. Jeremiah was to meet her there when he was finished having two of their horses shod. Lucy and Anna climbed onto the buckboard with their purchases and started toward the Bennings' farm.

CHAPTER SEVEN

THE SCOUTS—2

The men arose at daybreak. Frank threw some dried sticks on the few hot embers that remained in their campfire. The fire soon revived and flames once again blazed enough to heat water for a pot of fresh coffee to go with their breakfast. Their first cup of hot coffee was exactly what the men needed, as the early morning air had a chill to it. Within a short time they had eaten, saddled their horses, gathered their bedrolls, scuffed out the campfire, and continued northward. They rode alongside the river at a steady pace without much talking, Brady trailing the rest of the men.

Brady was lost in his own thoughts, harboring an uncanny feeling that this was exactly the same path that his grandfather had been on years ago. He had heard the stories of his grandfather's adventures from his father. Maybe this was the reason for the stirring Brady had felt about exploring new territory. Brady wanted to be successful ... to leave a legacy for his children and grandchildren. He knew he could eke out a minimal living on the few acres that he was now farming. But, if he could secure enough acres of good, fertile land to support his family and build a nice home and barn, then he would be satisfied. His thoughts turned toward Anna Marie and Patrick. The sinking feeling in his stomach was a feeling of guilt for leaving them there alone on the farm while he rode off to fulfill this yearning to explore beyond his small world. *Big Al and Lucy will look after the two of them, and they will be all right*, he consoled himself. He was not doing this for himself alone, but for Anna Marie and Patrick and the next child. Oh, how he missed her already. If he could only hold Anna close and caress her right now. His thoughts were interrupted when he heard the men ahead talking.

"Hey, fellas," said Joker, "look ahead. I think we're at the edge of Frankfort. Are we going to stop and look around?"

The men all drew their horses up together and stopped. They were high on a bluff overlooking the river. The scene before them was breathtaking. They could see the whole town and far beyond. The river water was flowing below them, clean and clear, and all around was thick, lush, green growth of grasses and wild flowers. Trees of all sizes lined the riverbank on both sides as far as the eye could see. They sat there together, quietly looking and listening. The woods around them were occupied by scurrying chipmunks, fluttering birds, butterflies, and bees, all busy with their own particular appointed tasks.

After a few moments, Charlie quietly said, "There are some beautiful trees here—some of the biggest and oldest I've ever seen. I'd say a person could get some good boards for a cabin out of one of them. I wonder if there are trees like this in Indiana."

Brady replied, "Yes, I believe there are, especially trees growing near a river."

Frank spoke up, "This is one nice place, but I don't think we should stop today. We need to keep moving along. What do the rest of you think?" Brady and the others looked to the horizon at the town before them.

Brady brought his thoughts back to their mission and said, "I agree with Frank. We can't stop now. We need to stay with our plan for now."

Joker spoke up. "I guess you're right. I'll have to use my imagination for now of how the streets and buildings look. I'll come back another day."

Jim and Charlie agreed with the others that it was more important to keep riding. Without another word being said, Frank and Brady led the men as they continued along the winding Kentucky River.

★ ★ ★ ★ ★ ★ ★ ★ ★ ★ ★ ★ ★ ★ ★ ★ ★ ★ ★

The men reached the Ohio River two days after they left the bluff at Frankfort. They decided to spend the night before making the crossing over the river into Indiana. It was necessary to replenish their meat supply and other food items. They had reached a small settlement called Oak Ridge located where the Kentucky River flowed into the Ohio River. The town seemed to be a growing community. The men found the general store where they purchased food staples. Then they went to the butcher shop for a couple bacon slabs and beef jerky. Oak Ridge seemed to be a prosperous town. There was a feed store on the outer edge of town where the men decided to get a bag of oats for their horses. Knowing that they would be pushing their horses each and every day of the journey, they wanted the horses to stay in good health. Located close to the center of the town was a good-sized gathering area with a roofed platform where people met for various occasions. Some bench seats had been built in front of the platform, and a there were a few more under some of the shade trees. Hitching posts, water troughs, and a well for drinking water made the grassy lawn and inviting spot. Children ran and played on the lawn while their mothers sat on the benches, visiting, reading, or knitting. It was a pleasant sight to see. The men rode their horses over to the hitching posts, dismounted, and let the horses drink from the trough. The scouts decided to walk down the street to find someone to ask permission to spend the night in the gathering area. They approached a full-bearded, older man who was sitting in a chair outside of the general store, whittling.

"Afternoon," Brady greeted him. "I guess you probably know about everybody here in town."

"Yep," he answered as he continued with his whittling.

"Could you tell us where we might ask permission to spend the night?"

"Probably could. Since it's about suppertime, you might find our sheriff eatin' with his wife over at Polly's Café. You can find it down the street here on the other side of the harness shop."

"Thank you for your help. You be careful, now, and don't whittle your fingers."

"Well, if'n I do, it sure won't be the first time," he said with a chuckle.

Brady and the other scouts walked on down the street and found the café. After a short discussion, they decided they could use a good hot meal, served on a clean plate, and they entered the café. They found an empty table big enough for the five of them and sat down. After a short time a waitress approached them. She was a buxom, full-figured lady with long, tawny brown hair, which was pulled back away from her face and wound up behind her head in a bun. Her face was round, and a few curly sprigs of hair had fallen across her forehead. She had hazel eyes that twinkled with life.

"Welcome to Polly's," she announced. "What would you like to eat? We have a special—beans cooked with pork and onions served with cornbread and a slice of apple pie."

The men all agreed to have the special. Before the waitress walked away, Brady inquired if the sheriff was there in the café. The waitress pointed him out and told them his name, Sheriff Burton. Charlie, being a bachelor, was impressed with the waitress. While the men waited for the food to be brought to their table, Charlie talked about how good looking he thought she was and how he would like to get acquainted with her. At last she came with the plates of food. Charlie watched her every move as she walked around serving the customers. He decided to talk to her before they left. The men thoroughly enjoyed their meal, especially the homemade apple pie. Brady, not wanting to disturb the sheriff's meal, watched until he finished eating before approaching him with the request to spend the night.

"Hello, are you Sheriff Burton?" he asked when he approached the mayor.

"Yes, I am. Who would you be?"

Brady stuck out his hand to shake hands with the sheriff and said, "My name is Brady Patterson. My friends and I are passing through your town on our way to Indiana. We'd like to know if it would be all right for us to spend the night down the street." He pointed to the grassy area he and his fellow travelers had admired. Then he gestured toward his friends. "Over there are the other four men I'm traveling with."

Sheriff Burton answered, "How long do you plan to stay?"

"We'll ride out in the morning. We've got a long trip ahead of us," Brady told him.

"Are you men armed?"

"We have rifles for our protection only. None of us has ever been in any trouble, and we don't plan to start any."

"We have a good, quiet town here. You men are welcome to stay the night."

Brady walked back over to his friends and informed them that the arrangements had been made to spend the night. Charlie left the group and stopped the waitress in a corner of the café. The men watched as Charlie talked to her and waited until he returned.

"Whatcha got goin' on, Charlie?" Joker teased.

"I'm gonna come back in about an hour and walk that gal home. She's the prettiest lady that I've ever met."

"Is that right? She's a good looker. Do you need someone to help you walk her home?" Joker snickered softly.

"I don't think so. You're so ugly, you'd scare her away," Charlie teased back.

After finishing their meal the men left and headed back to where they had left their horses. They unpacked their gear and their bedrolls. When the sun went down, Charlie returned to the café. The rest of the men talked a while then made their beds and called it a day. Charlie waited until the waitress, Rosalee, had finished her work. Rosalee lived about a half mile from the café. The two of them talked and laughed as they made their way down the road to her home. They sat on the edge of the front porch to her parent's cabin and talked for another hour or so. Charlie knew that he wanted to see her again. "Rosalee, I would like to see you again when I return from my trip. Would that be possible?"

Rosalee replied, "Yes, I think so. Do you know when that will be?"

"It won't be a long time. I'll come see you as soon as I can."

Charlie drew Rosalee close, kissed her softly and held her a few moments. "Rosalee," he said, "I hope you'll wait until I come back. I've never felt like this for any other woman."

"I'll be here," she said softly.

Charlie left Rosalee and went back to where his friends were camped. He spread his bedroll out and lay down, but all he could think about was Rosealee and how good it had felt to hold her close.

★ ★ ★ ★ ★ ★ ★ ★ ★ ★ ★ ★ ★ ★ ★ ★ ★ ★ ★

During the nighttime, the granddaddy of all thunderstorms rolled into the town. The men awakened to blowing gusts of wind, the hard cracking and roaring sounds of lightening and thunder. The horses were whinnying and snorting as they pulled against the reins, which were still tied to the hitching posts. The men all jumped up and pulled on their boots. They hastily grabbed their bedrolls and ran toward their horses as the rain began pouring down thick and heavy. They all saddled and untied their horses, then mounted as quickly as possible.

"Where can we go to find shelter?" Frank asked.

"I don't know!" Brady replied. "Does any of you have a suggestion?"

Charlie mentioned, "I don't know if it's a good idea or not, but maybe Rosalee's father would let us stay in his barn."

"Well, it's sure worth a try. Charlie, you lead the way. It's about the only option we have right now," Frank told him.

Charlie and the other riders pulled their hats down to try to keep the wind and rain off their faces. It was pitch black as the men rode as fast as possible through the mud and water puddles. It was a miserable ride. Charlie yelled out after a short time, "This is the place. I'll go find out what I can." It was with some hesitation that Charlie approached the porch and knocked on the front door. He heard heavy steps approach the door. His heart thumped hard with anticipation. Would he be greeted kindly or with a gun pointed toward him?

The man yelled from inside, "Who is it?"

"My name is Charlie. I am a friend of Rosalee's."

Rosalee's father, Jeb, opened the door holding a shotgun, but not pointing it at Charlie. "What do you want?"

"I have four men with me, and we need a place out of the rain. We won't bring you any trouble. Would you let us stay in your barn for the night?"

"Rosalee, come here. I need you," her father called out. Rosalee came and immediately recognized Charlie.

"Charlie, what are you doing here?" she asked.

"I need shelter for myself and my friends. We got soaked sleeping on the grass at the meeting place in town."

Rosalee turned to her father, "It's all right. I've met these men. They ate their supper in the café this last evening, and I visited with them."

Rosalee's father trusted her judgment. He turned and said, "I'll pull on my boots and put on a rain coat and I'll take you out there. There are a couple empty horse stalls you can use. Take your men on over there by the gate."

Within minutes Rosalee's father had opened the gate to the barn lot and led them and their horses inside the dry, musty barn. He visited with them and learned about their scouting mission then bid them good night. After taking care of the horses, the men quickly made up piles of straw to sleep on, and although they hadn't dried out from getting rain soaked, they weren't long in falling asleep.

The rainstorm continued throughout the night. The men were awakened the next morning when they heard the gates open and milk cans rattle and thump. Jeb had come into the barn early to check his livestock and milk his Jersey cow. Overhead the rain still pounded down on the barn. A few flashes of lightening were followed by the rumbling thunder. The men weren't too eager to get up as they felt groggy from the interrupted sleep of the past night. Jeb greeted the men and invited them to come into the house for some coffee and breakfast. As the men gave their horses some grain and water, they discussed what they should do next. Knowing that the heavy rains would affect the rivers, they knew they couldn't leave for a day or more. Charlie seemed to be the only one who was untroubled by the decision; in fact, he couldn't be happier. The men entered the home of Jeb, his wife, Tess, and Rosalee. Following the morning meal, the women cleaned up the dishes and the men sat and discussed their situation with Jeb. The men had gained Jeb's trust, and he told them that they could stay until the weather cleared enough for them to ride on. The scouts told Jeb that they would help out any way possible while they were staying there on his farm.

"Jeb, how did this town come to be called Oak Ridge?" asked Charlie.

"Have you noticed how many trees there are here?" responded Jeb.

"A good lot of them are oak trees. There are enough trees here for many homes and buildings."

"Is that right?" Charlie replied. "You know, I make my living cutting down trees. I cut poles and firewood. I use what I can and sell the rest. I could come here and make a good living."

"It would be possible. Our town is a young town, and the trees are plentiful," Jeb commented.

Charlie now knew what his future would be. He would come back to Oak Ridge and make a life. He would ask Rosalee to be his wife. Charlie spent as much time with Rosalee as possible. He walked her to the café before noon then walked back to the café in the evening to bring her safely home when her work was finished. They were becoming sweethearts.

So, that is the way the next three days went. Finally the rain stopped and the skies cleared. The men were now trying to figure out how they would cross the Ohio River. The heavy rains had swollen the river so the water overflowed its banks, and the current was swift.

Jeb told the men, "There's a ferry across the Ohio at the town of Milton, about ten miles west. It goes across the river to a town called Madison. It used to be called Madison's Trading Post many years ago."

"Wait a minute," Brady spoke up. "My grandfather spent some time there a long time ago."

"I'll tell you the history of Madison," Jeb continued. "A trapper, named T. J. Madison had a trading post there for a long time. He never married but he helped many a man who came by his way. I hear he was mostly responsible for the ferry starting up across the Ohio."

"Do you know if the trading post is still there?" Brady asked.

"I've been told the building is still standing somewhere in Madison."

Brady said, "That's something I have to see when we get to the other side of the river."

The scouts stayed there the rest of that day and night. When morning came they gathered their belongings and fed their horses. All the men shook hands with Jeb and Tess and expressed thanks for their kindness.

Charlie was having a hard time saying good-bye to Rosalee. He held her for a long time.

"I'll be back soon," he told her and he kissed her deeply. "Rosalee, I'm falling in love with you," he told her.

"I'm falling in love with you to, Charlie." she told him. "Take care of yourself and come back safe and sound."

Having readied their horses for the day's ride, they mounted. Once again, the men told Jeb and Tess how much they appreciated their hospitality.

"You men must be careful now, you hear?" Jeb hollered as the men rode away. "Come back any time to see us!"

Jeb, Tess, and Rosalee watched the men ride away until they were out of sight. Rosalee had tears streaming down her face, not knowing if she would ever see Charlie again.

CHAPTER EIGHT
THE SCOUTS—3

The five scouts headed for Milton, Kentucky, hoping to reach there within an hour. They rode westward away from Oak Ridge, following a wagon trail. The trail was muddy and had grown up with weeds. There was brush growing along the sides of the road and numerous tree branches hung low over their heads. Danger could come at them in any form, so they had to be watchful as they rode along.

Joker was talking to Charlie, telling some outlandish story, gesturing wildly with his head facing his comrade rather than where he was going. Suddenly, Charlie hollered, "Watch out!" But he was too late. Joker ran into a willow branch. At his indignant yelling, the others stopped riding and looked back.

"What happened?" Brady asked.

"Joker met a tree limb," said Charlie. Charlie couldn't help but laugh. "He was wound up talking to me and forgot to duck when we rode under that willow tree. Joker rode right into a big branch hanging down over the road. I thought he was going to pop right out of the saddle!" Charlie and the others were all laughing. Joker wasn't. He was rubbing his face. The branch had hit him hard enough to leave a welt.

"That wasn't funny, fellas. It stung like hell," Joker said curtly. He wiped his hand over his face and looked to see if he was bleeding. "Well, it didn't cut me, but I'll have a dang welt on my face for days!"

The men couldn't help but laugh. Brady gave a wave with his arm that meant "let's go on." The tree branch sting quelled Joker's talking for some time. The men arrived at their destination around noon and went directly to the river where they found the ferry dock. Two men were sitting in large wooden chairs next to the dock. The first man was stocky and built like a wrestler. He sported a full, shaggy beard and a head of rumpled hair that reached his shoulders. He had a wad of tobacco in his mouth and a spit can next to his boots. A younger man, possibly his son, with a similar build, hair and complexion, was sitting alongside him. The five scouts paused and looked at each other, not sure how to approach this pair. They got off of their horses and hitched them on a rail located next to a small shack of a building built on the riverbank. There were four mules hitched on a separate rail beside a water trough, shaded by a rough-built type of shelter.

"Well, men, let's see what we can find out about the ferry business," said Brady. They all walked down to the two men sitting in the wooden chairs. The men looked up as the scouts approached. The big man spit a wad into his spit can.

"Hello, fellas," Brady began, "is this where we catch the ferry across the river?"

"Yeah, this is the place," the big man answered. "The ferry is over on the other side right now. It'll be back over here in a couple hours."

"That sounds good. We'd like to get over to Madison this afternoon if we can."

"The ferry will make one more round trip today. Be sure to be here when she's ready to go."

Frank spoke up, "That won't be any problem. We're not going anywhere."

The scouts walked back up the bank toward their horses. They took some food out of their saddlebags and went to the shade to eat. The afternoon wasn't as hot as it had been, but the air was humid ... heavy feeling. Perspiration ran down the men's bodies. Weeds and brush lined the riverbank and grew up the side of the small shack. The mules had left their dung here and there, and where they had stood for a length of time, it was piled thick. Flies kept pestering the men's faces and settling on their food. As they ate and talked, they decided that the mules had been kept around so long that their stench was attracting the pests. A horse fly bit Jim on his left ear. He uttered a few nasty words as he wiped the blood off. Brady told the others that when they arrived on the other side, he wanted to spend a little time looking for the old trading post.

They agreed to go with him. It was a little later that they saw activity on the water and realized that the ferry was coming in toward the dock. The two ferrymen got out of their chairs and walked out on the dock to wait for it to arrive. The scouts were happy to leave the bugs and smell of manure for a whiff of the cleaner air coming off of the water.

The ferry was transported back and forth across the river by means of a pulley system and mule power. The mules were hooked to opposite ends of a horizontal pole that was attached at its center to a perpendicular pole to which was attached a rope that was, in turn, attached to the ferry. When the mules walked in a circle, the rope was wound around the perpendicular pole, and the ferry moved along. The ferry had now arrived and was secured. Two other horsemen and their steeds along with a horse and carriage carrying a man and his lady disembarked. The young ferry worker gathered the mules and hitched them to their harnesses.

The older man hollered out, "Get ready, fellas. This ferry will leave shortly." Brady and the others immediately led their horses onto the ferry. The horses were tied to the side rails, some on each side to balance the load. There were two other men going and another two men who manned the ferry; that made for a full load.

"Stand as still as you can while we cross," the ferry captain announced. "This here river's running fast. With all of the rain this past week, the ride will be real rough today. It'd be best if you men stand by your horses to help keep them quiet."

The captain gave the signal to the man working the mules, and the ferry started across the swiftly flowing river. The ferry struggled to keep an even keel, which caused the horses to shift their weight often as the boat moved. There were tree branches and logs floating along on the swift current. These obstructions smacked against the ferry at irregular intervals. When the ferry was halfway across, one large forked log hit the boat, bounced up, and hit Frank on the calf of his left leg. He let out a whoop, which caused his horse to rear up and lose its balance. Frank grabbed his leg and the ferry railing, hoping to catch his balance, but he slipped and fell into the water. Just at the last moment, he grabbed onto the floorboards of the ferry and held on for dear life. His horse faltered with his balance but managed to stay on all four feet. Everyone on the ferry called out while Frank struggled not to be torn loose by the river current. When he was hit once more by river debris, he was forced to let go with one hand, but he quickly recovered. Jim went to his side and grabbed Frank's arm and pulled him back onboard the ferry. Frank was soaked, of course, but otherwise only bruised. He got up and stood beside his horse as before. Thankfully, the winds weren't gusting, or the ferry might not have been able to cross the river. The men stood by their mounts and reassured them by stroking their necks and talking into their ears until they arrived on the other side to the shore of Indiana. As soon as the boat was secured, the passengers without horses disembarked followed by the five scouts and their horses. All remarked that they were happy to have arrived safely to solid ground.

"How's your leg, Frank?" asked Brady.

"It's got a lump on it where the log hit, but I'll be all right."

Jim asked the scouts, "Are we ready to ride? We still have a few hours of daylight left."

"The ferry captain said Vernon was north of here two or three hours," Brady stated. "Before we leave town, let's see if we can locate the old Madison Trading Post. I guess we'll have to talk to someone here to see if they know where to find it."

The two men who were manning the ferry had heard Brady talking. One of them spoke up. "Maybe we can help you with that, fellas," he said. He pointed eastward and said, "Follow that path over there by those trees and go around the bend. Go up the bank to the clearing and you'll see the old trading post."

The men mounted their horses and rode on the path they had been told to follow. They then rode up the riverbank toward the clearing. The rundown remains of a building stood toward the back of an opening in the wooded area. It was overgrown with brush and weeds, and tree limbs were scattered about on the ground. The porch, which had been built on the side, had fallen in and was, it seemed, only a haven for wild animals.

Brady spoke up, "Fellas, this place belonged to a good friend of my grandfather, T. J. Madison. Once, my grandfather and his men were attacked by Indians. My grandfather was seriously hurt as were a few other men. They made it here and T. J. helped them out with food, shelter, and medicine for nearly a week. My grandfather never forgot this man. He told my father about T. J. Madison, and my father told me. I have always wanted to see this place ... to stand on the same ground where my grandfather stood many years ago."

"That's quite a story," said Charlie. "I can see why you wanted to come. Knowing who lived, worked, and slept here on this same ground that we now stand on ... well, it makes the past come to life." The others agreed with him.

The men stayed a short while longer and discussed the possibilities of what they might do if they owned this piece of property. Charlie looked around and remarked on the many trees that could be harvested.

They would have enough daylight to reach Vernon if they didn't have any difficulties. The men mounted their horses and rode back to the riverbank where the ferry landed and continued north up the bank. They trotted through the main street of Madison, looking over the town and the businesses it offered. Brady's mind was still holding onto his memories of his grandfather. He thought, *If Grandfather had stayed here, it's possible that this would be my home right now. I would never have met Anna Marie, and we wouldn't have had Pat. I probably wouldn't have become a farmer. I might have become a businessman, a blacksmith, a boat captain, a banker, or maybe a lone trapper. Who knows?* Brady knew one thing—as soon as he and his men found a good piece of land, he planned to head back to Kentucky and his family. His feelings for Anna Marie stirred inside of him and he wanted to hold her right now. He remembered the words that the minister spoke at his and Anna Marie's wedding: "Therefore shall a man leave his father and his mother, and shall cleave unto his wife: and they shall be one flesh." Genesis 3:24, he remembered.

He wanted that oneness right now. Here he was miles from his family, riding into unknown territory without the slightest idea of what he would see or what would happen. Brady asked himself, *Am I doing the right thing? Should I forget the whole idea of looking for a new place to move my family?* Brady was lost in his own thoughts, remembering that Anna

Marie had told him that love endures all things. He rode through the town but didn't see a thing.

Frank tried to break his reverie. "Brady, do you think we'll reach Vernon before sunset?"

Brady hadn't heard a word Frank had said.

Frank raised his voice and said, "Brady, are you here or somewhere else?"

Brady looked at Frank, "What? Did you say something to me?"

"Yeah, I was asking if you thought that we'd reach Vernon by sunset."

"That's the plan, isn't it, Frank?"

"Yep, we'll try to get there by evening. Looks like a good road to travel, mostly farm country."

The men rode at a steady pace going past small farms where corn crops ripened in the fields. Some farmers and their grown boys were out cutting hay with scythes and piling it on a wagon hitched to work horses. They all wore wide-brimmed, straw hats that helped keep the hot sun from burning their faces. The men were mopping sweat as they worked out in the summer heat. Each farm had a large barn, while another section of the farm held a few head of cattle, some with calves. Their homes were basic log homes. There were clotheslines out beside the homes where the day's wash flapped in the breeze. Small children ran around barefoot as they played in the dirt and grass. Brady noticed how contented they all seemed as they lived their daily lives. He felt a pang of desire to be home again. He couldn't let himself get caught up in that feeling because he knew he had to keep focused on his quest. He brought himself back to the moment. He could see that his horse was getting lathered up from sweat and mentioned to the others that they should give their horses a rest.

The scouts stopped on a bank beside a pond nestled between a couple rolling hills. They dismounted and led the horses to the water and let them drink their fill. The sun was dropping in the west behind a few drifting clouds, which produced an array of colors across the sky. The men discussed that maybe this would be a good place to stay for the night, and then they could rise early and ride in the coolness of the next morning. Joker sat on the pond bank and watched for fish, and remarked to Frank that maybe he could catch some for a meal.

Frank replied, "That's a good idea. What do the rest of you think? Should we camp here tonight?"

"If we are here for the night, I'm goin' fishin'," said Joker. "We'll have a good hot meal tonight."

It was agreed by the group of scouts that this was where they would eat and rest.

CHAPTER NINE

MEMORIES

Pat lay down on his quilt on the floor, playing with a toy wooden horse that he liked. The minute he became quiet he dozed off asleep. Anna Marie was resting in her rocking chair. These days of being without Brady were taking a toll on her. She managed to get most of her work done in the mornings, which left the afternoons and evenings long and lonely. Pat, of course, was her whole life now since Brady had left, but that only fulfilled her maternal instincts. It had been over three weeks since Brady had gone; to her it felt like months.

The summertime heat seemed to be closing in on her today. She had opened the windows and both doors to allow some air movement inside the cabin, but what breeze moved through didn't offer much relief. She removed her shoes and unbuttoned several of the top buttons of her dress to cool off her neck. She hadn't put on her petticoat today, knowing the day would be hot, and she hiked her dress up to her knees. She took her kerchief and wiped the perspiration from her brow and face. She made another swipe down her neck and between her breasts then tossed the kerchief on the little light stand beside her. She let her head fall back onto the back of her rocking chair and closed her eyes.

She was remembering the time Brady and she were alone for the first time. He had driven her home from a Sunday evening hymn sing at the church. The church choir had sung two special songs, and Anna Marie had a solo part on one. She couldn't help but notice that he had looked at her the whole evening, until she was beginning to blush. Then he had winked at her! She had remained flustered during the rest of the program. Following the hymn sing the members gathered for refreshments. The church ladies had all brought in fresh baked cakes and lemonade. Brady picked up his cake and drink and went over to Anna Marie's side and sat down on the empty chair next to her. He was grinning from ear to ear. She remembered feeling flustered. He tried to visit with her, which at first was a bit uncomfortable, until she relaxed. They had had a lively conversation after they got past the awkwardness.

At the end of the social hour, he had asked to escort her home in his buggy, which she readily accepted. They were trotting along at a moderate pace when Brady pulled the buggy over to a level place just off of the road. Brady held both of her hands and told her that she was the prettiest gal in the county. He right away kissed her on the cheek, wrapped his arm around her shoulder, and pulled her close. She rested her head against his shoulder and he kissed her again, this time full on the mouth. That hadn't been her first kiss, but it was the first kiss that made her feel all warm inside. She had thought, *Should I make him take me home right away? Yes, but will I?* He made the decision by saying that he had better take her on home. He released her and took the reins of the horse, clicked his tongue, and they started on down the road. They had shared another kiss after he had helped her out of the buggy at her home. He held her close a few moments and told her that he wanted to see her again. She knew that she wanted to see him also. That had been three years ago.

During the following weeks, Brady and Anna were together as much as possible. They were together at the Fourth of July celebration held in Lexington, in a park located a short distance from the center of town. The place had been alive with a carnival atmosphere. There were pie and cake baking contests for the women, horseshoe pitching contests for the men, races for the children, as well as tables of food, drinks, and deserts. There were plates of fried chicken, homemade breads, and corn on the cob. A big pot of stewed vegetables hung over a fire. A group of men formed a band and played lively tunes on a stage in the center of the park. It was a wonderful day. When the afternoon drew to a close and twilight came upon the festivities, a group of men set off a fireworks display.

Everyone watched from a blanket or rug they had thrown on the ground. Brady and Anna sat together with their arms around each other on this perfect, cool, and calm evening. It was there that Brady had asked Anna Marie to marry him. Oh, she remembered perfectly. He'd given her a heart-shaped locket when she said yes, and then he'd kissed her passionately. It was too late in the day when the festivities ended to travel home, so they spent the night with one of Brady's uncles who lived in the area. Anna Marie slept in the spare bedroom, and Brady slept on a pallet on the floor in the parlor. Anna Marie, her mind flooded with memories of that day, sat there and smiled with her eyes closed. The house was quiet except for the ticking of the clock and the sounds of the outdoors filtering inside.

Anna was jolted back to consciousness when a rapping knock came from the front door. When she looked up she saw a man standing in the open doorway holding a rather large bag. He was dressed in a brown coat and weather-beaten hat, both covered with dust. His appearance was rumpled as though he had slept in his clothing many times. Pat awoke from his sleep and started crying, as the loud, rapping noise had scared him. Anna quickly flipped her skirt down to her ankles and started buttoning up her dress as she called for Pat to come to her. She was hesitant to acknowledge the man's presence, yet she did not want him inviting himself inside. She cautiously walked to the door.

"What do you want?" she asked him.

He replied, "Madam, I have here in my bag a selection of new pots and pans that I would like to show you. This is the finest cookware you will find anywhere—straight from Richmond, Virginia. Would you allow me to come in and demonstrate this fine cookware?"

"No, you can't," she replied.

"Well, I could show you out here on the porch—if you like?"

"Maybe I could do that. Just give me a minute to put my shoes on and I'll be right out."

She stepped inside, donned her shoes, brushed her hair back with her hands, and picked up Pat before returning to the porch. The salesman began unloading his bag near her rocking chair. Anna Marie was quite flustered with a strange man standing on her porch, as Brady had always been around when anybody unfamiliar showed up. How she wished he were here now. To say that she was comfortable with the situation would be an obvious misstatement. She scooted the rocking chair back away from the man, as she felt the need for added space, and sat down. The salesman was kneeling down beside the pans, which he had arranged on a crumpled cloth on the wooden boards. He looked up at her, and she felt his eyes assessing her. No doubt he could see that she was carrying another

73

child and that her breasts were large. He presented several different pans—a new skillet and a stew pot. As he finished his sales pitch, he moved closer to her and took her hand, which was gripping the rocking chair armrest. She jerked her hand away immediately, which threw him off balance and he landed on his bottom with a thud.

"What the hell got into you lady?" he yelled.

"You need to leave right now!" she shouted in a high-pitched voice. "I don't need your cookware."

The salesman collected himself, stood up, smirking, and stated, "You don't have a man around here, do you?"

"Yes, I do," she replied. "He'll be home any minute now, so you best go." She started to shake, and she stood and moved a couple steps back away from him.

"No, I don't think so," he said as he moved closer to her. "I think I'll just make myself at home here. You can make me a nice supper, and then I'll do something to make you happy."

Anna Marie was beside herself. She grabbed Pat and headed for the door, but the man blocked her way. She went down the porch steps and headed for the barn, intending to hitch up the horse. He grabbed her by the arm and held her firmly. "Now just where do you think you're going? I suppose maybe you were trying to leave, right?"

She didn't answer; she only glared at him as she tried to figure out her next move. He held her arm and guided her back toward the house. She pulled against him. At that moment, Big Al rode down her path. "Al! Help me!" she cried out. Al dismounted even before he stopped his horse. The salesman released Anna and gave her a little shove into the house. Before the salesman could draw back for a punch, Al hit him hard in the stomach and knocked the wind out of him, then down they both fell on the porch floor. Al pounded the man soundly two or three times then got up.

"You good-for-nothing scoundrel! What do you think you were going to do?" Al yelled. "Get yourself up and hit the road. Don't you ever come back, or I'll pound you again!" He turned from the intruder to Anna Marie. "Anna, are you and Pat all right?"

"Yes, we're all right. A little shaky, but we'll be okay."

"What was his business here?" Al asked Anna.

"He peddles pots and pans."

"Well I think he owes you whatever new pot you would like to have, considering the circumstances. Anna, you come and pick something out." Al gave a hard look at the salesman. "I'm sure he won't mind givin' you a gift for your hospitality." Anna chose a large stew pot and took it inside.

The peddler got up, gathered up his remaining merchandise, and dropped it into his sack. He limped to his horse, mounted, and headed out, never looking back. Anna Marie and Al watched as he disappeared beyond the lane. They could hear him uttering profanities as he rode off.

Anna said, "You sure came at the right time, but what brought you here?"

"Lucy sent me over. She was out working in her flower garden and she saw the peddler ride by. At first she didn't give it much thought. After a little time passed, she became concerned that he would stop at your place. Nothin' would do but I should check on you. I'm mighty glad I came."

"So am I. I don't know what I would've done."

"Do you want to come home with me and spend a couple days? That no-good critter of a salesman may try to come back later."

Anna Marie thought a few moments about her situation. "Al, I appreciate your thoughtfulness. I really don't want to leave. Could you have one of your boys come and spend the night for two or three nights? I think we'll be all right."

"Consider it done if you're sure that's what you want. My Matthew will be here before sunset. "

"Thanks, Al, for everything you do for me. You are the best neighbor anyone could ask for."

"It's just a neighbor helping a neighbor. See you later." Confident that Anna Marie would be all right, Al got back on his horse and headed home.

CHAPTER TEN

THE SCOUTS AND THE PREACHER MAN

The men sat around the campfire for nearly an hour after they ate their fill of fried fish and corn cakes. Joker took the fish heads and scraps and threw them several feet away from the campsite to keep the bugs away. Charlie had walked around and gathered enough firewood to last the night with the hope that the smoking logs would help keep the mosquitoes away.

Brady said to Frank, "We made good progress traveling today, don't you think?"

"We sure did," Frank replied.

"How far are we going to try to go tomorrow?"

Jim spoke up. "I think we're only a few miles from Vernon. Isn't that where we follow the road west?"

"That's right," Frank replied. "From Vernon we'll go west to a town called Seymour. If things go well, we could have lunch there then we'll keep riding west till evening."

Charlie turned to Joker. "Maybe you can catch some more fish to feed your saddle-sore friends."

"Talk about saddle sores! I've got blisters on top of blisters. By the time we reach new farmland, I'll have blisters not only on my butt, but on my knees, ankles, and elbows."

All the men laughed except Joker. Charlie said to him, "You'll toughen up in a couple more days. Maybe you should sit in the river water to cool your saddle sores while you're fishing."

At that the men laughed even harder. Joker replied, "That's all right, fellas. I'm glad you're getting a laugh out of my misery. You'll laugh more when you're sitting in the water right beside me."

It was a remarkably clear summer night, and the stars twinkled brightly above the men. The moon, which rose slowly in the east, was nearly full, and a light breeze stirred the air, making for a good night's sleep. They could hear lonely howling sounds from off in the distance, but the noise didn't keep the men from sleeping soundly. During the middle of the night, a pack of wild dogs wandered toward the camp. They had picked up the scent of the raw fish heads and entrails that were lying on the ground. The pack came into the camp, prowled around the men, and started growling.

The men awoke immediately, looked around for their rifles, and realized they were out of reach. The dogs surrounded the men, bared their teeth, and growled. Two of the dogs lurched toward the men and snapped their jaws, ready to attack. Charlie grabbed a chunk of burning wood from the campfire and waved it wildly in front the fierce dogs, which forced them back for a brief time. Joker hurled a large stone and hit one. Frank reached for his rifle as a dog lunged toward him. Brady stood and hit the dog on its back with his work boot, and the animal turned, jumped on him, and knocked him down. His powerful jaws snapped at Brady's shoulder and neck area, ripping his clothes and tearing some skin on his shoulder. Jim and Joker yelled at the raging animals and waved their arms wildly as they moved toward their rifles. The dogs approached the two men slowly, their lips curled up. Snarling sounds came from deep inside their throats. The men grabbed their rifles and quickly fired at the dogs. The dogs yelped as the bullets found their marks. The campsite was chaotic.

In the melee, one dog had sunk his teeth deep into Charlie's left thigh, torn open the skin, and exposed the underlying muscle. A piece of flesh was hanging, and blood was spewing out. Joker hit the dog with the butt of his rifle and knocked it off of his friend; he then fired and killed the attacking animal. Frank and Jim fired upon the remaining dogs, and they all left, running and yelping.

The attack ended. It was a quiet night once again. The campfire crackled, and sparks floated skyward. The men were dazed. Had they shared some freakish common nightmare or had this really happened? Brady and Charlie held their hands against their wounds as the blood ran over their fingers and soaked into their clothing. Frank brought himself back to reality and walked over to Charlie first. Joker was already tending to him, putting a tourniquet above the open wound on his leg. Jim went to his saddlebag and grabbed cloths and medicine. Charlie was hurt the worst and needed the most immediate attention. Frank went to see Brady's injury, which was bad enough that it needed to be treated.

Frank spoke, "How are you doing, Brady?

"Not so bad, considering how much worse it could've been."

"I've got some whiskey I could pour on your shoulder if you think you could stand it. It might keep your wound from getting infected."

"Go ahead."

Frank opened the bottle and splashed whiskey on Brady. Brady winced when the alcohol hit his open flesh. "Yeow! Damnation!" he hollered. "That whiskey bites hard!"

Frank proceeded to apply a cloth, which he had folded to make a thick patch, onto the ragged wound. He then took a long strip of cloth and secured the patch by wrapping it around under Brady's arm a couple of times and tying a knot. Jim threw few more dried branches on the fire, and the men all sat down around it and watched the flames flutter upward as they engulfed the wood. There wasn't much conversation for a while—it was like the calm after a storm.

Finally Frank spoke up. "Men, do you think you can go on?"

Charlie spoke first, "I don't think I can. I need to see a doctor, and I probably need someone to go along with me."

"I'll go with you, Charlie," Joker offered. "I say we should start out first thing in the morning."

"I agree," replied Charlie.

"What about you, Brady?"

"I'm not going back now. I want to go on. I've come too far to quit."

Frank sat quietly for a few minutes and looked at the men and said, "Tonight has taken its toll on us, but it shouldn't keep us from going on.

We told our families we'd find new farmland to live on, and by golly we're goin' to do it!" Brady and Jim nodded in agreement. The scouts calmed themselves down as they sat and talked and discussed the future. One by one they went to their bedrolls with the hope of catching a few more winks of sleep before sunrise.

★ ★ ★ ★ ★ ★ ★ ★ ★ ★ ★ ★ ★ ★ ★ ★ ★ ★ ★

Morning seemed to come earlier than usual the next day due to their lack of sleep. Joker was the first to rise up out of his bedroll. He stirred the live ashes remaining in the campfire and threw in some dried branches. Within minutes, the flames rose up and lapped the sides of the coffee pot. All except Charlie were now up and moving about.

Joker said, "What do you think, boys, wasn't that an exciting night?"

"You call a wild dog attack exciting?" remarked Brady. "Count me out for another night like that. I couldn't go to sleep thinking that some wild animal would sneak up on me. "Ow, my left arm isn't working too well this morning," he said as he tried to move his arm around.

The men had their morning coffee with some biscuits and jerky, then broke camp. Joker helped Charlie with his horse, saddle, and bedroll, and then helped him onto the horse. The men all shook hands and wished each other well then went their separate ways. Joker and Charlie headed south, back to Madison. Frank, Jim, and Brady headed north toward Vernon, bent on finding some farmland. They passed through Vernon, then followed a dirt road westward toward Seymour, a span of about fifteen miles. The day was a normal, hot summer day without danger or hardship. After having been in the saddle for close to three hours, the men stopped to rest and have a bite of lunch. They rested for about an hour under the shade of a huge oak tree growing along the side of a cemetery. The cemetery was across the road from a small church called The Country Blessings Church, which was located in the corner of a cornfield.

Jim commented, "Do you suppose there's any corn over there ready to eat?"

Frank said, "What do you think? Should we go see?"

Brady said, "I'm staying right here. You two go if you want."

Frank and Jim looked at each other, grinned, and started getting up off of the ground at the same time.

They walked over to the field, checked a few ears, and simultaneously began tearing ears off the stalks until each of them had half a dozen ears in his arms.

"We'd best not shuck this corn here in front of the church," Frank said. "That just doesn't seem right. Let's put them in our saddlebags and ride on out for a while. They'll sure taste good for a meal later today."

Once more the men mounted up and continued onward. They hadn't ridden far—about a quarter mile—when they came upon a small cabin with a cross fastened over the front door. A middle-aged man with white hair and beard was working out in front of his house, hacking at the weeds around his hitching post with a hoe. He stopped his work and waved as the men approached his place. He called out, "Stop and visit a while. Have a cool drink with me."

The three scouts pulled up and greeted the stranger. They hadn't planned to stop this soon, but it seemed as if the old fellow needed to talk. The old man was stooped over and held his back as he shuffled to the bench beside a beautiful grape arbor. He motioned for the men to come over to him.

"How are you doing, old man?" Frank asked.

"Guess I'm doing fair. I live here by myself. My wife died last year and, you know, it's hard to get along without her."

"I'm sorry, but why are you still here living alone? Don't you have family to live with somewhere?"

"Yes, I do. My son and his wife moved to Louisville. My daughter went to Cleveland, Ohio, to work as a school teacher. My other three children are married and living far away from me."

Brady asked him, "So, why don't you go live close to one of them?"

The old man replied, "I can't leave. I still work for a living. I am the minister of that little church that you rode past as you came this way. That patch of corn between the church and here belongs to the church congregation. We use the corn to raise money to keep our church building in repair."

The three scouts glanced at each other as pangs of guilt hit them when they realized they had taken from the church.

"How does that work? Do you sell the corn?" Jim asked.

"Yes. We pick it when it's ready and bundle up the good ears. There will be a county fun day coming up in about ten days, so we'll take the roasting ears over there. The men from the church will build a big fire and cook the corn in a large kettle then serve it on a tin plate with fresh butter. Everyone for miles around will come to enjoy the food and play games."

"How much would a dozen ears of corn make for your church?" Brady asked.

"We get five cents for each ear," the old man told him. "Say, why don't you fellows stay the day with me and you can bunk here tonight? I haven't had visitors for a long time."

"Oh, I don't know," said Frank as he turned toward the other two. Jim and Brady looked at each other and shrugged their shoulders then nodded their heads yes. Frank introduced himself and the other two and asked, "Do you have a name we can call you, preacher man?"

"I'm Preacher O'Reilly. Good to meet you gentlemen."

The four men sat and told tales all afternoon. The preacher told about marriages he had performed and all the sweet little ladies who brought him special food as they tried to impress him with their cooking talents, especially after he lost his wife. "I practically have my own harem," he joked. The men rolled with laughter as they listened to the preacher.

The sun was sinking in the western sky and all the men were getting hungry. The preacher said, "Would you young men like to have some of the church roasting ears tonight? I've got a big pot we can use if one of you can make us a campfire. There may be enough ripe ears in the patch next to my yard a couple of you could fetch for us. I've got a few tomato plants behind my house. I'll go pick a few ripe tomatoes for us to eat with our meal."

"That's mighty nice of you, preacher," Frank told him. "We didn't expect you to feed us tonight."

"It would be my pleasure. You fellas can tell me all about your families and what you plan to do."

They all agreed to stay the night. Brady said, "I'll help with the campfire and Frank, you and Jim can get the corn. Before you leave to pick, I've got a good story to tell. There was a farmer who raised a field of corn every year. Every year the raccoons would get into the field and get the ripe corn from the outside rows. When a friend, who wasn't too smart, came by one day, the farmer told him how he always lost the 'outside' corn to the pesky varmints. The friend said, 'That's easy to figure out, just don't plant any corn on the outside rows.'"

The old preacher man slapped his thigh, leaned backwards and hollered, "God bless me, that's the best story I've heard in years!" And he laughed until his eyes squinted and tears rolled down his face. Frank and Jim laughed at the joke, but they laughed even harder as they watched the preacher enjoying himself. Finally, the men went about gathering corn. It was soon cooked, and they enjoyed the delicious repast. They visited together until long after sundown before they decided it was time to bed down.

★ ★ ★ ★ ★ ★ ★ ★ ★ ★ ★ ★ ★ ★ ★ ★ ★ ★ ★

The men awoke a little after daybreak. They went about readying their horses for the day's ride by giving them water and grain and placing the blankets and saddles on them. The old preacher stepped outside and hollered, "I've got a big pot of hot coffee ready for you. Come on inside and have some hot mush with me before you move on."

The men hitched the horses and went inside the cabin. They all sat around the preacher's kitchen table with their cups of coffee and their bowls of cornmeal mush. The preacher had put a bowl of jam on the table to share with his new friends.

Frank looked at the old man and said, "Preacher man, you've been mighty kind to us. We were complete strangers, and yet you were kind and trusting of us. We've shared a piece of our lives with you, and you've shared with us. We'll always remember you. But there's something we must tell you before we leave. We haven't been totally honest with you. Yesterday, before we rode up to your place here, we took a dozen ears from the church's corn patch. The three of us talked about this, and we would like to give you a donation for the church. We regret that we stole the corn." Each of the men placed one dollar on the kitchen table. The preacher replied, "You know, that's not the first time someone has helped themselves to some ripe corn from our little corn patch, and it probably won't be the last. God always provides for his church, and I'll be glad to put your money in the church fund. You men have been a blessing to me at a time when I felt an overpowering loneliness. I'll carry the memories of the past day with you fellows for the rest of my life."

The three scouts shook hands with the preacher when they left his home. They mounted their horses. Brady said, "Thank you, Preacher O'Reilly. The past hours that we've spent with you rested our bodies and renewed our spirits. We'll always remember you."

"Don't take any chances," warned the preacher. "God bless all of you on your journey."

CHAPTER ELEVEN
CHARLIE AND JOKER

Traveling on horseback proved very difficult for Charlie. It wasn't that he couldn't ride, but the jarring rhythm of the horse trotting along the road caused sharp pains to shoot from his wounded thigh. It was a long ride to reach Oak Ridge, but that was his goal. Joker had wrapped his thigh really well that morning and had made sort of a sling for his leg. The sling looped around the saddle horn and held his leg out in front of him. He would have to rest when they reach Madison. The events of the preceding night were still preying on his mind—and Joker's too—consequently, they road along in silence for some time.

Joker suddenly spoke up, "Charlie, old buddy, how are you getting along?"

"Not too bad, considering that I've got this bum leg."

"My friend, you'll be back on both legs before you know it."

"Yeah, well I need to heal as quickly as I can so I can dance at my wedding. I'm going to ask Rosalee to marry me."

"Can't say that I am surprised. You two were sparkin' pretty good back there in Oak Ridge. You seem to be made for each other."

"Joker, I want you to be my best man."

"No kiddin'! It'd be my pleasure. I ain't ever been a best man before." Joker laughed.

The men arrived in Harrison in time to eat lunch. Joker helped Charlie off of his horse and into a café they found on the main street. Charlie struggled as he tried to walk normally, but the look on his face reflected his pain. The people who were eating in the café couldn't help but notice his injury. One stooped-over, old man watched the two men as they came in and sat down. Joker and Charlie ordered their meal and chatted as they waited for it to be brought to them. Charlie propped his hurt leg on the empty chair next to their table.

The old man spoke up, "It looks like you got yourself a bum leg, young man. What happened?"

Charlie and Joker looked at each other and shook their heads. The memories of the past night rushed into their minds.

"It's quite a story. One you've probably never heard before," replied Charlie.

"Go ahead and try me; I like a good story." As Charlie began telling what happened, several others in the café turned their attention to the conversation. Charlie told his side of the story, and Joker added in tidbits of his own. The café became quiet as the story unfolded. Some of the listeners gasped as they heard the details.

"You lived through a wild dog attack. You're very lucky men to be here today. We've heard that wild animals are out there, and some farmers have lost chickens and lambs recently. It looks like maybe you and your friends took care of the problem. Tell you what ... I'll buy your lunch today."

"That's not necessary," Charlie said.

"No, I want to. You helped out the people who live around here," he stated. About that time, the waitress brought them their food.

"Here you are, enjoy your meal. I'll have a piece of apple pie for both of you when you are ready, compliments of the owner." The two men accepted the kindnesses offered to them. When they finished their meal, they asked the people in the café if there was a doctor who might be able to look after Charlie's wound. They received a name, Dr. Hawkins, and directions to his office. They left immediately to find him.

Joker helped Charlie onto his horse, and the two men rode off to see the doctor. His office was just a short ride to the end of the main street, and was situated right across from the livery stable. A wooden shingle hung over the doorway of the office: Dr. Jacob Hawkins. The two dismounted. With help from Joker, Charlie struggled up the wooden steps and they knocked on the office door. A middle-aged man with a dark, but graying hair and mustache, opened the door. He wore his glasses low on the bridge of his nose. His britches hung loosely from his waist, and the sleeves of the checkered shirt he wore were rolled midway up his forearm. He had bushy eyebrows and soft brown eyes that reflected caring and patience.

"Afternoon, gentlemen, how can I help you?" the doctor asked and then he noticed Charlie's bum leg. "Come on inside and I'll take a look at that leg of yours."

As Charlie lay on the examining table, Doc Hawkins had a good look at his leg. It was the first time Charlie had actually been hurt badly enough to qualify being flat on his back on a doctor's table. He had grown up like other boys, enduring skinned knees, knife cuts, and bee stings, and he had had his share of colds and fevers during the cold winters. He observed the doctor's certificate hanging, somewhat tilted, over his desk, which sat next to the only window in the room. Pens and papers were strewn across the desk along with a couple stacks of what he supposed to be medical books. Charlie's attention was quickly drawn away from the desk when the doctor pressed painfully on his thigh as he assessed the size and depth of the wound.

Charlie let out a moan. "Easy doc," he urged.

"Charlie, I'm going to have to sew you back together. It'll be painful. To do this, I'm going to have to use chloroform to put you to sleep," the doctor said. "Have you ever been put to sleep?"

"No, I sure haven't."

"Here's what'll happen. I'll just put a cloth with some chloroform on it over your face, and after a couple breaths you won't feel anything. Then, when you wake up, it'll be all over. Do you agree?"

"Yeah, I guess so. Joker, I'm countin' on you to see that the doctor sews me up nice and purdy."

"Don't you worry, pal. I'll watch every stitch. I might even have him stitch a dog's paw pattern on that bum leg of yours," Joker told him as he laughed. "It'll look just like grandma's counted cross-stitch pillow."

"Thanks a lot. That's just what I've always wanted," he replied. Joker laughed and patted Charlie on the shoulder.

The doctor gave Charlie the chloroform and went work cleaning the tear on his leg and stitching him back together. While Dr. Hawkins worked, Joker told him about the dog attack. Doc Hawkins finished dressing the wound. Charlie was still asleep, so Joker and Doc went over to the little table in the office.

"How long have you been doctorin' here in Madison?" Joker asked.

"Oh, I guess about fifteen years or so. My wife and I came here from Columbus, Ohio. She didn't want to leave her parents and three sisters as their family was very close. I finally convinced her to come west with me. We got as far as Madison and decided to stay here and rest a week and we ended up staying."

"What made you decided to stay here?"

"The people were so darn friendly, and I was the only doctor in fifty miles. They put us up in a boarding house until we could find a place to live. About that time my wife got sick and I discovered that she was in the family way. We really couldn't travel with her in that condition. So, here we are."

"I guess it was fate, right?"

"I guess it was. We like it here; couldn't imagine livin' anywhere else now."

Charlie began to come around and started moving on the table. The doctor went over to check on him to be sure that he didn't fall. Charlie was naturally groggy and wasn't able to speak much.

The doctor asked Joker, "Where do you plan to spend the night?"

Joker replied, "I don't have plans as of yet. What do you suggest?"

"I have another room here in the back of the office. There's only one bed, but you're welcome to stay the night if you want."

"Yeah, that would work for me. When Charlie wakes up I'll check with him, but I don't think he'll refuse. He needs to rest. He can have the bed and I'll use my bedroll."

When Charlie awoke he agreed to spend the night in the back room. Dr. Hawkins instructed Charlie, "Stay off of your leg until the soreness and swelling lessen. I don't advise you to sleep out in the night air because we don't want you to take a chance of getting sick."

Joker brought their bedrolls and saddlebags into the building then proceeded to take their horses across the street to the livery stable. Doc Hawkins helped Charlie into the back room where he was quite satisfied to stay. He hated to admit it, but he was still groggy from the chloroform, and his leg throbbed.

Joker spent the afternoon walking down the main street and browsing in a few of the shops. As the day faded toward evening, Joker went to eat his evening meal. He brought a bowl of stew and two slices of bread and butter back to Charlie. Charlie roused himself enough to eat his meal and drink some water, but he soon went back to sleep. Joker rolled out his bedroll on the rug that lay alongside the bed. He then went outside and sat on the porch to watch the activity along the street. It was a clear, starry evening with a soft breeze that blew away the heat of the day. As he sat there he realized that the two of them would most likely need to stay a few more days until Charlie healed enough to be able to ride.

Three horsemen disturbed the peace of the night as they galloped down the street, waving their hats in the air and howling. It seemed obvious that they had spent time in the saloon. As soon as they passed by, two more men on horseback came along at a fast pace, as if they were chasing the first three men. The horses kicked up swirls of road dirt. No doubt a fight would soon ensue. Joker had passed by the saloon earlier in the day and it had seemed like a lively place, filled with loud, boisterous talk and laughter. He wasn't a drinking man, so he hadn't gone inside. As he sat there observing life there in Madison, Joker wasn't sure what direction his life was going to take. Did he really want to leave his home back in Reeds Crossing and start all over? He sat there and pondered on the subject until he realized that the moon had moved far above his head. Its glow dimmed now and then whenever a few scattered clouds passed in front of it. The town had gone to sleep and the streets were empty of men and horses. The only sounds to be heard were the usual sounds of a summer night—a few barking dogs, hoot owls off in the distant trees, chirping crickets, and the yowling sounds of a cat fight. Joker got up and went inside to the doctor's back room to retire for the night.

Both men were awakened the next morning when Doc Hawkins

slammed the door as he entered his office. Joker sat up quickly and looked at Charlie. Charlie's eyes were wide open. "Mornin'," he said. "I made it through the night! Slept like a baby." He laughed. He sat up, put his legs over the side of the bed, grunted, and looked down at the bandage. "Old feller," he said to his leg, "I ain't done with you yet. We've got a lot to do here in this lifetime."

Joker got up and rolled up his bed. "You take it easy here and I'll see if I can rustle up something for us to eat this morning."

Doc Hawkins entered the room about that time. "How's the leg doing this mornin'?" he asked Charlie.

"Well, I haven't tried to walk this mornin' but it feels mighty sore."

"You probably should walk with a crutch for a few days before you try to put all of your weight on it," Doc told him. "I've got one somewhere here that you can use. I'll check the wound later this afternoon to see how the stitches are holding. You just keep your leg up most of today and rest. You can stay here for now." The doctor went back to the front office.

Joker went back to the same place for breakfast that he had eaten at the day before. He ate a plate of eggs and fried potatoes and had a big mug of coffee, and then he ordered the same to take back to Charlie.

When Joker entered Charlie's room with the food he said, "Best that you get better soon 'cause I'm not gonna keep being your nursemaid." And he laughed.

Charlie retorted, "If I was to get me a nursemaid *she* would be a *female*, not an ugly coot like you!"

"Glad we got that straight. That pretty gal, Rosalee, would fill the bill, wouldn't she?" Both men laughed. They had been buddies for several years and they knew each other well.

"I can't wait to see that gal and set a wedding date. My future plan is to be with her," Charlie admitted.

Charlie and Joker spent five days in Madison before Dr. Hawkins decided that Charlie was healed enough to ride.

CHAPTER TWELVE

OAK RIDGE REUNION

Joker was glad to be leaving Madison. He had walked the streets, visited with strangers, watched young adults acting like fools, and listened to old folks talk about the good old days. He'd had so much time on his hands that he'd made an acquaintance with and old fellow who lived in a small, older home just past the livery. The old fellow, called Guff, spent most of every day sitting in a chair out in front of his house whittling, and he had become an expert whittler. Joker had become so interested in whittling that he'd bought a knife with a sharp, pointed blade and started learning the craft from the old fellow. This was an art that he planned to continue.

As Joker and Charlie were securing their saddles and bedrolls on their horses, Charlie remarked that he wanted to get a gift for Rosalee. Joker said, "I made friends with an old man who whittles. Let's go see him before we leave town. He might have something you'd like to buy."

"Okay, I'll take a look. Let's go right away."

The men rode over to see the Guff. "Mornin'," Joker said. We're ready to leave town, and my friend here would like to see some of the things you have made."

"Sure thing. Come inside. I've got a few things to show you that you might like."

Charlie went to the table to look. He saw a small horse, a dog, some birds, and some boxes—boxes of all sizes. The carvings on the boxes were made in fine detail. Charlie picked up each item and examined it carefully. He saw one box that struck him as one that would appeal to Rosalee. He asked the old man, "Would you sell me this box with the flower carved on it?"

"If you care to buy it, its price is one dollar and fifty cents."

"That seems a little high but, since it's for a special lady, I'll pay your price." Charlie took the box and shook the old whittler's hand.

"Let me wrap the box in a paper for you to protect it," the old man offered.

"That's a good idea," Charlie replied.

The old whittler took the box into the next room where his wife was busy working. He soon returned and handed Charlie the box, which had been wrapped in sturdy brown paper.

"Now that looks real nice," Charlie remarked. He shook the whittler's hand and thanked him.

The two men went out to where they had left their horses, and Charlie carefully put the wrapped box in his saddlebag. The men got on their horses and rode out of town. It had been a week since the two men had crossed the Ohio River into Indiana, and now they were about to cross back over into Kentucky. The Ohio River had settled down. It was no longer the raging river it had been only ten days before. Charlie and Joker had no problem getting to the ferry, boarding, and crossing over. Even though Charlie's leg was weak, he was able to walk now without a crutch and to mount and ride his horse. Knowing that he would soon be back to Oak Ridge, he could hardly contain his desire to see Rosalee once more.

Joker asked Charlie, "Are you going to be able to ride all the way to Oak Ridge?"

"A team of wild horses wouldn't stop me." Charlie laughed and said, "I would go to Oak Ridge if I had to walk from here."

"Buddy, you've got it bad!"

"I know Rosalee is the woman for me. I knew from that first day I saw her in the café. I'm planning to give her the box I bought when I'm with her tonight."

The men rode at a steady pace following the road eastward. It seemed like nothing had changed from the previous week. By the time that they had ridden an hour or better, Charlie's bad leg started to pound. "Do you think we could pull over for a short time? My leg needs a rest from riding," he asked.

"Sure we can. There's a shady spot over on the right," said Joker.

The men dismounted and sat on the thick bluegrass, letting their horses graze beside them. Charlie leaned against a tree and stretched his bad leg out. He closed his eyes and drew in a big breath. He called to mind events that had happened since leaving Reeds Crossing. The ride through Lexington, the view of the Kentucky River from the bluff near Frankfort, the rainstorms, and crossing the wildly running Ohio River. These were only a part of his search for a new home. The image of Rosalee's face crossed his mind. He recalled walking her home after she finished working. He had held her close and kissed her. Just the thought of his arms around her body made his heart beat faster and his temperature rise. He felt a tingling desire in his groin as beads of perspiration appeared on his forehead and upper lip. A soft groan escaped his throat as he raised his arm and used his sleeve to wipe the sweat away.

Joker took a big drink from his canteen. "We might as well have a little jerky to eat while we're stopped here. I'll get it while you rest your leg."

"You know, Joker, we didn't make it all the way to claim a new farm, but we've sure had an adventure, haven't we?" Charlie said.

"You bet. The past two weeks gave us enough experiences to tell for a long time. It seems calm and peaceful today. I hope it lasts all the way to Oak Ridge."

"No doubt. Oak Ridge and Rosalee are my goals for today. Just thinking about her makes me sweat."

"You're hooked, partner. You'll be staying in Oak Ridge, and I'll be going home by myself."

"Yeah, you're probably right. I'll have to go home later and get my tools, clothes, and whatever else that I think I may need so I can make a living in Oak Ridge."

"Maybe I should hang around Oak Ridge and find a woman who will make me sweat."

"That sounds like a great idea. Rosalee might know somebody just right for you."

"No, I don't think so … not yet anyway. I'll do my own looking. Are you up to riding on now?" Joker asked.

"Let's go. I've rested enough. We don't have all day, and I've got a date to keep."

The two scouts got back on their horses and continued the ride toward Oak Ridge. They were of one mind in that they appreciated Kentucky more now than ever before. To them, Kentucky offered everything a man could want—plains and hills, rivers and cliffs, wild game for hunting, forests and cropland, pretty women and good horses. They rode only about another hour when they reached the edge of Oak Ridge. In five minutes they would be riding down the main street and tying their horses in front of the café. Charlie had a grin on his face that made Joker laugh.

"So, what do you find so funny?" asked Charlie

"That grin you're sportin' makes you look like a love-sick calf!"

"Does it now? Well, when I get a chance to be alone with Rosalee, I'll be a happy man."

It was suppertime and the café was getting quite busy. The two men were ready for a hot meal, so they hitched their horses, walked inside, and sat at an empty table. Charlie had told Rosalee when he last saw her that he didn't know when he would be back to see her—probably two or three weeks. He knew that she wouldn't be expecting to see him just days later. Charlie anxiously watched Rosalee and waited for the inevitable eye contact and recognition. Once again his heartbeat accelerated and tingling feelings rushed through his body. Rosalee carried two plates of food to the table next to Charlie and Joker, talked politely to the couple seated there, turned to go back to the kitchen and it happened—she saw Charlie and stopped in her tracks.

"Hello, Rosalee," Charlie said to her.

"Charlie! What are you doing here?"

"We're hungry. We want to eat," Charlie said, toying with her.

"Yes, but, you're supposed to be in Indiana." Suddenly she noticed that he had his leg stretched out in an unusual manner. "What's wrong with your leg?" she asked.

"Oh, it got hurt about a week ago, but it'll be all right. I'll tell you about it later. I'm glad to see you, Rosalee. Could I see you tonight after you finish work?"

"Of course you can. I'm so happy to see you. Let me bring you some coffee and tonight's special, if that's okay?"

"That's all right with me. How about you Joker?"

"That suits me just fine."

"I'll be a few minutes," she told them, and she went about her work.

★ ★ ★ ★ ★ ★ ★ ★ ★ ★ ★ ★ ★ ★ ★ ★ ★ ★ ★

Charlie and Joker had finished their meal and left the café. Charlie and Rosalee had talked and arranged to meet up later. The two men mounted their horses and rode toward the farm owned by Rosalee's parents. As they dismounted and tied their mounts outside the cabin, Rosalee's father appeared at the open door. "Hello, boys. What brings you here?" he asked.

Joker replied, "Charlie was injured back in Indiana, so we had to turn back and come home."

"Come inside, both of you, where you can rest."

"Thank you," Charlie responded. "It's been quite a ride today." Charlie hobbled up the steps and into the cabin. Being tired and sore from the day's ride, he leaned on his rifle, using it as a cane. The three men sat at the kitchen table where they were joined by Tess, Jeb's wife. Charlie began telling them everything that had happened since the scouts had left Oak Ridge—the flooding river, the delays, and the wild dog attack. Jeb and his wife could hardly believe the hardships the men had gone through in such a short amount of time. Charlie explained that the other three men had gone on with their search for farmland.

"You men are welcome to stay and rest here," Tess stated. "You can bunk in the barn again, if you don't mind. Rosalee will be happy to have you around."

Joker responded, "I plan to leave for my home town when morning comes. I need to visit Brady's wife and tell her that her husband will not be coming home when she expected. He was also injured, but he insisted on continuing his search."

The four continued to visit for a time, and soon Rosalee came through the front door. She was all smiles. Charlie jumped out of his chair and nearly lost his balance when he saw her.

"Careful, partner," Joker exclaimed. "Don't hurt your good leg," he teased.

Charlie wanted to embrace Rosalee and give her a kiss, but because her parents were right there, he didn't do it. He took both of her hands and looked into her eyes. His heart pounded as he felt his body become excited. He found it hard to breathe. "You are a beautiful sight to behold. I feel like I've been away a month and it has been only a short time. I've missed you so much," Charlie told her.

"And I've missed you. Will you be staying here with us?"

"I'll stay a short while, but I have to go back home and take care of some business. Come outside with me. I have something for you in my saddlebag." Rosalee looked at her parents for permission, and the two turned and went outside on the porch.

Charlie hobbled to his horse, felt inside his saddlebag, and took out the small, wrapped package and limped back to the porch where he had left her standing. "I hope you enjoy this small gift. It's not a lot, but it reminded me how lovely you are."

She opened the gift and saw the intricately carved box. She ran her fingers over the carved flowers and leaves and turned her face upward toward Charlie and said, "This is beautiful, Charlie." Before she could say another word, he took her in his arms and kissed her passionately. He then held her close to his chest and caressed her hair. "Rosalee, you are all I could think about since we've met. I want to spend the rest of my life with you." He lifted her head so that their faces were only inches apart and he looked deeply into her eyes. He continued, "Rosalee, will you marry me?"

"Oh, Charlie, I feel the same way about you. Yes, I'll marry you." The two embraced once more. Charlie took Rosalee by the hand and said, "Let's go inside and tell the news."

When Charlie and Rosalee walked back into the house, their beaming faced reflected that they were in love.

"Well, what is it?" Jeb remarked. "You look like two kids who got caught with their hands in the cookie jar."

"Daddy, Mamma, Charlie gave me this beautiful carved box, then he asked me to marry him. I said yes," Rosalee announced.

"Oh, my goodness," her mother exclaimed. "Our daughter is going to be married!" She stood and hugged Rosalee.

Charlie went over to Rosalee's father and the two men shook hands as Charlie asked, "Is it all right with you?"

"You know darn well it's all right. Welcome to the family."

★ ★ ★ ★ ★ ★ ★ ★ ★ ★ ★ ★ ★ ★ ★ ★ ★ ★ ★

After breakfast the next morning, Joker said his good-byes to Rosalee's family and Charlie. He said to Charlie, "You keep in touch with me, you hear?" Then he turned to Rosalie's family. "Best of luck to all of you."

"I'll let you know when the wedding will be," Charlie said as he gripped Charlie's hand.

They all said good-bye and wished Joker a good trip home. Joker left Oak Ridge hoping to reach Reeds Crossing soon.

CHAPTER THIRTEEN
TRAPPED

It was a nice, sunny morning with a cool breeze blowing in from the west. Big Al came into the kitchen after completing his chores and sat down at the kitchen table to eat his breakfast with the family. "This looks like a good day to go fishing," he stated. "I think I'll go dig some worms and see if I can catch us enough fish for supper tonight. How does that sound?"

Lucy replied, "Sounds good to me. I've been hungry for a fish fry. Did you remember that Anna and I are going into town this morning to sell our eggs and buy supplies?"

"Oh, that's right. I remember. When I catch enough fish, I'll come home and the boys and I can dress them. Matthew and Jack, I want you two to cut hay in the section east of the house. When we get the fish dressed, we'll work together and put the hay in the barn."

"Pa, why can't we come with you? We would catch more fish. We could cut hay tomorrow," Jack said.

"It's true, we would probably catch more fish, but I need you boys to cut hay. If it'd rain, you know wet hay is no good! We'll all go fishing together another time. I think that a little time alone will be good for me."

"All right, Pa, we'll go next time for sure," agreed Jack. "In another two weeks, we'll have most of the hay cut."

Lucy put the last two biscuits left from breakfast in a small bag and dropped some sugar cookies in with them. She handed them to Al and said, "If you're gone more than two hours you'll probably get a little hungry." She gave him a quick kiss on the cheek and ruffled his thinning hair.

Before leaving on his fishing trip, Al went out by the pigpen next to the cattle barn and dug worms from under a rotten log. In only ten minutes he had half a can of nice-sized worms for bait. It was now mid morning, and Big Al mounted his horse and was on his way to Muddy Creek, his fishing pole strapped to his saddle. He carried small box of extra hooks and the worm can in a pouch he'd hooked onto the saddle horn. He knew a spot on the river where there was a curve—actually a wash that went back to a grove of trees. He considered this to be his own special fishing spot. The creek water had splashed back on its bank and worn away the dirt, which made a separate pool of water, a perfect place for fish to feed. It was upstream from the road crossing nearly half a mile. He had checked this spot earlier in the week and thought that he saw some big fish swirling the water where cattails were growing.

Al arrived at the creek crossing and turned northward, riding along the little, crooked trail on the creek bank. It was a trail that he knew well for he had traveled it many times during the cold fall and winter months when he was out setting his beaver and fox traps. He stopped once when movement across the water caught his eye. He realized a family of otters was playing in the water, probably feasting on the minnows. *This river provides for all species, man and many other animals of creation*," he thought. He remembered a Bible verse that he learned as a child, "O Lord, how manifold are they works! In wisdom hast thou made them all; The earth is full of thy creatures."

He rode on up to his fishing hole, dismounted, and tied his horse to a sapling that was growing under a shade tree. There was plenty of grass for his horse to graze on. He walked over to the cattail pool and found a place with room to stand and a place for his worm can and fishing box. He got right to business. He baited his hook and threw the line out toward the river next to the cattails. A few minutes passed and his line began wiggling, then he felt the sudden jerk. A fish was definitely interested in the bait. He waited ever so patiently, and the next time the line jumped, he jerked it and set the hook in the fish's mouth. He flung the line up on the bank and hauled in a large catfish. He took his rope stringer and ran it through the gill and mouth of the fish, then removed the hook. "You're a mighty fine catfish," he said out loud. He fastened the rope to a tree root, which allowed the fish to be in the water but remain captive on the stringer. He baited the hook once more and continued fishing. After a little over an hour, he had landed three more fish—two more catfish and, lastly, one mid-sized wide-mouth bass. Big Al was standing on the sloped edge of the riverbank as he struggled to remove the hook from the bass. The grass and dirt were soft and a little slick. The bass gave a mighty wiggle, and he lost his footing. He fell sideways, tripped on a tree root, and fell backwards into a thicket of thorny bushes. As he struggled to his feet, he veered sideways and put his left foot down. Suddenly, there was a popping sound and pain shot through his foot and up his leg.

"What the hell!" he exclaimed. He fell back into the bushes and groaned in agony. The sharp teeth of the trap had pierced through his worn boots. When he looked down, he could see blood oozing out, staining the worn leather. There were deep scratches on his arms from the bushes, and some of the thorns had cut into his back and shoulders. The thorns scraped and poked him each time he struggled to get out of the bushes. He let go of his fishing pole and the bass on the hook flopped, struggling for air.

After some painful struggling, Big Al made his way onto the soft grass. He felt weakened, but he knew he had to try to free his foot from the agony of the trap. He sat up slowly as the pain in his ankle surged into his toes and up his leg. Every beat of his heart was matched with throbbing pain in his leg. *I should have let the boys come with me today,* he thought. *They would've been here to help me.* He grabbed each side of the trap and pulled with all his might. He managed to pry the trap open just a bit. The metal bit into the flesh of his hands, but he managed to pull his injured leg a short distance toward his body. Just as he got his foot halfway out, he lost his grip and the trap snapped again; lower this time, across his instep. "Oh, Lord Jesus," he yelled aloud. The new surge of pain pulsed through his foot. Why this had to happen he couldn't figure out. He fell back to the ground. The pain now roared like fiery pokers stuck into his foot. He lay still for a minute and gazed heavenward. He studied the cloud formations, perhaps waiting for God to send an angel. Realizing he was in a situation that he must get himself out of, he struggled to sit up. He worked once more to pry the trap open, and managed to pull his foot free. He had broken out into a full sweat from his exertion. Al's mind was full of questions: *"How will I get home? Should I try to get the fish rope off of the tree root and take my catch home? Can I get to my horse? Can I get onto my horse?*

★ ★ ★ ★ ★ ★ ★ ★ ★ ★ ★ ★ ★ ★ ★ ★ ★ ★ ★

Anna Marie and Lucy arrived in town and went directly to the mercantile store, each one carrying a basket of eggs to sell. Anna Marie was planning on buying some material to make a new dress to wear to the church picnic … maybe even a bonnet to match. Pat was toddling along beside her as they walked along the board walkway and into the store.

"Morning, ladies," spoke the store owner. "How may I help you today?"

"Morning," they both replied. Lucy spoke up, "We've brought in some fresh eggs that we'd like to trade in on our purchases today, if we could."

"All right," he said. "I'll count your eggs while you look around." He looked at Pat and said, "Good morning, young fellow, did you come to the store to get something?" Pat quickly scampered away from this stranger and went to his mother's side.

The two women examined the dry goods for quite some time. Lucy and Anna Marie each picked out the bolt of fabric that suited them, and then picked out matching ribbons and lace. Finally, they gathered their food staples. Pat had wandered around the store and spotted a small, carved pony sitting on a shelf. "Mama!" he exclaimed. "See, see!" Anna Marie walked over to see what he was looking at.

"What do you see?" she asked. He pointed to the pony. The miniature pony was running with its mane and tail flowing out. She picked it up and said, "Okay, I'll get you the pony." Pat clapped his hands and smiled a wide smile. "Here, you hold it," she said.

Anna Marie and Lucy completed their shopping. After settling their bills, they walked out of the mercantile and placed their purchases into the buggy. They decided to go into the boarding house for some hot tea or lemonade and maybe a roll before starting back home. They walked the short distance to the boarding house and went inside. They stayed a while longer than they had planned as they visited with other ladies they knew. The ladies enjoyed seeing Pat, and commented about how he was growing.

Lucy glanced at the clock on the mantle and said, "Goodness, look at the time. We had better start toward home. It's past noon already." Anna Marie agreed. They left their friends, walked outside, and crossed the street toward the buggy. Anna Marie lifted Pat up and placed him on the seat. Then she stepped up into the buggy. Lucy unhitched the horses, got on the buggy seat, and the three were on their way home.

"Do you think Al will have any luck with his fishing today?" Anna asked.

"That man can always catch fish when he decides to go fishing. He is the luckiest man. Why, he'll probably have a string of fish as long as his arm."

"Well, we haven't had any fish since before Brady left on his trip. I'm sure it would taste good." The ladies chatted as the horses trotted along the road. The summer day seemed to be hotter than usual, and the perspiration was running off of their brows. The horses had worked up quite a sweat as well. Suddenly, however, everything changed as a dark, ominous cloudbank approached from the west. The wind had picked up, causing the tree limbs to sway as gusts blew through the leaves.

"Do you suppose we're in for a storm?" Anna Marie asked Lucy.

"Well, that black cloud could very well be bringing heavy rain." Lucy snapped the reins on the horses' backs and they picked up their gait. "We'll get home as soon as we can."

★ ★ ★ ★ ★ ★ ★ ★ ★ ★ ★ ★ ★ ★ ★ ★ ★ ★ ★

Big Al scooted his body to where he had fastened his fish and untied the stringer. The big bass was lying beside him, the fishing hook still attached inside its mouth. The fish had little life left in its body, so Al had no problem removing the hook and adding the fish to the other fish on the stringer. He took hold of his fishing pole and used it as a support as he struggled to stand. With the stringer of fish in his right hand and the pole in his left hand, he headed toward his horse. Although his wounded foot was excruciatingly painful, he managed to limp along to where the horse stood. He untied the patient animal. He didn't know how he was going to mount his horse because his left foot, which was injured, was the foot that he normally put into the stirrup first before throwing his body into the saddle. He tied his catch to the saddle horn and walked around to the right side of his horse. As awkward as he felt, he attempted to mount by putting his good foot into the right stirrup so he could swing his left leg over the horse. Unused to this most peculiar procedure, his horse stepped sideways away from Al, who struggled with his balance and the moving horse. After a few more attempts, Al finally landed awkwardly in the saddle. His next thought was that he had to get home.

Al had lost track of time. As his horse walked slowly back down the trail toward the road, Al noticed a threatening, dominant black cloud in the western sky. It was rolling eastward at a fast clip, kicking up gusts of wind. A storm would be upon them soon. The wind suddenly increased; tree limbs rustled and bushes swayed. Big Al bent his head downward as he rode against the force of the upcoming storm. It was hard for him to protect his injured foot as the bushes along the side of the path kept swatting it. He checked the fish stringer to make sure it was still tied tightly to the saddle horn. After what seemed a long time, he arrived at the road and guided the horse toward home. He felt a few large drops of rain splash against his face and upper body. The strength of the wind had increased, blowing and gusting stronger. He was still a good thirty minutes from the protection of his barn and house.

★ ★ ★ ★ ★ ★ ★ ★ ★ ★ ★ ★ ★ ★ ★ ★ ★ ★ ★

The buggy was headed for home, and the two women were intently watching the bank of storm clouds rolling toward them. The wind was blowing the brims of their bonnets, and the dirt thrown up by the horse's hooves was hitting their faces and bodies. Pat started crying as he tried to cover his face with his hands. Anna Marie took him into her lap and turned his face against her body as any protective mother would do. It wasn't long until large raindrops pelted down on the threesome. The two horses pulling the buggy struggled against the wind and rain, heads bent down, and breaths coming heavily. As the buggy topped the last hill before the Bennings' home, Lucy and Anna saw a man riding a horse coming toward them in the distance, but they couldn't make out who it was through the heavy downpour. They saw the horseman ride into the lane that led to Lucy's home and then Lucy realized that it was her husband. Only a few moments later they followed the same path toward the barn. Lucy saw Big Al limping as he struggled to open the barn door to get inside. They all went inside the dry, musty barn at nearly the same time. Lucy dropped the reins, jumped off of the buggy, and headed for Big Al.

"You're limping and there's blood on your boot. What happened?" she asked him as she went to his side.

"I made a fool mistake and caught my foot in my own trap. I'll tell you more about it when we go inside the house. I did manage to bring home a small stringer of fish though. Anna Marie, you and the boy come on inside the house with us until this storm passes. We're all soaking wet as it is."

"Thank you," replied Anna Marie. "We'll gladly go inside with you. I don't care about riding home in this weather."

The four left the horses, buggy, and supplies where they were in the barn for the time being. Big Al made his way toward the house by steadying his weight as before with the fishing pole on his left side. Stubbornly, he carried the fish stringer with the other. They trudged their way to the back door. The rainwater dripped puddles on the kitchen floor as they entered. Anna Marie took Pat's jacket off him and hung it on a peg by the door to dry. Then she did the same with her own jacket. Lucy put water in the teakettle and set it on the cookstove to heat. They would all enjoy a hot cup of tea in a short time. All of the Bennings' children came into the kitchen to see what was going on. Al had sat down on a chair to take the boot off of his injured foot. He cringed with pain as he pulled on the boot. Everyone in the room gasped at his bloody foot injury.

"How did you get hurt?" Lucy asked.

"Oh, I stepped into my own animal trap," Al answered. "It was my own fault because I wasn't careful—with my traps *and* with where I was stepping! Sit down and I'll tell you all about it."

Lucy and Anna Marie had seated themselves at the kitchen table as Pat toddled around to see the other children. Big Al ran his fingers through his hair and stroked his beard as he began telling about his day. When he had finished, everyone was amazed that he had managed to retrieve his fish catch, walk to his horse, and make the ride home. The boys promised to go retrieve his box of extra hooks when the weather cleared.

"I'll tell you one thing," Big Al stated, "it sure was different trying to mount up from the right side of my horse. Chester did a do-si-do with me on his wrong side!" Everybody laughed, even Al. Lucy got busy and located some clean cloth strips to wrap around his foot after she cleaned it. The family settled down as the children went on their way to play games and the adults sat and drank their hot tea. The storm rumbled on, but it made no difference to the ones inside, warm and dry, and looking forward to a fish fry for supper.

CHAPTER FOURTEEN

SALOON STOP

Frank, Jim, and Brady rode westward, optimistic about their intended goal. They talked about the past hours they had spent with the preacher man and laughed again as they retold his stories. They all agreed they should come back past his home to visit him again. The men urged their horses onward until they came upon a large settlement. The signpost at the edge of town said Welcome to Seymour.

Frank remarked, "My father knew a man named George Seymour when he worked for a logger back in the mountains of eastern Kentucky. Pa would be gone two weeks at a time logging high in the mountains. The men would roll the big logs down the hills or hitch a couple of horses and use ropes to pull the logs to a clear spot. When they had a big stack of logs, they would roll them into the river and float them to the next large town. They didn't log any during the freezing cold winters, but they worked all the rest of the year, rain or shine. George and Pa worked two years together cutting trees with a crosscut saw. After the two years of hard work, both of the men decided to find another way to make a living. It was then my father bought the twenty-five acres that I lived on until I left home to make my own way. Pa never knew where George went after they parted ways."

"Did you want to try to find George?" Brady asked.

"I didn't really know the man. Heck, he could be anywhere in the country. I think we need to keep heading west. We've already lost valuable time on our trip."

"You're right. We'd best keep going."

The three men rode at a slow trot down the main street of Seymour. The town seemed prosperous and was bustling with activity. Even with the hot summer weather, many people were on the streets going in and out of the businesses. The finely dressed ladies walked under frilly parasols. The more ordinary women wore sunbonnets and long-sleeved dresses to protect themselves from the hot sun. The horses and buggies kept the dust stirred along the streets, and when the breeze picked up, dust swirls engulfed everybody and everything. The men noticed that there was a saloon at the end of the street—The Raccoon Saloon. Frank and Jim looked at each other, nodded their heads, and rode up to the hitching post in front of the saloon and dismounted.

"What do you say we go inside and wash some of the road dust out of our throats?" Frank said.

"That sounds like a great idea," Jim said. "I'm so thirsty I could drink a well dry. Are you with us, Brady?"

"You know, boys, it's not in my nature to drink. My Pa was a real teetotaler. He'd have disowned me if he found me in a saloon." However, Brady didn't want to stay outside alone, so he decided to join his friends. The three scouts went inside a few steps and looked around. They decided the saloon was aptly named. The inside was roughly decorated with raccoon skins, some of which were tacked to the walls, while others were draped on the backs of high-backed chairs placed around what appeared to be a card table. Deer heads with large antlers hung on the walls behind the bar. Old battered leather hats hung from some of the antlers, probably placed there by drunks; raccoon tails decorated others. There were a few raggedy-looking men standing at the bar drinking whiskey and an older woman talking with them. Her hair was piled high on her head, and straggly locks fell softly around her face. She wore thick makeup, no doubt in an effort to cover the years of a hard life. Her dark lavender dress fit quite snugly and had obviously been worn and laundered quite often; some of the lace around the neckline had come unstitched.

The three scouts walked up to the bar. Frank and Jim ordered beer, but Brady told them he would wait a while. Frank and Jim quickly emptied their glasses.

"Whew, that tasted mighty good," Jim remarked. "I think I'll have to have another. What do you two think?"

Frank answered, "I'll have another with you. Let's go sit down at one of the tables." Frank and Jim got their beers and Brady followed them to a table by the wall. The three men sat at the grimy table, which was covered with cigar stubs, tobacco pieces, and sticky beer spots. It was obvious that nothing had been cleaned since the past Saturday night. The men relaxed as they sat at the table and drank their beer. After a few minutes had passed, Brady looked toward the back of the room and saw the door open. Two younger women came into the room dressed in bright-colored, mid-calf-length dresses. They had flowers in their hair fastened on a raccoon tail, and they wore black garters trimmed in red lace. They walked toward the table where Brady and his friends were sitting. Brady avoided any eye contact with the women and looked down at the dirty table.

The woman dressed in red said, "I don't think I've see you men in here before. Where do you come from?"

Frank answered, "We're all from Kentucky."

"Is that so? Now why would three handsome men leave Kentucky and end up here in Indiana?" she said in her best beguiling voice.

Jim answered, "We're on a business trip."

The other woman wore a blue dress. The white sash at her waist was decorated with blue buttons. "Why don't you buy us a drink and tell us all about your business trip?" she said.

Frank replied, "Sure, I'll buy you both a drink. Pull up a chair and sit with us." The saloon women obliged, pulled up two more chairs, and sat down, one beside Frank and one beside Jim.

Brady stood up and said, "Excuse me, fellas. I need to go check our horses." As Brady started to leave, he turned and looked at the other two men and shook his head, as if say "don't do this." They just grinned back at him. The two women were moving closer to Frank and Jim, both using their feminine guiles. Brady went out the saloon doors and left the men on their own. Frank and Jim drank their second beers more slowly than the first ones. They sat and made some conversation with the saloon women. During this time, other men started drifting into the saloon and ordering beer and whiskey. One of the fellows was the local fiddler. He had a handlebar mustache and a bald head. He wore bright-colored suspenders to hold up his saggy britches. He tuned up his fiddle, started tapping his foot, and away he went with his music. He played tunes like "Oh! Susannah," "Turkey in the Straw," and "Yankee Doodle," and the business really livened up.

As all the partying was going on and the consumption of alcohol increased, the men started throwing their hats at the deer heads in an attempt to hook them onto an antler. At the start, the drunken men were betting drinks as who could land his hat in one try. Then as the competition increased, they were betting dollars. As is human nature, the men who were losing the contest were becoming angry and belligerent, and soon a brawl broke loose. One scruffy-looking man was getting right into the face of another rough-looking man, spouting "You're a cheat. You bumped my arm when I tossed my hat." "You're a liar," the other man fired back. The first man swung at the second, stumbled, and missed. The second man grabbed the first man and knocked him across the room. He hit Frank and Jim's table with his shoulder. Frank and Jim rescued their beers just in time. The bartender came barreling out from behind the bar. "That's it, fellas! Hat throwin's over for today! Stop your fighting or leave!"

★ ★ ★ ★ ★ ★ ★ ★ ★ ★ ★ ★ ★ ★ ★ ★ ★ ★

Brady led the three horses to the nearest watering trough, which was located in the shade of a large tree, and let them drink their fill. He didn't want to put the horses back on the street in the hot sun, so he walked them to a shady hitching post at the side of the saloon building. He looked at his pocket watch and decided to give the men some time before going to look for them. He was unsure as what to do during that time. He decided to find the local doctor to see if he could get a fresh bandage put on his shoulder. He walked down the boardwalk and asked a local businessman where to find the doctor's office. Within a few minutes he found the building. Standing under a sign that said Office of Dr. Murphy, M.D., he knocked on the door.

"Come on inside," Dr. Murphy said. "How may I help you?"

"I think you should look at a shoulder injury I have," Brady answered.

"Let's have you take off your shirt and I'll take a look at it." Brady removed his jacket and shirt, and the doctor saw the crude, bloody bandage wrapped around his shoulder.

"You must have quite an injury. Let me remove this old bandage. You need to tell me how this happened." When the old bandage was removed, Dr. Murphy saw blood and puss oozing out of the torn flesh. "It's a good thing you came by my office," he remarked. "Your shoulder is getting infected."

Brady told him all about the scouts and their encounter with the wild dogs. While Brady was talking the doc cleaned his wound. He put disinfectant and a clean bandage on it.

"Those dogs that attacked your camp, they weren't rabid, were they?"

"No. They were just mean dogs looking for food and a fight."

"I sure hope you're right. Young man, you take care of that shoulder and try not to break that wound open."

"Thanks, Doc. How much do I owe you?"

"I guess a dollar will do. Here, take some fresh bandages with you and this bottle of disinfectant."

"By the way, Doc, would you happen to have some paper and an envelope I could buy? I've been gone from home nearly four weeks, and I want to write my wife a letter."

"By golly, I sure do. There's some right here on my desk."

"Thanks again, Doc. You're a good man."

"Well, it's my job to help people. You and your friends take care of yourselves."

"We're sure going to try, if the wild animals will just leave us alone," Brady joked. They shook hands and Brady left. He walked out of the doctor's office and went to the post office where he wrote a letter to Anna Marie. When he was finished, he asked the postal agent, "When will the mail go to Kentucky?"

The agent replied, "It goes south every Friday without fail."

"That'll work just fine."

A few minutes later Brady was at the saloon doors. Somebody was playing an out-of-tune piano, and there was loud talking and laughter inside. He saw that another half dozen men had gone into the bar. He went inside and looked over to the table where Jim and Frank had been sitting, but they were no longer there. He spotted them dancing with the saloon girls who were providing laughter and amusement to all in the room. He stood there a few moments taking in the whole scene, the likes of which he had never seen before. He could tell from the way that Frank and Jim spoke and their sluggish movements that they were drunk. The people inside were singing a Kentucky folk song accompanied by someone playing the dulcimer. Jim looked up and saw Brady watching.

"Brady, ole pal, come on and join the party," Jim called out loudly. Several of the saloon customers paused to look at Brady. Brady ran his fingers through his hair and decided that he couldn't do too much at this time to stop the good time his friends were having.

"I'm not much for this kind of party, fellas. Why don't you come on out in a few minutes and we'll ride out of town?"

Frank picked up his beer from the table. "Brady, my friend, we'll stay just a little longer and then we'll be ready to move on. We're just havin' a little fun. I need to have one more dance with this little darlin'. Is that all right with you?"

"Yeah, I'll be waiting outside for both of you." The smoke and smell inside the saloon was overpowering to Brady so he turned and quickly went back outside and stood on the boardwalk. He thought, *Pa, you were right. Drinking and saloons are not for me.* Brady decided that he should retrieve the horses and bring them back to the saloon hitching post so when the men decide to come out, the horses would be ready and waiting for them. He crossed the street to sit on a bench out in front of the post office. He sat there, thinking about Frank and Jim, hoping they would come out soon and not end up in some brawl. Brady was disgusted. *What am I doing here? I'm sitting on a bench in front of the post office, waiting for my friends who are partying in a saloon. They don't have any business stopping for the afternoon to drink beer when we're supposed to be finding a new place to live. But, here I am in a strange town while time passes. I've come this far, and I can't and I won't quit now.* He thought of Charlie and Joker. *They must be back in Kentucky by now. What about Anna Marie and Pat? Are they all right? Of course they are,* he consoled himself, *Big Al and Lucy are looking out for them. We have been gone three and a half weeks already; one delay after another and we haven't gotten close to finding new farm ground.*

Brady saw the saloon doors push open and watched Frank and Jim come outside with the two women hanging on to them.

"You don't have to leave so soon do you?" cooed one of them. "We can have more fun if you come back inside. You could even stay all night if you want."

Frank replied in a slow, deliberate voice, "Sorry, pretty gal, my friends and I have to leave to do business west of here. I will say, though, that I've had a mighty fine time." Frank gave her a squeeze around the waist. She turned to Jim and said, "I suppose you're also goin' to leave us." Both saloon women hugged up to Jim. One stroked his stubble beard and said, "Sweet Jimmy, you want to stay with me, don't you?" It was obvious that Jim had had more than his share of liquor and didn't have much control over himself. Jim wrapped his strong arms around her and planted a big kiss on her lips.

Brady watched his friends in their drunken state and he wasn't impressed with their actions. He yelled across the street to them, "It's time you fellas came out of the saloon. We need to ride out of here."

"We're comin'!" yelled Frank.

"Good-bye girls. It's been a most entertain'n afternoon," Jim told them.

Frank and Jim released their hold on the saloon women. The women tried to get the men back into the saloon, but the two scouts resisted the offers, stumbled their way off of the saloon walk, and went to their horses. Brady got up from his chair and joined his friends. All three men proceeded to mount up and head out. Jim removed his hat and waved good-bye with it. They said very little to each other as they left the town of Seymour that afternoon.

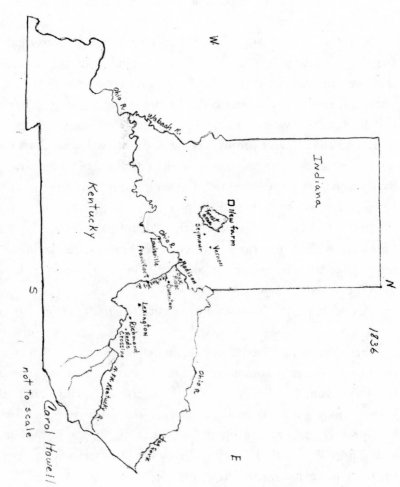

A Map of the Travels of the Scouts

not to scale

Carol Howell

1836

Indiana

Kentucky

Ohio R.

Wabash R.

New farm

Seymour

Vernon

Madison

Ohio R.

Louisville

Frankfort

Lexington

Richmond

Reeds Crossing

N. Fk. Kentucky R.

Ohio

Red Fork

W

S

N

E

CHAPTER FIFTEEN
SUNDAY PICNIC

The past week had gone by fairly swiftly as Anna Marie had picked and prepared several batches of fresh vegetables from her garden. Lucy's two oldest boys had come over one day and helped her weed her garden. At that time she had found that her two rows of green beans were ready to harvest. She picked a small basket of beans that she cooked with some pork—enough for three or four meals for her and Pat. Pat came into the garden with her one day when she decided to try to find some beets big enough to cook. One by one, she pulled the beets and gave them to Pat. He did his toddler best to brush the dirt from them before he put them in the basket. Giggling, he ended up getting dirt all over his hands and face. Suddenly, he bent down and grabbed two handfuls of dirt. With a defiant look at Anna, he tossed the dirt high in the air and then laughed. Anna's first instinct was to scold him, but then she ended up laughing with him. She thought, *They say a little dirt is good for everyone.* Pat had such a good time playing in the garden that day.

Sunday arrived, and not too soon for Anna Marie. She had been looking forward to getting off the farm and being with her friends. It was the church picnic day and it looked like a perfect, sunny day. She had hitched Mandy to the buggy and completed the other chores early that morning before Pat work up. She picked up her picnic basket, which held the chocolate cake and hard-boiled eggs she had prepared the day before. Pat was toddling around in the kitchen while she was putting on her bonnet. They both walked out of the cabin.

"All right, little fellow, let's put you in the buggy. We're going to church, and then we'll have a picnic. You'll be able to play with your friends. Won't that be fun?" Anna Marie had learned to tie a tea towel around Pat and the wagon seat to keep him from being bounced out.

He'd nearly fallen off of the seat once when she ran over a hole at the edge of the road.

Pat nodded his head and said, "Go, Mama, go."

"Yes, we're ready to go," Anna Marie replied when they were both comfortably seated and the food was safely stored. She flipped the reins on Mandy's back. "Giddy up, Mandy," she said. They trotted down the lane and onto the road leading to town. As they went past Big Al and Lucy's place, she saw all of their family getting into their two buckboard wagons. Anna thought about how much food Lucy had to prepare every day for such a large family. She knew the work involved cooking for two or three. Could she imagine cooking for eight or ten people every day? Not yet, she couldn't. She waved heartily at all of the Bennings, and they waved and hollered back to her. Anna Marie and Pat continued on down the road. She felt safe with her friends following a short distance behind. The rhythmic clippity-clop, clippity-clop of the horse's hooves was soothing to her ears as the buggy moved gingerly down the dirt road. Pat made talking attempts and pointed at things as they rode along. Anna Marie was amused with his jabber, but at the same time it filled her with joy. It seemed but a short while before she was pulling up to the churchyard. She hitched the horse to a post in the shade of a large, old oak tree and lifted Pat out of the buggy onto the ground. Several other buggies had already arrived, and families were gathered in the shade of the trees. No doubt they were talking about the past week before going in for the Sunday morning service. The children were running around, and mothers were calling for them to not to get dirty. It was a typical setting of families and friends who were gathered together.

"Good morning, Anna Marie," the ladies called out. Pat hadn't been with other children his age very many times, and he was excited.

"Good morning," she replied back. "It's good to see all of you."

Pricilla walked over to Anna Marie and they shared a hug. "It's so good to see you today. How are you doing? Are you feeling all right?"

"Yes, of course, I'm doing fine. I keep busy caring for Pat, along with the chickens and garden. How are you?"

"I have good news. Jeremiah and I are expecting our first child."

Anna Marie hugged Pricilla. "That's wonderful. I'm so happy for you. I hope you haven't been too sick."

"No, I haven't. Anna, are you planning to come to the ladies quilting this Wednesday?"

"Yes, I think I could. You'll have to tell me later what I should bring. I don't have much in my sewing basket."

"Don't worry a thing about it. With what the other ladies and I have, we'll have enough to share. Bring Pat and a smile, that's all you need. We'll sew and talk the afternoon away."

The church bell began to ring. Anna said,"We'll talk more at the picnic." She took Pat by his hand and led him into church.

★ ★ ★ ★ ★ ★ ★ ★ ★ ★ ★ ★ ★ ★ ★ ★ ★ ★

When the church service ended, the ladies went to their picnic baskets and quickly placed the food on the tables, which had been arranged at the back of the church, just inside the main door. Within moments, the preacher blessed the food and the hungry men and children filled their plates. Some took their food outside and sat on blankets while others, like the older women or women with young children, sat on a church pew inside where they visited and supervised the little ones.

Pricilla sat alongside Anna Marie. "Brady has been gone a while now," she observed. "When do you expect him home?"

"I'm looking for him to come home by the end of this week. He said he wouldn't be gone longer than four weeks, and he has been gone four weeks now."

"It must seem like a long time for you to be alone out there on your farm."

"Yes, it does. I have good neighbors, Lucy and Al, who watch out for me. Al and his boys come by and help when they can. Lucy and I come into town for supplies about once a week, so it's not really too bad. Now if he were to be gone for months, I wouldn't like that."

When people were finished eating, the women began gathering up their dishes. They were all distracted when they noticed someone riding up to the church. He dismounted and asked the men, "Is Anna Marie Patterson here today? I have word about her husband to tell to her."

"Why, yes, she's inside with the women and children."

Joker walked inside the church, removed his hat, and said, "Who is Anna Marie Patterson?"

She turned from her picnic basket and looked at him, wide-eyed and apprehensive. "I'm Anna Marie," she stated. "What do you want?"

"My name is Johnny Reed. I'm known as Joker. I was one of the scouts who rode with your husband, Brady. I came to tell you that he is still in Indiana. He was injured about ten days ago when a pack of wild dogs attacked our camp after dark."

Anna Marie grabbed the back of the pew tightly. She swooned a bit, as if to faint, and said to him, "Oh, no! Is he going to be all right?" Pricilla went to her and held her by the waist. The other women around heard the conversation and gasped at the news.

"Yes, he'll be all right. A dog bit into his shoulder. We dressed the wound, and he should heal just fine. Charlie was hurt worse in his thigh, so he and I headed back to Kentucky. He stayed up north in Oak Ridge with a lady friend and her family. The other two men, Frank and Jim, are still with Brady. They are going on to Indiana, still looking for new farmland."

"When do you think he'll be back?" she asked.

"I don't know. It'll be at least another couple weeks or more. They're still searching for the right place to settle. Try not to worry, ma'am. Brady is a tough man, and he can take care of himself."

"Would you like a plate of food? I'm sure you're hungry after your long ride."

"Yes, I would. I appreciate your offer," he replied.

Anna Marie quickly fixed his plate. Joker ate his food in a short time and got up to leave.

"I should be going. Thanks for the meal."

"Thank you. It was kind of you to stop by to tell me about my husband."

"It wasn't a problem for me 'cause I wanted to be sure to let you know what happened. I promise that he will return in good shape as soon as he can. If I can be of any help, please call on me." Joker placed his hat back on his head and walked outside. He waved good-bye to the rest of the church folks, remounted his horse, and rode on his way.

Anna Marie went through the motions of gathering her food basket, even though she felt weak in the knees. She said good-bye to her friends and walked to her buggy. Pricilla followed her.

"If you would like, you could come and stay at my home for a while," Pricilla told her.

"Thank you very much, but I should go on back to my home." She lifted Pat into his seat. "I'll see you at the quilting this Wednesday. Pat and I will be all right." The two friends hugged good-bye.

Lucy and Al came over to Anna's buggy as she was climbing into her seat. Al told her, "Now don't you fret none. That man of yours is a survivor, and I know he will take care of himself." Al and Lucy both invited Anna Marie and Pat to stop by their house on her way home. Anna turned down the offer. All she wanted was some time alone to think. She didn't need help or pity at this point.

"I'll do just fine," Anna replied. "Lucy, I'll go with you to the quilting on Wednesday. I'll come by about mid morning."

"Good. I'll expect you then. Remember to call on us if you need anything—anything at all."

"Thanks, I will. You two are my best friends."

Anna Marie tied Pat onto the buggy seat and took up the reins. The ride home carried with it a more somber tone for Anna Marie than the ride coming to church had. For Pat, it was a happy, fun day. Nothing had changed. He tried to say words as they trotted along the road, making some words up, which was amusing to Anna Marie. Her mind was twirling. Oh, how she longed for Brady's touch ... just to feel his strong arms holding her close and caressing her hair. Had she been a fool to agree to his wandering? A month ago it seemed all right. Today, it was not. Tears started to trickle down her face as she realized how very lonely she now felt. Two, three, maybe four more weeks until Brady would return. She felt her throat tighten as the tears now flooded over her cheeks and dripped onto the collar of her dress. She rubbed her eyes with the sleeve of her dress, and the buggy veered into a rut and bounced hard. She regained her focus and checked to make sure Pat was all right. He squealed a happy sound as he pointed at a squirrel running across the road in front of them and said, "Look, Mama, look." Anna Marie saw the smile on her little boy's face as she looked at him. She wrapped her arm around him and his joy eased her pain. Her sadness and tears withdrew deep inside of her and she smiled with her son.

"You and me, little man, we'll be all right. We'll wait for your daddy to come home," she said to him. Pat clapped his hands and said, "Daddy come home, Mama." Anna Marie clicked her tongue and said to their horse, "Take us home, Mandy."

★ ★ ★ ★ ★ ★ ★ ★ ★ ★ ★ ★ ★ ★ ★ ★ ★ ★ ★

The afternoon drifted into early twilight. Anna Marie and Pat walked out to the chicken house and shut the door, making sure that all the hens had roosted for the night. Pat called out, "Chickee, chickee."

"The chickens are roosted and going to sleep now," said his mother. "Let's go up on the porch and we'll watch the birds fly to their nests where they go to sleep. As Anna Marie and Pat went up the porch steps and she lifted him up, she noticed how much he was growing. He was certainly getting heavier. She suddenly realized how her midsection had grown with the child inside—she had to hold Pat high above her rounded belly.

She sat in the rocking chair and held Pat where he could look out toward the sun. "See the sun? The sun goes down over there just past the trees and we know it's time to rest. Everybody in the whole wide world can watch the sun go across the sky and, in the evening, watch it go down in the west. Your daddy has probably stopped to rest for the night. I think that he is watching the very same sunset that we are seeing right now. Isn't that wonderful?"

"Daddy see?" chattered Pat as he pointed.

"Yes, little boy, it makes the three of us closer together. Go to sleep now little one." Anna Marie held Pat and rocked him until darkness closed in and he was sound asleep. She stood up and carried her son inside, into the warmth and safety of their home.

CHAPTER SIXTEEN
THE QUILTING BEE

Today was Wednesday, the day of the quilting bee. It was quarter past eight in the morning, and Anna Marie was busy trying to organize herself for the day. She had made some molasses cookies the day before and this morning she made egg salad sandwiches, both which she would take for their lunch. She had already gathered items for her sewing basket and had taken it out to the buggy. Pat could sense that his mama was getting ready to leave, so he was staying very close to her. She sat down to rest a few minutes and said to Pat, "Come over here to see Mama." Pat climbed up on her lap and gave her a hug around the neck. "Would you like to go with me on a buggy ride today and see some friends?"

Pat nodded his head affirmatively.

"Well then, let me wash your hands and face and we will get into the buggy and go. We will go by and get Lucy to go with us."

Anna Marie and Lucy arrived for the quilting bee about an hour or so before lunchtime. Pricilla was hosting the gathering for the first time, and she was all aflutter, trying to do everything just right for her friends. All the women were full of chatter and hugs. Some of the women brought older children to help take care of the toddlers and to play games with them. It was a time when women could be away from the day-to-day wearisome work patterns of their lives on the farm and they could socialize and relax, yet they would make good use of their time together. Women had been making their own bed quilts for decades. Now, the quilt patterns in America were evolving into more than just random squares of fabric sewn together, and the women were discussing what pattern they wanted to use for the new quilt they were going to start today. The choices were varied— Log Cabin, Dresden Plate and many more.

Including Pricilla, there were eight women gathered together for the quilting bee. As soon as the ladies were all seated in the living room, the preacher's wife, Naomi, stood up and said, "Welcome, ladies to our quilting bee. It's so good to see all of you, especially our newest member, Anna Marie Patterson." With this unexpected introduction, Anna Marie blushed and smiled, then turned her head slightly to the side. Naomi continued, "Over the next few months we will make a quilt choosing a pattern, choosing colors, cutting the pieces, and sewing them all together. Yes, we will create a one-of-a-kind, original quilt. The best part of the experience is the weaving together of the threads of our lives as we share the pieces of our everyday living with each other. As we finish the quilt blocks and bind the quilt, we, ourselves, will be bound closer to each other. So, there you have it." She laughingly added, "I almost made a sermon out of a quilt talk, didn't I?" The women joined in the lighthearted laughter and humor.

The women took out the fabric they had brought, laying it out on the long table that had been set up in the large room. They grouped the materials according to color then stacked the colors together, matching and coordinating colors together. The business of the women was interrupted as Pricilla announced, "Come to the kitchen, ladies. Our lunch is ready." The children had already been gathered in and were lined up, eagerly looking at the banquet of food waiting on the large kitchen table. "Naomi, would you kindly offer thanks for this meal?" Naomi nodded her head and said, "Let us all join hands together." Anna Marie held Pat's hand as she smiled lovingly at him.

Naomi prayed, "Lord, we thank you for this food. Bless each one here as we take nourishment for our bodies and minds. Keep all of our families in your loving care. Amen."

Pricilla said, "Ladies, attend to your children's plates first and then the rest of us will fill our plates." Anna Marie took Pat by the hand and filled a small plate with food and sat him down where she would be sitting. Pat picked up the egg salad sandwich his mother had made and began eating. Anna Marie and the others all settled in to enjoy their meal, while stories and laughter filled the household.

There was one lady named Rebecca Lancaster, whom everyone called Becky. She was a little over five feet tall and quite plump. Her grey hair was pulled into a bun at the back of her head and secured with two fancy hair combs, one on each side of the bun. Becky had a jolly spirit about her. She had married a man who was a foot taller than she and he also had a happy attitude. They had two children, a tall son and a short daughter, mirror images of their parents. She was by nature a jolly gal who cared for everyone, and thereby always agreed with everyone. She wore a big grin on her round face, which was now weathered looking with age spots and wrinkles in the corners of her hazel eyes. A person could look at her eyes and see the beauty and kindness coming from them.

Becky was sitting in a rocking chair, giggling, and enjoying the day. Lucy asked Becky, "Do you have a story to tell us today?"

"Yes, I do," she replied in a high-pitched voice, "This is a true story!" And her body shook all over from her accelerated giggling. And then she began her story. "It was Saturday night and everyone in our family was to get a bath in the big tub. We kept it out on the closed-in porch. I bathed the two children first and got them upstairs to bed. My husband hadn't come home from checking a new baby calf in the pasture, so the children and I were home alone. It was dark, they were asleep, and I was enjoying a bath in peace and quiet. When I was finished, I dried myself with a bath towel and then I pulled on my nightie and started to go into the house. But the hook had come down and locked the door, so I was locked out. What was I to do?" Becky stopped telling her story as she was laughing so hard she could hardly breathe and her whole body was shaking. Like ripples going out in the water all the women began giggling with her.

Finally, she continued, "The windows were too high for a short person like me to open and get inside. I had to figure out a way to get inside. There was a woodpile next to a window, so I decided to crawl up on top of the logs, open the window, and go through into the house. But as I began climbing up the wooden logs, some of them began rolling and I almost lost my footing. I finally reached the window and open it. Just as I was going through, the logs rolled again and left me hanging there halfway in and halfway out. The wind had blown my nightie up when I was pulling myself into the house, and my bare bottom was sticking right out for anyone to see and I couldn't get my arms out to pull it down!'"

At this point at the telling of her story, all the women were laughing hard. Becky continued, "I was kicking my legs and sucking in my stomach—anything I could think of to try to wiggle myself into the house. I was about two-thirds of the way inside when my husband came home. He couldn't believe what he was seein'. He stood there on the porch and laughed until he cried. I yelled, 'Aren't you goin' to help me?' He didn't know whether to push or pull! He said, 'Wait a minute.' He put his shoulder against the door and knocked the lock off. He went inside, wrapped his big arms around me and pulled me through the window. It was sure good to have my feet down on the solid floor of the house."

The ladies laughed and laughed about Becky's story as they pictured her situation in their minds. They finished the noon meal and were ready to continue the afternoon with the task at hand, starting a new quilt. Pricilla and Anna Marie visited together during the afternoon while working on cutting out the quilt pieces.

Anna Marie asked Pricilla, "How have you been feeling lately?"

She replied, "I'm over most of the morning sickness. However, I do get a little dizzy from time to time."

"I understand," Anna said. "You need to be careful. You don't want to have a fall and risk losing your baby. I slipped once going down the porch steps when I was carrying Pat. I sat down hard on the top step, and it gave me a jolt, but luckily I was fine."

Pricilla quietly asked, "Anna, how are you really getting along with Brady being away for so long?"

Tears quickly filled Anna's eyes. "I haven't had any big problems, but I've been worried about Brady since I heard that he was injured. I haven't heard another word."

"I'm sure he'll come home as quickly as possible. After all, he has traveled a long way. You know, if he needed help, there are doctors in Indiana who would help him." Pricilla took Anna Marie's hand in hers and gave it a squeeze.

"You're right. I miss him so much, and I can't help worrying about him." Anna Marie dabbed her eyes with her kerchief. "You're a good friend, Pricilla."

The ladies worked diligently through the afternoon and made a good start on the new quilt. As they worked, they shared their lives, until it was time to gather their children and leave for their separate homes. They shared hugs and pleasant good-byes as they agreed to meet again in two weeks.

CHAPTER SEVENTEEN

THE BEAR

The scouts had about three hours of daylight left to ride that day. Brady had visited with a few local residents in Seymour while waiting for Frank and Jim to come out of the saloon. He had learned that there was a large forest area about fifteen miles west. They would have to ride another ten or fifteen miles through the forest to the other side to find prime farmland that was still available to claim.

The men stopped after about an hour and a half to rest their horses and themselves. Jim, feeling quite thirsty, drank half a canteen of water. As soon as it hit his stomach, he stepped away from his horse and puked up everything that he had drunk or eaten that day. He grabbed hold of the nearest tree, wiped his forehead, and let out a groan.

"Are you going to be all right?" Brady asked him.

Jim replied, "Lord, help me. I promise to never drink that much again the rest of my life. My whole body feels terrible."

"I hope that means that we won't be making any more saloon stops," Brady stated. "What about you, Frank?"

"I had enough to last me. I'm sorry we went in there, Brady; it's just that we were so hot and dry. We intended to have only one beer and be on our way. Those two saloon women were very persuasive. They sure showed us how to party. I've got to admit that I had a real good time."

The three men sat on the cool grass in the shade of a tree and rested a few minutes. Brady spoke, "You know, before I left Kentucky, I thought that two or three weeks would be plenty of time to go to Indiana and back. We've already been gone over three weeks, and we haven't made it one way, let alone back to Kentucky."

"You are so right," remarked Frank. "We lost most of a week because the Ohio River flooded."

"Because of that stop, Charlie got hooked!" Jim said laughingly.

"He's caught all right. That waitress gal has him wrapped around her little finger," Frank agreed.

"That wild dog attack wasn't good for us either," Jim added into the conversation.

"How is your shoulder doing?" Frank asked Brady.

"It doesn't feel bad right now. You know, I went to see a doctor while you guys were in the saloon enjoying yourself. He told me the wound is infected. He cleaned it good and put a new bandage on it for me."

"You were lucky that the dog didn't grab you by the throat or you wouldn't be here today," Frank stated.

"That's no lie, but I believe it's still my destiny to keep going to find a new home for my family." Brady stood up and stretched. He faced his companions and said, "I'm ready to ride. I guess it was worth the stop in Seymour if the two of you learned that this saloon stuff is not for us. I wasn't a bit happy that we lost riding time today, but we'll make it up. What do you say, friends, are we going to ride today or sit here and talk about it?"

Both men rose from the ground. "I'm good enough to go," answered Jim.

"Westward ho!" Frank said laughingly, as he mocked a wagon train call. All three men mounted their horses again with renewed spirits. They needed to make miles during what was left of the daylight.

★ ★ ★ ★ ★ ★ ★ ★ ★ ★ ★ ★ ★ ★ ★ ★ ★ ★

The men were riding westward, following the road, when they met another horseman riding toward them. As the man neared, the scouts halted. The rider stopped and said, "Afternoon. Where are you men headed?"

Frank answered, "We're heading to western Indiana to find farmland. We want to move there with our families."

"Is that so?" the horseman replied. "Do you know the lay of the land west of here?"

"No, I can't say that we do," Frank replied. "Isn't it farm land?"

"There's not much farmland for quite a ride. It's mostly trees, steep hills, and gullies. You might want to change your route."

Brady spoke up, "What route would you suggest?"

"It'd be easier travel to cut up north a day's ride and go around the forest and hill country. There's good land up there and plenty of water."

Jim spoke up, "Is there a road up that way?"

"Sure 'nough," he replied. Keep ridin' till you reach the pine forest and you'll come to a crossroad. Take the road north and you'll be all right.

"We sure appreciate your help. Glad we bumped into you today. We hadn't heard of a mountain range around here. You've probably saved us time as well as some hard riding," Frank told him.

"I'm glad to be of help. I've lived here in Indiana all my life, and it's a good place to settle down. I hope you find your land—and best of luck to you fellas," the stranger said. He nudged his horse and rode on his way.

"I'm sure glad that we came across that stranger," Brady told his friends. "It would've been a hard ride for our horses through the trees and big hills."

The men agreed as they started riding again. The scouts reached the edge of the forest and chose a place to bed down for the night. They would've liked to ride longer, but they weren't familiar with the territory and the darkness of the night was upon them. They built a small campfire and made a pot of coffee. They had relieved the horses of their burdens—saddles, food, guns, and other gear. They pulled some food out of their saddlebags, which they ate hungrily with their hot coffee. The wind had increased, and the campfire smoke was swirling all around them. They were keenly aware of the sounds of the night coming from the forest. Owls were hooting and crickets were making annoying, high-pitched chirping sounds by relentlessly rubbing their legs together.

The men were quiet, not having much to say to each other. When they finished eating they took their bedrolls, laid them close to the campfire, and prepared to sleep. They were a little uneasy as they lay on their blankets, recalling the wild dog attack. They watched the clouds move overhead, blocking the moon rays in erratic patterns, causing strange shadows that seemed to move through the trees and across the grass. The wind blew with increased speed, and the normally hot summer night became much cooler. The men relaxed as they lay quietly, listening to the sounds of the sticks crackling in the campfire. Finally they all succumbed to a restful sleep.

The three men rose as the sun peered over the eastern horizon, an orange glow sending out the promise of a bright, clear day ahead. They added some dry wood to the low-burning campfire and managed to heat up last night's leftover coffee. The horses were grazing on the fresh morning grass. Frank gave them some water and grain. The men chewed on some jerky and called it breakfast.

Frank finished most of his coffee and gave the rest a pitch. "This coffee has cooked so long it tastes like tree bark!" And he dumped the rest of the pot on the campfire.

"How is your shoulder today?" Jim asked Brady.

"It feels better." Brady raised his left arm and worked it up and down. "I think it is healing. Could you help me change the bandage before we ride this morning? I'll get the antiseptic and bandage out of my saddlebag."

"Sure thing, pal," he answered.

In a short time, Jim had the wound redressed. Frank and Jim cleaned up what little mess was left at their campsite. They finished putting out the campfire by kicking dirt over it, rolled up their blankets, and saddled their horses. The three men began their trek north through the edge of the forest, riding carefully on the narrow trail.

They had ridden eight or ten miles when they came upon a small pond of water and decided to rest for a spell. But, before they dismounted, they saw a sight that sent fear into their hearts. Just a short distance in front of them, a black bear was reared up on his hind legs and growling viciously at a young Indian boy who sat astride a black horse. The horse was skitterish, and the boy was pale with fear.

"Would you look at that!" Frank shouted. "A black bear right here in the woods!"

The black horse suddenly reared up and threw itself around in fear of the black beast. The young boy came to his senses. Holding on to the reins with all of his might, he shouted, "Whoa! Whoa now." But he was unable to control the large animal, and he fell to the ground. The horse ran off.

Brady reacted instinctively. He urged his horse toward the bear. "Hey, bear!" he yelled loudly. Meanwhile, Jim drew his rifle from his saddle. The bear turned around and faced the men and growled loudly, then loped toward them. Jim's horse reared up and bucked, throwing him off before he could get off a shot. His rifle was thrown out of his grip when he left his saddle. He rolled when he hit the ground. Brady and Frank tried to get their guns ready to shoot the bear, but they underestimated how fast that the bear could run. The bear was on Jim in a flash, and Jim was no match for the strength of the bear. Frank and Brady couldn't take a chance. If they fired their rifles, they might hit Jim.

They turned their horses toward the bear, and beat on the bear's head with the butt ends of their rifles. The black beast turned toward them, and they pulled their horses back. The bear reared up on his hind legs and roared furiously. He was hurt and angry. This gave Jim enough time to reach for his rifle. He struggled as he moved toward his gun. The bear caught a glimpse of the movement and turned. He dropped down on all four legs and moved toward Jim. He took a swipe with his huge paw, striking Jim across his back and ribs, ripping through his cotton jacket with his powerful claws and sinking them deep into his flesh. Frank had the bear in his gun site, waiting for any chance to fire. The bear turned away from Jim and reared up again. At that very moment Frank shot the bear twice in the head and dropped him on the path next to Jim.

Frank and Brady quickly dismounted and ran to Jim, who was groaning and writhing with pain. The blood from his wounds had already soaked his shirt and jacket. Frank looked closer at Jim's back and ribs. The bear had actually torn his flesh down to the bone—two of his ribs were plainly visible.

"My God, Brady, look at his ribs! We have to get help for him, but where?"

Brady remembered the boy and turned to look for him. The boy had gotten up off of the ground and had managed to capture his horse. He was standing in the road, holding the reins, and stroking the horse's neck to keep him calm. "Boy, are you all right?" Brady yelled. The boy responded by nodding his head. Brady said, "I'll go talk to the boy. He may know who could help us." Brady walked over to the boy. The boy took a couple steps back, not knowing who Brady was.

Brady drew closer to the young boy. "Do you have a name, young man?" Brady asked.

"I'm called Running Fox," he answered.

"Do you have a mother around here or someone who could help my friend?"

"I live with my mother and grandmother. My grandmother has strong medicine." He pointed back behind himself and said, "We live in a small house down that way."

Jim lay on the dirt road, continuing to make groaning sounds. "Fellas, I need help. I'm hurt bad," he said out loud.

"Show us the way to your place," said Brady. "We'll take our friend, and maybe she can fix him." The boy nodded his head.

Frank sat Jim up and put him up on his horse. Frank then mounted on the same horse and held Jim as they rode down the path, following the boy and Brady.

Frank told Jim, "Hang on, buddy, you're going to get some help. I'll try to keep the horse from any sudden jumps."

Frank's horse trotted along, following Brady, who held its reins. The men rode a short distance—a mile or so—and the young boy led them up to a small cabin, nestled among some pine trees. A small curl of smoke drifted out of the chimney and melted among the pine needles above the cabin. The perimeter of the cabin showed Indian influences. Animal skins were stretched to dry on wooden frames near an outdoor clay oven. Large clay pitchers sat beside the door, and clothes hung to dry on a length of twine that was strung between two trees.

A woman who appeared to be about thirty-five, came out the door when the boy and the others rode up. She was of medium height with straight, dark hair and dark eyes. Right away the men noticed how good looking and shapely she was. She was dressed in a deerskin skirt with a colorful blouse and beads. She wore moccasins on her feet.

"I am Little White Feather. What is wrong?" she asked.

Frank replied, "Our friend was attacked by a black bear down the road. He was trying to save your boy, and the bear turned and attacked him. He's hurt real bad."

"Bring him inside."

As the men dismounted, she went inside and then an older woman—the men assumed she was the boy's grandmother—came to the door. The medium-framed woman had black hair streaked with gray and adorned with colorful bird feathers woven into the braids that fell down her back. She wore a dress made completely of animal skins, which was cinched with a beaded belt. She also wore moccasins on her feet. Her weathered, wrinkled face reflected the hard work and times she had endured.

Frank had gotten Jim down from his horse when the old woman peered from the cabin door. "Is it all right to bring him inside?" Frank asked. She gave a small waving gesture and turned back inside the cabin. Frank and Brady held Jim by the arms as Jim half walked, and was half carried, as he groaned with each step. They followed the Indian woman inside.

The old cabin didn't have much to offer. There was a fireplace on the side with a blackened pot hanging from a hook over the low flame. Various large cooking utensils hung from an antler, which was fastened to the nearby wall. There were four crude seats cut out of large tree stumps. Built onto the sides of the cabin were two bed-like structures, each made to fit one adult, with deerskins hanging between them for privacy. The floor was dirt, strewn with twigs and straw-like thatch. Clumps of dried herbs were tied together and hung from pegs that had been driven in between the logs of the cabin close to the fireplace.

Various other items such as bones, feathers, wooden carvings, and stones were placed around in the cabin. There was one small window, with a board shutter. A single oil lamp hung by a rope over a roughhewn table, apparently the only inside light. The men could see two shelves where dishes and food were stored.

The medicine woman pointed to one of the beds, indicating that Jim should be put there. Frank asked the woman, "Can you help our friend?"

The old woman spoke in her native language, and the younger woman said, "She will call on the Great Spirit and He will tell her what to do." Then she said, "She won't do anything for your friend if you stand around watching. You must go outside. Don't worry. I'll come and talk to you later."

The men obliged and went outside. Brady and Frank checked their horses and tethered them a short distance from the cabin where they were protected from the hot sun. The men removed the saddles and put them in the shade. They proceeded to sit down and lean against a tree. They waited silently together.

CHAPTER EIGHTEEN

THE LETTER

Every day since the Sunday that Joker told her Brady had been hurt, Anna Marie thoughts were of deeper concern about her husband. Questions filled her mind. *How badly is he injured? Where is he now? When will we see him again?* Her life was too routine, too lonely, and too empty. Even with her little boy to care for, she needed more. The baby inside her was growing, and she realized that she was getting clumsy. She waddled as she walked around, especially as she went outside to do her few chores. She couldn't bend over easily to pick the vegetables in the garden, so sometimes she would just sit down between the rows, then struggle as she tried to get back on her feet. This was not the way she was supposed to be living, her husband gone off on some venture. She started to work herself up into a dither. *Maybe I should just pack up everything and go back and live with my parents,* she thought. *It would serve him right to come home to an empty house.* The thought caused a little grin to come to her face. She knew in her heart that she wouldn't do that because she loved him and didn't want to hurt him. She would stay.

Today was Friday, and Anna Marie thought that she needed to talk to somebody to relieve her loneliness. She decided that she and Pat would go to Big Al and Lucy's place for a morning visit. She would take her basket of fresh eggs; maybe they could go into town. She gathered up Pat and the other things that she normally took along, readied the horse and buggy, and in no time at all, they were on their way. As they travelled on the road, Pat talked, pointed his fingers, and waved his hands. His vocabulary was increasing by the day. They saw grey squirrels gathering nuts and running up the trees to their nests. Many of the wildflowers were blooming along the road and beyond out in the grasses. The blue cornflowers were one of Anna Marie's favorites.

When they crossed the Muddy River, they could see fish jumping around in the water and a family of raccoons that had gathered on the bank. "Look over there, Pat. The fish are jumping and the raccoons are trying to catch some to eat."

"Fish," said Pat. "Look. See fish?" The horse trotted up the hill away from the river, past the last patch of woods, and around the bend toward the Benning home. Anna's spirits were already lifted up as she watched Pat. She was so proud of her handsome, healthy little boy. Anna Marie had weaned Pat from her breast these past few weeks knowing that she needed to give the new baby inside herself all the nourishment possible. Pat was able to eat mashed vegetables and drink the cow's milk quite well. She had brought along some crackers for him to eat to keep him from wiggling around too much in the buggy.

Anna Marie and Pat arrived, unannounced, in front of Big Al and Lucy's home. The children were playing in the yard and waved heartily at their arrival. She and Pat waved back. By the time Anna had hitched the horse, Lucy was at the door.

"Land's sake, come inside. Good to see you two," Lucy stated. The two women hugged. Anna Marie held Lucy especially tight. "Are you all right? Is there anything wrong?" Lucy asked.

"I'm all right. No, nothing's wrong. I've been alone too long. Since I had word that Brady was injured, he has been on my mind, and I've had trouble sleeping. If I'm not constantly working, I sit and worry about him. I'm just beside myself." Lucy's children had already taken Pat by the hand and led him off to play. Lucy and Anna Marie went inside. Lucy apologized for her messy kitchenl as she had been busy snapping fresh green beans from her garden. The bean stems and leaves were strewn on the table and floor. The two women sat together at the kitchen table as Lucy finished with the vegetables.

Lucy said to Anna Marie, "You and Pat must and eat lunch with us."

"I brought along a basket full of eggs. I thought maybe we could ride into town this afternoon."

"Sure thing. Pat can stay here and play with my children. It will give you a good break from him."

Anna Marie missed seeing Al around the house. "Where's Al?"

"Do you remember when Al hurt his foot some time back? Well, his foot hasn't healed. It's swollen and red looking, like it has fever in it."

"You don't want him to lose his foot. Has he been to see a doctor?"

"I can't get him to go to a doctor. He's being pigheaded about it." Lucy choked back a few tears.

"Let's just get him to go to town with us this afternoon and then we'll devise a way to get him to see the doctor. What do you say?"

Lucy wiped a couple tears from her eyes and held Anna Marie's hand. "Thank you. Al means everything to me. I don't want to lose him over a sore foot."

About that time Big Al hobbled into the kitchen. The two women looked up and watched him make his way to a chair.

"You're not walking too well today, Al," Anna Marie remarked.

"No, this gimpy ole leg of mine hurts." Anna Marie could see his furrowed brow and the drawn look on his face.

"It's been a couple weeks since you got your foot in the trap; it ought to be healed by now."

"Yeah, it should be, but it stays swollen and sore. I can't bear any weight on it."

"Well, you probably ought to go see a doctor. You don't want to lose your foot or leg, do you?"

"Hell no," he blurted out. "I don't want to be a cripple the rest of my life."

Anna Marie was a little astonished by his outburst, yet she understood why he seemed cross. "You know I care for you just like my own family, Al. You think about going to town with Lucy and me after lunch," Anna calmly said to him. Al looked down at his aching foot and rubbed his thigh. He didn't say much then or during lunch.

★ ★ ★ ★ ★ ★ ★ ★ ★ ★ ★ ★ ★ ★ ★ ★ ★ ★ ★

When they all finished eating, Al told Lucy, "I've been thinking about what Anna Marie said, and I think she's right. I'll go to town with both of you and see about getting my foot looked at." The two women looked at each other and smiled.

"I think you've made the right decision," Anna Marie told Al.

After Lucy sorted out her children, she, Al, and Anna Marie got into the Bennings' buggy and headed toward town. Al was a little surly when they first left the farm. However, after they had gone only a short distance he calmed down and the three began to laugh and talk together. In no time, they were on the main street. They stopped at the mercantile first and the two women took their baskets of eggs inside. Al sat on a chair in front of the store while the women shopped. He propped his bad foot on the empty chair beside him and watched the activity of the shops and the busy street. Several townspeople walked by and asked him about his leg. Al led them to believe that he was just fine, not to worry.

The local doctor approached Al and spoke to him. "What's wrong with your leg?" he asked.

"Hi, Doc," Al replied. "It's a little sore. I caught it in a trap."

"Let me look at it, if you don't mind," Doc said. Al nodded his approval and removed his boot. The doc looked at Al with a serious look of surprise. "You need to come to my office right now. That foot needs immediate attention—if you intend to keep it."

"I suppose you're right, doc. I've had about all the pain I care to endure. Let me say something to my wife. She's inside the mercantile." Al limped to the store entrance. "Lucy, come over here and talk to me," he called out. Lucy turned from her shopping and went to the entrance door. "Doc saw me out front and wants me to go to his office so he can have a better look at my foot. I guess I'd better go."

"I think I should go with you." She turned to Anna Marie. "I'm going with Al to the doctor's office. We'll see you a little later over at the boarding house. Is that all right with you?"

"Of course it's all right," Anna Marie replied.

Anna Marie finished getting her groceries and dry goods, paid and left the store. Outside on the sunny street, she made her way to the Bennings' buggy and put her purchases away. She stood beside the buggy a few moments and looked down the street. She decided to go

135

over to the post office on the outside chance that there might be some mail. It felt strange going into the post office alone. Brady had always been with her other times. She walked inside and found that she was the only one inside besides the clerk. "My name is Anna Marie Patterson. Do I have any mail?"

"I'll look for you, ma'am," he replied, and he disappeared through a door. When he came back, he handed her a paper that announced the fall harvest festival, an envelope from the tax office—and a letter. It was from Brady. She couldn't believe her eyes. A letter from Brady. She just stood there a moment and stared at it. Finally, she thanked the clerk and went out the door. She went to a bench in the shade of the boardwalk and read Brady's letter.

> *My dearest Anna Marie,*
>
> *I have been away from you a little over four weeks now, and it feels like a year out of a lifetime.*
>
> *We've had many delays since leaving home. We haven't found farms here in Indiana where we could move our families. Charlie was seriously injured by a wild dog, consequently he and Joker decided to return to Kentucky. My shoulder was hurt but it is healing. I found a doctor and he fixed me up. We have met many friendly and helpful people while we have been gone. If we move our family here, I know we'll be happy.*
>
> *I'll come home as soon as possible. I pray that God will help me return safely so I may hold you close once again. Take good care of yourself and Pat.*
>
> *I send you all my love.*
> *Brady*

Anna Marie stared at the letter and reread it. She had had feelings of loneliness earlier today; they were now multiplied tenfold. Oh, how she ached for Brady as tears stung her eyes. *How long?* She thought. *How long must I wait?* She tucked the letter into her purse and held the purse close to her body. She stood up and walked slowly toward the boarding house, still feeling a little off balance emotionally. She was perspiring from the heat of the day, and the extra weight from her unborn child made the heat even more unbearable. *Only two more months to go until the baby will be born,* she thought. *Surely Brady will come home long before that time arrives.*

Anna Marie entered the boarding house and seated herself at the large table. She responded graciously to the kind greetings from the other customers. She asked for a cool glass of water and sat quietly, listening to the conversations going on around her. Much of the talk was about the incessant heat and the need for more rain for the crops. She became lost in her own thoughts as she sat and stared at the sun rays caught on the bottles placed on the windowsill. The colorful patterns held her gaze. She was unaware how long she had been captivated by the various color splashes when Big Al and Lucy walked up to the table and sat down beside her.

"Oh, hello," she managed to say when they sat down. "How did your doctor's visit go?" she asked Al.

Al replied, "It was a good thing you two women convinced me to come to town. My foot was infected and blood poisoning was ready to start up my leg. I need to come back to town in about three days and let the doc take another look at my foot. I guess I owe you both a big thanks."

Lucy asked, "Did you get all of your shopping finished?"

"Yes I did, and I put my packages in your buggy," she answered. "Then I went over to the post office to see if, perchance, there was any mail." She pulled the letter from Brady out of her purse and said, "There was a letter from Brady."

"A letter from Brady!" Lucy said with an astonished tone to her voice. "What did it say?"

"He said that he has had delays and he hasn't found a farm for us yet. He will be home as soon as possible."

Al stated, "Brady is a determined man. He always does what he says he'll do. He'll find a good farm and return to his family."

Lucy encouraged Anna Marie by saying, "Brady is a good husband. I'd say, he'll be home within two weeks. Just mark my words!"

The three sat and talked while they enjoyed a refreshing drink and a sweet dessert together. Then they went back home.

CHAPTER NINETEEN

LITTLE WHITE FEATHER AND THE MEDICINE WOMAN

Jim didn't know the Medicine Woman by any other name than Grandma, which is what the boy called her. As soon as he was laid upon the wall bed, she started moving around the cabin gathering objects, which she placed on the table. She came back over to him and beckoned her daughter, Little White Feather, to come over.

The Medicine Woman spoke in her Indian language only. She said, "Remove his jacket and shirt. I will clean his wound." Her daughter, Little White Feather, did as instructed and carried the clothing off.

The Medicine Woman took a clean, but ragged, cloth and wiped the wound with cold water. She then went to the small table. She placed herbs and animal fats in a small wooden bowl and mixed them with care. When the concoction was finished to her satisfaction, she carried the bowl to Jim's bedside. She set the bowl on the floor, then lifted her hands up toward the ceiling and began to chant. Her voice was high pitched and made sounds which one might interpret as pleading. This ritual went on for some time. When she finished chanting, she covered Jim's wound with the ointment and motioned for the daughter once more.

She spoke to her daughter again, "Bind his ribs and back with clean cloths and cover him. I will prepare medicine tea for him to drink."

Little White Feather looked into Jim's eyes and said to him, "You must trust my mother. She's a great healer." She went about covering Jim's wounds and then skillfully wrapped several layers of soft cotton fabric around his torso. The Medicine Woman brought the tea for Jim.

She spoke to her daughter, "Have him drink all of it. The juice of the healing plants will make him strong."

Little White Feather lifted Jim's head and instructed him, "You need to drink all of this tea. It is powerful medicine."

Jim started drinking. When the bitter tea entered his mouth he could hardly swallow it. He grimaced and turned his head away after the first swallow, but Little White Feather put the cup back to his mouth and said, "You must drink it all." He forced himself to finish the repugnant liquid and lay his head back down on the bed. She said, "You rest now." In a short while Jim fell into a sound sleep.

Little White Feather went outside. She spoke to Frank and Brady, "Your friend is resting now. Grandmother put medicine on his wounds, and I bandaged him. He also drank some of Grandmother's healing tea. Now we wait."

Frank and Brady looked at each other. Brady spoke, "I wonder how long we will have to stay here. It's one more delay we didn't expect."

"We'll wait until morning" Frank replied. "If he has to stay very long, we may have to go on without him." The men gave their horses some water and grain. They noticed a small shed behind the cabin and decided to take a look at to see if it would work for a place to sleep the night. They walked around to the front of the building and peered inside. It didn't appear to be infested with bees, bugs, or rodents. Apparently the Medicine Woman had placed dried herbs and various other items, like hedge balls, inside, which had repelled unwanted insects and animals. "Unless we have us a big storm," Frank decided, "we should be able to rest here." They walked back to the front of the cabin and sat on a fallen log in the shade. After an hour or more passed, Little White Feather came outside and walked over to the two men.

"How's our friend?" Frank asked her.

"He's having a good sleep. The medicine given to him by my mother will heal his wounds as he rests. He will probably sleep all night."

Brady spoke up, "We will stay the night in your building in the back if you don't mind. Tomorrow we will make a decision about when we should leave."

"Yes, you can sleep there. I will fry corn cakes and cook some greens with onions for your meal tonight." She turned to see her son, Running Fox, who was leading his horse to some water. Both boy and horse seemed to have calmed down from the encounter with the bear. She walked over to him and, speaking in her native language, talked to him, gesturing to his horse. He nodded his head affirmatively and smiled at her. She walked back toward the men.

"Running Fox wishes to thank you for saving him from the bear. He asked if he could have the honor or riding with you to the edge of the forest when you leave."

Frank looked at Brady, who nodded his head, and replied, "We would like for him to ride with us. Tell him he's a brave young man."

"Thank you. I will tell him." With that she turned and walked back inside the cabin.

★ ★ ★ ★ ★ ★ ★ ★ ★ ★ ★ ★ ★ ★ ★ ★ ★ ★ ★

Frank and Brady were awakened the next day at daybreak by a chorus of chirping birds, welcoming the new day. They had rested well. They hastily gathered some dry pieces of wood and made a small fire to brew their coffee. They led their horses to water then brought them back where they had been hitched the day before. Brady dumped some grain on the cool grass in front of them, and they eagerly began eating. The men went over and sat beside the campfire, drank their coffee, and discussed what they should do. They were anxious about Jim.

"I wonder how Jim is feeling this morning," Frank remarked.

"If the Medicine Woman is truly a healer, he'll be better today," answered Brady. "As soon as we see movement about the cabin we'll ask to see him."

"Do you think that he'll be able to travel with us? I'm thinking that he'll have to rest a few days before he'll be able to ride and keep up with our pace."

"I agree with that. That bear sure made a deep gash in his side. We probably need to consider going on without him. We can find our land

and then come by on our way back home. I think he'll be all right here with the two women and the boy."

"Yeah, that's for sure. They'll take good care of him."

They noticed Running Fox when he came out of the cabin and went to his horse to care for him. He then fetched a bucket of fresh water and took it back inside. The men knew that the day had begun for all of them. While they waited for an invitation to go inside, they watched the forest area come to life. Half-grown grey squirrels chased each other around the base of a shagbark hickory tree, then they sprinted up the tree trunk and ran out on a limb midway up the tree. The leaves of a group of sugar maples located down the road were beginning to show some orange color, an indication of the changing weather. Striped wooly bear caterpillars crawled intently along dead, moldy logs. Whenever they came across a large leaf or a pulled up piece of bark, they quickly checked the barrier, took evasive measures, and continued their hurried pace. A pair of cardinals made quick flights from limb to limb on an oak tree, as if they were on a secret mission. Then they flew to a grove of pine trees and disappeared within its branches. The sounds of chirping birds and the various buzzing sounds of insects filled the morning air.

The attention of the men changed when Little White Feather came outside carrying a small woven basket. She had pulled her hair to one side and fastened it with a beaded leather strip. Her black hair was long and glistened in the early morning sun as it cascaded over her shoulder. She looked beautiful as she walked over toward the small garden patch. She put the basket down and raised both of her arms skyward and looked toward the heavens. The breeze blew against her soft leather skirt, which caused it to cling to the shape of her body as if caressing her. Her breasts were fully outlined as were the curves of her hips and legs. Wisps of her hair danced around her face and neck as she stood motionless, lost in her own world. The men were mesmerized. As they both experienced arousals in their groins, they inhaled deeply, held their breath, and exhaled slowly. She knelt down to gather some fresh vegetables, which she placed in her basket. The whole world seemed to pause as the men absorbed all that nature had created in this moment of time.

"Holy cow," Frank exclaimed. He looked at Brady, who had beads of sweat on his brow. "What do you say, friend?"

"I have no words to describe it. I don't think I could stand being around here a long time. I have to remember that I'm a married man."

"I'm not married, but I understand. She sure is a beauty."

Little White Feather stood up and started back toward the cabin. Brady managed to ask her, "How is our friend doing this morning?"

"He is awake. Mother is feeding him. You are welcome to come inside."

Frank and Brady stood up, followed her into the cabin, and walked over to Jim's side. He was sitting in one of the crude stump chairs.

"Mornin'," they both said to Jim.

"Hey, fellas," he replied. "I slept like a rock all night. Whatever the Medicine Woman gave me was good stuff!"

"How does your side feel today?" Frank asked him.

"It's pretty sore. I think I'll be laid up for a few days. It won't be so bad with Little White Feather taking care of me. You know what I mean?"

"Yeah, she is one nice-looking woman," Frank answered. "Maybe I should have an accident of some kind so she could take care of me," he joked.

"I get first chance," Jim said. "I could get very interested in courting that gal. She needs a good man to take care of her, and I could be the man."

"Remember, she has that young lad to care for also."

"That won't be a problem with me," Jim stated.

The Medicine Woman was busy with her herbs and potions while Little White Feather cooked some sort of grain porridge with wild berries for all of them to eat for their breakfast. After their meal, Frank and Brady went outside to talk.

"What do you think we ought to do, go or stay?" Brady asked Frank.

Frank answered, "Jim shouldn't ride. I think we should go ahead to find our land. He's in good hands with the two Indian women nursing him."

"I agree," Brady replied. The two men went back inside and told Jim of their decision. He sat quietly for a few moments, knowing that they were right. He looked disappointed, then he smiled and spoke, "You're right. I'd hold you back, even if I could ride my horse. You two go ahead. Will you come back by this way, or will I go home on my own later?"

"We'll come back for you. You can count on it, friend. You concentrate on getting well. We'll be back as soon as possible," Frank reassured Jim.

Frank and Brady thanked the Medicine Woman and Little White Feather for their kindness. They readied their horses with their gear and mounted up. Running Fox got on his horse, and the three rode on the trail to where the main road went northward. They halted at the road crossing.

Frank turned to Running Fox, shook his hand, and said, "You be careful, young brave. Your mother and grandmother need you to watch out for them." Brady reached out and shook his hand.

Running Fox held his arm high and said, "May the Great Spirit keep you safe until you return." They waved good-bye to the young boy as he turned and headed toward home.

The wind had picked up and the leaves were swirling down from the trees. Puffy white clouds were moving quickly overhead, but they didn't look like storm clouds. They saw a doe with twin fawns eating the fresh morning grass. The deer lifted their heads, alert, with ears pointed up as they watched the men ride along.

After several hours of steady riding, the men stopped to take a break and rest their horses. They knew there was no time to waste. They had been gone a month due to all the delays and accidents. The five scouts were now down to two able-bodied men who were still determined to reach their goal.

CHAPTER TWENTY

LAND AT LAST

The two remaining scouts rode along on the road north past the forest area then turned west. The land had leveled out; there were no more forests or large hills to go through or cross. They rode past many acres of what appeared to be untouched, fertile farmland. The grasses grew thick and tall from the road for as far as they could see. Every once in a while they would see a flock of wild turkeys feeding in the grass. When the turkeys noticed the riders, they would quickly turn and run in zigzag patterns toward the cover offered by the bushes and trees that grew along a creek bank. The scouts rode along the narrow road most of the morning.

At last they came across a small settlement of cabins. They decided to stop and visit with the settlers and make inquiries about the land. Brady first saw a farmer and his wife. The couple looked to be about ten or fifteen years older than himself. They were out working on a corral fence. Their young boys were running around, playing amongst the trees. Brady and Frank rode up to the farmer and dismounted. They observed the weatherworn faces of the man and his wife. Their tattered clothing showed signs of having been washed many times. She wore a sunbonnet to protect her face from the hot sun. The farmer wore a hat and a long-sleeved shirt that had patches on both elbows where the material had either torn or worn through. His trousers were the same, either ripped or patched in several places.

"Mornin'. How are you today?" Brady asked the two.

"Mornin'. We're doin' pretty good," the farmer replied. "Why did you men stop by?"

Brady answered, "My friend and I have come a long way from the middle of Kentucky to look for farmland. Do you happen to know if there's any available here in this part of the state?"

"Could be," the farmer replied. "It would be best if you talk to our town recorder. We're a very small community of settlers, but we're tryin' to keep records of our neighbors—marriages, births, deaths, land ownership, and that sort of thing. Ride on down the road and stop where you see a cabin, a big barn, and another cabin all lined up in a row. Foster Browning lives in the last house. He makes buckboard wagons, and his wife, Beulah, sews clothes for people. She keeps the records of our settlement. I think she could help you."

"Much obliged for your help," Brady told him. Frank and Brady remounted and waved good-bye as they urged their horses down the road. They followed the farmer's directions and in a short time arrived at the Brownings' home. They saw a white-haired, bewhiskered man working under the shade of an old maple tree, apparently repairing a set of broken wagon wheels. They rode up to the hitching post located near the barn where they dismounted and fastened their horses. The horses were thirsty from the day's ride and began drinking from the watering trough in front of them. Frank and Brady walked over and stood in the shade of the large tree. The man looked up from his work. The scouts observed the face of a friendly, hardworking man.

"Hello. It looks like you've got yourself a job there," Frank said to the wheel maker.

"This gosh darned wheel had about four broken spokes and I can't seem to get the new ones to fit into the rim right," he replied.

"Here, let me help hold the rim while you work on the spokes," Frank said. Brady stood and watched the two men working together, not offering any advice. Within a short time the spokes of the wheel were secure and the job was finished.

"I sure do thank you, young man. Say, what made you two young fellas stop by here anyway?"

Brady answered, "We've heard that the farmland in Indiana is fertile and ... well, we're interested in bringing our families from Kentucky and homesteading up here. A man down the road told us that you and your wife keep land records. Would you know of any land in this area that hasn't been settled?"

"Let's go inside my home. My wife is the one you should talk with. She's very organized and does a good job of keeping the records of our little settlement here. She talks to most of the women and hears all the news. If someone new comes here and decides to stay, she finds out who they are, gets a list of their children, and learns where they plan to live. Yes, she'll know."

The three men walked into the Browning home. Mrs. Browning, needle and thread in hand, was sitting next to the window working on somebody's shirt.

"Beulah, I'd like you to meet a couple young men who need to talk to you." He turned to the men and said, "I'm Foster Browning, and this is my wife, Beulah. I don't know your names."

"I'm Frank Justice and this is my friend, Brady Patterson. It's nice to meet you, ma'am."

Foster turned back to his wife and told her, "These men are looking for land to settle on. Can you help them?"

Beulah went into the bedroom and returned with a journal. She went into the kitchen and placed the book on the long kitchen table and started looking through it. The men had followed her into the kitchen and leaned over the table to see what was in the book. She had drawn sketches of the perimeter and approximate size of each family's land. Some of the sketches included waterways and wooded areas. They looked carefully at each page. She had devised a number and letter system that she used to identify the separate parcels of land. After carefully studying the pages, she was able to tell the men what they needed to know.

"I don't know how much land you want to settle on, but there seems to be plenty available not too far from here," Beulah told them. "There's a large parcel of land west of here about three miles that you could settle on. If it's too big, you could divide it. My husband could take you there, and you could look it over."

The men asked Foster, "Do you have the time to go show us this land?"

147

"Of course I do. We could go right away, but maybe we should have something to eat. Beulah, would you have enough food for the four of us before we go?"

She shook her finger at him and smiled. It was obvious that the two had bonded with a mutual love through the years. She said, "Now that's a foolish question. You know we always have enough to share. You men need to give me just a little time, and I'll let you know when it's ready." The men went back outside to the shade and helped Foster with his wheels. It wasn't long before Beulah rang the dinner bell.

Half an hour later, the three men felt refreshed from the home-cooked meal. Foster offered to take Frank and Brady in his buggy. They were happy to have a rest from their saddles. He drove the horse and buggy about three miles west and a mile north where he stopped in the shade of a grove of trees. He explained that the land started there at the grove of trees and went northward. Frank and Brady got out of the buggy and took a look around, taking in the lay of the land, then they walked across it toward the west. They walked until they came to what appeared to be a waterway; a small but steady stream of water flowed inside its banks. That was good; they needed water. They came across some large rocks that would have to be cleared and several dead trees among a large grove of trees. They decided to walk back to the buggy.

When they arrived, Brady asked Foster, "Could we go farther north so we can look at more of the land?" Foster obliged, and they traveled another half mile or so. At that particular place was a crossing over what was probably the same waterway. A big, old oak tree stood on one side of the crossing, and on the other side stood a few cedar trees. The two scouts again got out of the buggy and walked across the land as they followed the curves of the waterway. They found patches of cockleburs, thistles, and some wild grapes.

"It'll take a good long while to clear the rocks off of this land," Frank said to Brady. He added, "It'll take a few years to get rid of the thistles and cockleburs 'cause they seed themselves down every year."

"You're right, but I think this is where I want to build my cabin and raise my family. It looks to be about eighty acres. In time it will make a good farm. I'm going to try to get it, how about you?"

"I don't think I want this much land. Maybe I could get about twenty acres adjoining you."

"Sure, that's a good idea. We could share the water and help each other with the work."

"I'll take you up on that offer, pal. Let's go back and we'll make our arrangements."

Frank and Brady walked back to Foster. Brady spoke up, "This place suits me just fine. I'll talk to your wife and see about getting my name on it. Frank, here, wants a smaller section beside my place."

"We'll head back home and you and Frank can discuss what you need to do," Foster said.

The three men climbed aboard the buggy and retraced their way back to the Browning home. Frank and Brady excitedly discussed the possibilities of the new farm as Foster managed the buggy along the bumps and holes in the road. The older man smiled as he listened to the men, probably recalling his own first home when he was a young man.

The two could hardly contain their enthusiasm as they entered the Browning residence. They talked and talked as they made plans for their farms. Beulah and Foster sat and listened to the young men.

Brady spoke to Beulah, "Tell me how I can claim land here in this territory."

Beulah answered, "First you decide what size farm you think you can handle. Then you must mark the corners; usually with large stone piles. You should cut some trees where you plan to build your cabin. All these things will establish that you intend to live there and work the land."

"I can do that," Brady said.

"When that is done, I will enter into the record book that you are the intended land owner. After you have built your cabin, moved your family there, and get your farm established, the record book will note that you are the official land owner," Beulah said.

"Frank, how soon do you think we can get started marking the land?" Brady asked.

"Hold on there! I thought you wanted to go home as quickly as possible."

"You're right, I do, but I need to claim my land. How much do you think we can get done in a week?"

"Well, I think that together we can do a lot. If we could get two or three more men to help us, it would go quicker. I guess you have your heart set on this, right?"

"Yes, I do. That's a good idea to get some help," Brady answered. He looked at Foster, "Foster, would you know where we could get some men to work for us?"

"I could probably rustle up some strong men who would be willing to work a few days. The crops aren't ready to harvest, so they should have the time. I'll finish fixin' that wagon and then we'll take the buggy and go visit some friends. How does that sound?"

Of course that was quite agreeable with the two scouts. They were so anxious to make progress toward securing their land that they would go along with most any suggestion.

Foster and the two men went outside and worked. When the job was finished, they went on their search for workers. Within an a little better than an hour they had secured three strong, able-bodied men who were willing to work the next morning. Brady and Frank felt another rush of excitement as everything seemed to be falling into place. After the men returned to the Browning home, Brady and Frank sat outside and talked and planned until it was time to sleep. The Brownings had offered them the comfort of their cozy barn.

The men awoke the next morning to the sound of the rat-a-tat-tat of a woodpecker pecking away at the tree just outside of the barn. The woodpecker was relentless with his mission to peck a hole in the trunk of the tree. The men groaned as they sat up, stretched, and rubbed their eyes. The sun had just risen above the horizon into a cloudless sky. The world had awakened with the crowing of roosters, while off in the distance they could hear a single barking dog. The men pulled on their boots, stood up, re-tucked their shirts into their pants, and cinched their belts. It wasn't long until they heard the familiar dinner bell being ringing, signaling mealtime.

Beulah put out a hearty breakfast for the three men. Frank told her, "Beulah, this has to be the best breakfast I've had all year. Your biscuits were delicious with that apple jelly you made."

"Thank you, young man. Could be I've had years of practice," she replied.

"She's always been the best cook from the day I married her," Foster said as he smiled at her.

"Oh shoot!" she replied. "He'll eat anything and tell me it's delicious. He says burnt fried potatoes are his favorite!"

They all had a good laugh. Foster went over and squeezed Beulah around the waist. "See you later today. We've got work to do," he told her. He reached back and patted her backside. She handed him a basket packed with cooked sausages, biscuits, and apples for their lunch, her eyes twinkling with a knowing look. He gave her a peck on the cheek and turned to leave.

The men went outside, and a few minutes later the three hired men arrived. They all left for the land that Brady and Frank had decided to homestead. Foster rode in his buckboard, which he had loaded with digging tools, ropes, saws, and anything else they might need that day. Frank, Brady, and the hired men rode their horses. It looked like a good working day with partly cloudy skies and a nice breeze. The men hoped they would make a significant start on the work necessary to claim the land.

They worked steadily with shovels and prying poles from the time they arrived at the homestead, digging up rocks and marking the boundaries. One man would dig around the rock as the others would pry with a large wooden pole, all using their brute strength to loosen it. When the men loosened the stones, Brady or Frank would tie ropes around the larger ones and, using their horses, pull them to the nearest marker pile. Some of the rocks they tried to dig up were far too big to move. Those were left for another time. They placed the smaller rocks onto the floor of the buckboard.

When midday arrived, the five men welcomed a rest in the cool shade of a large tree where they ate Beulah's hearty lunch. Even though the air temperature wasn't too high, all of the men had soaked their clothes with sweat from their hard work. They visited during their lunch break and became more acquainted with each other as they talked about their families and some of their life experiences. After eating and resting, the men went back to their tasks. All of the men except Brady worked steadily for another three to four hours. Brady's shoulder had given out on him. He was suffering from his injury, and all he could do was supervise the rest of the day.

When mid afternoon rolled around, Foster called out to the men, "What do you say we call it a day now? You've all put in a full day's work."

"I'm ready to quit," Frank stated. The other men agreed. They reloaded the buckboard with all the gear, and they started back toward the settlement.

This ritual of working the raw land continued for five days. During that time they succeeded in marking off the eighty-acre lot and the twenty-acre lot with piles of stone big enough so that anyone would recognize that they had been put there intentionally. They had chosen sites for their cabins. They had cut down trees and stacked the logs near the house sites where they would remain through fall and winter to cure. All of the men shook hands when they had finished, knowing that they had made long-lasting friendships. They loaded the wagon for the last time, mounted their horses, and headed back to the settlement.

Beulah was sitting in a rocker on the porch when the men came trotting up the road. She waved to them, and when they had stopped she hollered out, "Come on inside. I've made some oatmeal cookies and a fresh pot of coffee. I'm sure you've worked up an appetite this afternoon."

Everyone sat at the big kitchen table and talked about their day, laughed and told stories while enjoying the fresh-baked cookies and coffee. Beulah enjoyed listening to the men and laughing with them as they kidded each other.

Frank started laughing as he brought up the time that he and one of the hired men were on a knoll working at loosening a large rock.

He said, "We dug and pried, pushed and tugged on that stubborn rock, then it let loose. It rolled down the knoll and stopped right in front of the wheel of the buckboard. We followed it to the buckboard 'cause we knew we had to move that darn thing again. We struggled to pick it up. Just as we got it a foot or so off of the ground, we lost our hold on it. It came down on our toes! Lordy me, that really hurt. Of course we had to lift it up *again* to get our toes loose. After we recovered from that, we had to pick the damn thing up one more time and put it in the buckboard. We both groaned and complained as we limped away."

Beulah and the men had a good laugh. After an hour or more had passed, the three hired men got up to leave. Frank and Brady followed them out of the house to settle their wages.

"Thanks for all your help," Brady said to them. "I'm real grateful for all you did."

"That goes for me too," Frank added.

"You're welcome. We'll look forward to seeing you both next spring when you come back to build your cabins."

"That's a promise," Brady replied.

★ ★ ★ ★ ★ ★ ★ ★ ★ ★ ★ ★ ★ ★ ★ ★ ★ ★ ★

Frank and Brady spent their last night in Foster and Beulah's barn. They awoke earlier than usual the next morning, probably because they were anxious to start their journey home. They pulled their boots on and cinched their belts. It didn't take them long to roll up and tie their bedrolls. They both walked outside as the first rays of sun shone onto the Browning property. The two men walked their horses to the water trough where the horses had a good long drink. As they waited for the horses to finish drinking, the men's attention turned to the variety of birds flitting around. Some had found worms in the grass and others hopped about, pecking at the grass as they searched for their morning meal.

"These past weeks have been quite an experience, haven't they?" Frank stated. "Now we're ready to start our way back home. What do you say?"

"It took much longer than I ever expected," Brady answered, "but

I wouldn't have missed it. We finally found the land we were looking for, and I can't wait to tell Anna Marie."

Beulah stepped out on the porch and began ringing the dinner bell. The men turned and waved at her. "Come in for breakfast," she called out.

The men were once again treated to a good, hot breakfast. Foster, Beulah, and the two scouts had a long, enjoyable conversation about the happenings of the past week.

As the time came for their good-byes, the men all shook hands and wished each other well until they would see each other next spring. Both scouts gave Beulah a little hug and thanked her for her kindness and hospitality.

"You cook as good as my ma," Frank told her.

"Come on now, I just cook plain food," she replied.

"Darn good plain food," he said back to her. Brady agreed and said, "Thanks for everything."

"You're welcome. We'll look forward to seeing you both next spring when you come back."

Brady replied, "I can't wait to bring my wife here."

In no time at all, the horses were saddled and the men were ready to mount up and begin riding back to their Kentucky homes. They knew they had made lasting friendships with these people. Months from now, when the bitter cold of winter passed and the rays of the spring sun began warming the earth, Brady and Frank would return.

CHAPTER TWENTY-ONE
HOMEWARD BOUND

The week of claiming his land had drained Brady's strength, but nothing could hold back his eagerness to head home to his wife and child. He and Frank had left Foster and Beulah's home directly after breakfast the day after the work had been completed to establish ownership on their farms. The two scouts had accomplished their goal satisfactorily. They talked the whole time as they retraced their previous path. There was excitement in their voices as they made their plans. If Frank hadn't been sure about the move, he was now. He talked about finding a lady friend to marry.

"You know, Brady, with the land I claimed, I think I'll get serious and look for a nice woman to marry. It'd be nice to have a wife in the home while I'm working. I'd like to have at least two sons to teach about farming and to leave an inheritance to when I'm gone."

"You've got the right idea, partner. I've got one boy now and another baby on the way. When a man has his own family, it just makes life worthwhile."

Brady and Frank reached the forest edge and turned south. They knew they had one more stop to make on their journey. They had left their friend, Jim, in the hands of the Indian healer, and they were anxious to see him. The two scouts arrived at the home of the Medicine Woman and her family in the late afternoon. As they rode up to the cabin they saw Running Fox under a tree, dressing a turkey. Running Fox waved heartily at the two riders and watched them as they dismounted and tied their horses.

Brady spoke, "Howdy, young man. Looks like you've got a nice tom turkey there. You must be real good with your bow and arrow."

"I've been using my bow and arrows since I was young. Mother will roast him in the outdoor oven," Running Fox replied.

"You're doing a good job taking care of your family. Are your mother and grandmother inside?" Frank asked.

"Yes, mother is weaving. Grandmother is washing the roots that she dug this morning. She will use them for her medicine."

Brady said, "We would like to go and see how our friend, Jim, is doing."

"He's better. Grandmother's medicine worked every day to help him. I'll go see if you can go inside." Running Fox walked to the cabin door and went inside. In moments he gestured for them to come. Brady and Frank immediately went to the cabin and entered. They saw Jim sitting on one of the crude chairs and noticed that he not only looked healthy, but he was wearing a smile that showed signs of a newfound happiness. The men shook hands with Jim.

"You're lookin' good, my friend. These women must have used some powerful medicine on you. Tell us about it," Brady said.

Jim answered, "I don't know what she used. The Medicine Woman mixed up different potions and spread them on my side. She also gave me strange things to eat and drink. I slept most of the time. Little White Feather also took care of me. She fed me and then sang a soft Indian song when she rubbed my head. They burned dried leaves in a small pot every evening, and the Medicine Woman chanted, going on and on with her singing. When Little White Feather woke me yesterday morning, I was fully alert. I felt like my old self, maybe even better."

"Are you going to be able to ride in the morning?" Frank asked.

"I think I can. Most of my pain is gone," he replied. All the while Frank and Brady talked to Jim they noticed that Jim couldn't take his eyes off of Little White Feather. He watched her every move inside the cabin.

"Do you feel like taking a walk outside?" Brady asked him.

"Sure. I need to find my boots."

The three men walked outside into the fresh air. Jim said, "Fellas, there's something I need to tell you. I think I've fallen love with Little

White Feather, and I'm sure that she feels the same for me. I'll go back home with you, but I plan to come back for her and her son."

"She *is* a good looking woman—and smart. Another plus, she knows how to cook," Frank kidded. "Congratulations. It's surprising how fate works in our lives. First Charlie finds Rosalee, and now you've found Little White Feather."

"Did you have any luck finding farm land after you left here?" Jim asked.

"We found some land north and west of here. I staked out eighty acres, and Frank staked twenty. We plan to come back next spring to build our cabins, and then we'll move up there," Brady told Jim.

"That's great! I'm happy for you," Jim said. "Guess I wasn't supposed to go with you and get land."

"We would like to leave early in the morning if you feel up to it. We've been away much longer than we planned, and we're anxious to get back home." Brady stated.

"I understand that. I'm ready to leave with you," Jim replied. "This has been a real experience. Just think of everything that has happened to us. We'll definitely have stories to tell our children."

Little White Feather came outside and started walking over toward the three men. Frank and Brady looked at each other as they watched her eyes connect with Jim's.

"Let's go check our horses," Frank said as he looked at Brady and winked. The two men walked away as Little White Feather went to Jim. He took her hand and they walked to the edge of the clearing away from the house. It was apparent that he was telling her of his plans, and then they embraced, and he kissed her.

As evening approached, Frank and Brady sat outside. The sun hung just above the horizon, a golden glow sifting through the tree branches and casting long shadows on the ground. The men planned to leave early the next morning to get as far as possible on their homeward journey. They had decided to retrace their original route as nearly as possible, hoping the trip would not offer as many detours and hardships. Brady found himself staring at the sunset with his thoughts on Anna

Marie and Pat. *I'm on my way home, Anna Marie. Oh how I ache for you. In a few days my arms will be holding you once again.*

★ ★

The men arose early, and after having their coffee and some corn cakes that Little White Feather prepared for them, they readied their horses. They filled their canteens with water and prepared to ride out. The Medicine Woman, Little White Feather, and Running Fox came outside to bid them farewell. Running Fox came over to Brady and Jim and said, "I want to ride with you like I did before, out to the road."

Brady replied, "You're welcome to ride with us."

Jim said to the Medicine Woman and Little White Feather, "You took me into your home and healed me. I'll always remember your help and kindness. When I return, you can count on me to help you any way I can." He held Little White Feather's hand for a moment then turned to mount his horse. He wanted to sweep her up into his arms and take her away, but he knew that this was not the time. He knew that he needed the Medicine Woman's approval to have Little White Feather for his wife. There would be many things that Jim would have to know about the ways of the Indians.

Brady and Frank mounted and waved good-bye, then the men, along with Running Fox, rode off. The group trotted their horses at a steady pace, and in a short time they had once again arrived at the forest edge and the main road. Running Fox halted his horse and said, "May the Great Chief give you safe journey."

"Stay well and care for your mother and grandmother. I'll return soon," Jim replied as he waved good-bye.

The men maintained a steady pace that day, and by late afternoon had arrived at the familiar Preacher O'Reilly's place. They rode up, dismounted, and before they could knock on his door, he came outside to greet them. He was waving his arms and grinning from ear to ear.

"Hello, boys. How in the dickens are you?" he enthusiastically hollered out.

"Well, we've had quite a time, but we found our land and claimed it. We're on our way back home," Frank told him.

"You *are* going to spend the night with me, aren't you?" he asked.

158

The men looked at each other, and they knew they were hooked. It was apparent that the Preacher man was so excited to have company, they couldn't refuse.

"Go ahead and hitch your horses, then come over to the shade and tell me all about your adventures," he said to the scouts.

So it was that the scouts shared lots of stories and laughs with Preacher O'Reilly. The preacher shared a pot of soup beans with pork pieces that he had made up the day before. He still had fresh tomatoes from his plants and an apple cake that one of the ladies from the church had made for him.

Brady said, "This food is just like Thanksgiving dinner." The other men agreed.

The preacher responded, "It *is* Thanksgiving. You are thankful for the food, and I am thankful that you returned safely and are sharing your time with me."

Brady added, "You've been a blessing to us. We've shared our lives together and made lasting friendships with each other." Once again Frank and Jim agreed. About an hour after sundown, they were all talked out and decided to bed down for the night.

★ ★ ★ ★ ★ ★ ★ ★ ★ ★ ★ ★ ★ ★ ★ ★ ★ ★ ★

Frank, Jim, and Brady stood with the preacher man outside in front of his cabin the next morning. It had clouded up during the night, and a brisk wind blew.

"Must be a storm coming. It hasn't rained for over a month," Preacher O'Reilly said. "We're due for a good one."

"If you're right, we'd better ride now. Maybe we'll keep ahead of it," Frank responded. "Thanks again, Preacher O'Reilly," said Frank as he shook the old man's hand.

Jim and Brady also shook hands with the preacher and expressed their thanks. "Take care, old fellow, and be careful of all the ladies baking cakes and cookies for you," Brady joked.

The men got on their horses, waved good-bye, and headed east. Preacher O'Reilly smiled and waved as they rode off. It was the goal of the three men to ride through Seymour and as much farther as possible that day. They set a brisk pace on their mounts and reached

Seymour by noon. They stopped at a place called Mom's Kitchen and ate a quick meal, then continued riding. The clouds had increased and the wind had picked up, causing each man to secure his hat tighter on his head. Along about mid afternoon, the men heard a crack of lightning. Thunder immediately rolled overhead. Within minutes a steady rain came down upon them. The persistence of the men was equally matched by the storm overhead. As they neared the town of Vernon, the scouts, along with their horses and gear, were completely drenched. Frank signaled the men to halt by a building that gave some protection from the rain.

"Men, I don't think we should keep going if we can find some shelter for the night," he suggested. "What do you think?"

Brady said, "I agree, even though I'd like to keep going."

Jim spoke up, "Boys, I'm plumb tuckered out. Remember, I haven't done much but rest the last ten days. Do you suppose we could rent a room somewhere instead of bunking outside?"

Frank said, "Let's find a general store and get out of the rain. We should be able to talk to someone and get some information."

The three rode along the main street and found a general store. They dismounted, tethered their horses, and went inside. The store was infused with the musty odor of ropes, animal feed, leather, and oils. Yet, mixed in with those smells were those of yard goods, soaps, candies, and dried herbs. There were several women and a few men inside looking at the merchandise. The store owner and his clerk were very busy trying to keep up with the requests. Nearly an hour had passed by before the store owner had enough time to visit with the travelers.

"Well now, what can I do for you men?" he asked.

Frank replied, "This storm came upon us while we were riding and we'd like to find a place to sleep tonight. Are there any rooms for rent close by?"

The store owner scratched his head as he thought. "There are rooms over the saloon, which I don't know if you're interested in. Then, there's the livery stable on down the street." He rolled his eyes and then spoke up, "I know a better place than that. An old man called Chester lost his wife last winter, and he lives all by himself in a big house. He's a friendly sort of a man, and he may welcome someone to visit with."

"Where's his place?" Frank asked.

"You ride down the street and you'll see the school house. His place is right across the road."

"Much obliged," Frank told him.

The men went outside and remounted their horses. They rode in the pouring rain down the street looking for Chester's house. A few minutes later they were at the big house where they once again tied their horses. They walked up on the large porch that hugged three of the four sides of the house. They stood under the shelter of the porch, pausing to let some of the rainwater drip off their soaked clothes. They looked at each other with apprehension, not knowing when they rapped on the door if they would be met with a loaded gun or not. Brady took the initiative and knocked loudly on the outside door. They heard heavy steps coming their way, and they stepped back a couple steps. A husky, middle-aged man peered through the window in the door before he proceeded to open the door.

Brady spoke up, "Sorry to bother you. My friends and I have been riding in the rain for several hours and would like to have a place to sleep for the night. The man who runs the mercantile said you might have a room or two to rent to us. We won't be any bother; we're riding back to our families in Kentucky."

"Step inside, take your coats and boots off, and we'll visit here a little bit," the man replied. "You're not carrying guns are you?"

"No sir, our rifles are on our horses. We use them only for protection."

The men went inside and removed their wet coats, hats, and boots. They observed a gentle man who had graying hair and wrinkles creasing around his lively eyes. He was of medium build and walked slowly with a slight limp, which favored his right leg. It seemed that he had no fear of letting three total strangers into his home.

"You can call me Chester. Come on in and I'll fix us all a hot drink. That sounds good, don't you think?" he asked.

"Let me make some introductions. I'm Brady Patterson." Brady pointed to his scout friends and said, "My friends are Frank Justice and Jim Bates."

The men politely said hello to each other and followed the kind

161

man into his kitchen. They relaxed in the warmth of the home that they had found. Chester busied himself getting the water hot and fetching the mugs out of the cabinet. The scouts sat quietly, still feeling chilled from the rain, which had soaked through all of their clothes. Soon Chester was filling the mugs with hot tea, and he sat down with the three scouts.

"This here's a big house for a man to live in alone," Chester began. "My wife died last winter. She first had a cough, then a sore throat. She coughed and coughed. Even the doc didn't have the medicine to stop it. Then she started running a high fever and took to the bed. She had quit coughing but she was having trouble with her breathing. She said she felt like a heavy sack of flour was pressing down on her lungs. The neighbor ladies brought chicken soup to feed her and helped me care for her. She tried, but after about two weeks she got too weak to even eat. I knew by that time that I wouldn't have my sweetheart many more days." He bowed his head and wiped away a few tears. The men stayed quiet so as not to interrupt him. They could tell that he needed to talk. He raised his head and looked at each of the young men and said, "I sure do miss her. She was the most wonderful woman a man could ask for. Are any of you married?"

"I am," Brady answered.

"I can tell you that a good woman is the best thing a man could ask for in life. He looked at Jim and Frank and said, "If you have feelings for a woman, don't waste time making her your wife. If you don't have anyone, try to find one."

Frank and Jim looked at each other and they realized that Chester was offering them words of wisdom that came from his own experience in life. They smiled and nodded affirmatively at Chester's suggestion. For some time the four men sat together sharing their lives. Chester then agreed that the men could stay upstairs. They would sleep in a real bed for the first time since leaving their homes in Kentucky.

CHAPTER TWENTY-TWO
TURMOIL ON THE RIVER

The men arose more rested the next morning than they had been for a long time. The comfort of a house and a real bed had been a luxury they hadn't enjoyed for weeks now. They looked out the windows and could see that it was still overcast and dreary, but the rain had stopped. They went downstairs into the kitchen where they found Chester drinking a large mug of coffee. He was standing in front of a long window watching a gathering of various birds as they pecked at some dry bread that he had thrown outside. A wooden bowl of water sat on a tree stump not far from the house. It was Chester's ritual during the early sunrise hours to watch the birds as they gathered around the food crumbs. They would peck on the ground with fervor then suddenly loft into the air and land on the tree stump where they would dip their beaks into the cool, fresh water, lift their heads skyward, and let the refreshing water run down their throats. He provided food and water every day possible. He enjoyed this ritual, the simple beauty that nature and God provides.

Brady joined Chester at the window. The activity of the birds caught his eyes. "Good morning," Brady greeted. He, too, looked out the window. "That's quite a sight out there," he commented.

Chester replied, "Mornin'. You know, I consider those little creatures as part of my family. My wife always had a special love for birds. Every morning after breakfast she would put some leftover dried bread or biscuits outside. If it was very dry or cold outside, she would be sure that there was fresh water for them to drink." He cleared his throat and took a drink of his coffee, as the thoughts of her caused him to become emotional. "Since she passed away, I feed them just like she did."

"It's a good thing that you're doing. More people need to be kind to our feathered friends," Brady told him.

Jim and Frank came into the room at that time. "Morning, everyone. Mm, I smell coffee," Frank remarked.

"Go ahead and help yourself to a cup," Chester said. "You too, Jim. There are cups on the table."

"Thanks, we will," Frank answered.

"Let's all sit here at the table and drink our coffee," Chester suggested. The three visitors agreed that was a good idea. Brady looked around inside the kitchen and he could see that Chester had left it exactly as it had been when his wife was alive. Her flowered apron and bonnet hung on a hook beside the back door. There was a crocheted doily placed in the center of the kitchen table with a blue sugar bowl sitting on it. The silvery white lid had a flower on the top for the handle. There was a small silver spoon lying beside it, no doubt a family treasure. Brady was sure that it had been very special to her. There were also some dried wildflowers in a vase on the cabinet. A twinge of loneliness touched him as Anna Marie's face briefly appeared before him.

Chester shared a bowl of apples and pears with the men. The four men talked and laughed together. Chester seemed to have gotten past his melancholy. He shared stories from his life that included a wagon train trip and fights with the Indians. The three scouts were engrossed with all that he told them. They weren't aware that the skies had once again clouded over and the kitchen had gotten darker. After a while Jim did notice the darkness and gestured to Frank to look outside.

Frank said, "Brady, look outside. It's clouded up again. Don't you think we ought to leave?"

"Look at that! Yes, we'd better ride." Brady stuck his hand out to shake hands with Chester. "Thank you very much for letting three strangers into your home and allowing us to spend the night. You're quite the old fellow, and I'm sure glad I met you. How much room rent do we owe?"

Chester replied, "It was worth a hundred dollars to me, having you men spend time in my home. You don't owe me a wooden nickel! It's been a real pleasure getting to know you."

"You're a good man, Chester. We'll never forget your kindness,"

Frank told him. Frank and Jim shook Chester's hand and said their good-byes.

The three men got their horses out of the small barn located behind Chester's house, saddled up, and rode away. Their goal was to reach Madison, cross the Ohio back to Kentucky, and cover as much ground as possible by nighttime. They had ridden about thirty minutes when the lightening flashed, the thunder rolled, the sky opened up, and the rain poured down hard. The men couldn't believe that another rainstorm was upon them, and once again they were drenched. The pelting rain and the muddy roads slowed down the progress of the threesome. At times the horses became spooked and reared up when a hard, crackling bolt of lightning pierced the sky and struck close. The riders urged their horses onward, making the best time possible.

The men finally reached Madison about one o'clock that afternoon. The rain had not only soaked them once again, but it had removed the joy from their spirit and replaced it with irritability. They were very hungry, having only chewed on dried meat during their ride, and they needed a good, warm meal. The men and their horses went through the town with their heads down, protecting their faces as much as possible from the relentless rain. They spotted a café, rode up to the hitching posts, and dismounted. They tied their horses securely and entered the business. After they removed their hats, they stood just inside the door and looked around. Their coats dripped puddles of water, and their boots dropped muddy globs of water. One of the women working there told the men to go ahead and sit down.

★ ★ ★ ★ ★ ★ ★ ★ ★ ★ ★ ★ ★ ★ ★ ★ ★ ★ ★ ★

A small band of six Shawnee Indians were still quite angry that the "white man" had taken over their land. They were vicious men on the warpath, and they would stop at nothing to kill anyone who wasn't an Indian. They were camped a couple miles west of Madison in a forested area along the Ohio River. They had been planning their next attack, and they weren't going to let the rain stop them.

★ ★ ★ ★ ★ ★ ★ ★ ★ ★ ★ ★ ★ ★ ★ ★ ★ ★ ★ ★

After a hearty meal, the men decided to see if the ferry would be making its three o'clock trip back across the mighty Ohio River. The meal had refreshed the energy and determination of the three scouts to reach Kentucky today. They got on their horses once again and rode down to the river's edge. They found a place to tie the horses that provided some shelter, and Frank poured some grain in a trough that was built just below the hitching rail. The horses began eating, and the men went to talk to the ferryman, who was sitting in a small structure about ten feet square. There was barely room for four chairs, a small table, and couple shelves. Large pegs lined one side where ropes and various tools hung. Brady, Frank, and Jim went inside the small building to check on the ferry's departure time.

"Good afternoon," Brady said to the ferryman.

"I don't know what's so good about it," he replied with a disgusted tone to his voice. "That consarned rain is causing the river to run hard and fast again. It's hard on the ferry business, you know. I can't risk the lives of people and their animals."

"Yep, I suppose that's right," Brady replied. "Are you going to run it back today?"

"It would be risky. I think it would be best to wait until mornin'. If the rain stops tonight, the river will be calmer tomorrow." The ferryman was irritated that he was losing money every time the river made it difficult for the ferry to make its crossing. "You fellas better find a place to stay tonight. Come back early tomorrow morning; maybe you'll be able to cross then. I'll plan to send it over to the Kentucky side around 8:30."

"All right, we'll come back in the morning. Thanks."

The scouts walked over to their horses and talked about where to spend the night. "We could camp out at the old trading post," Frank suggested.

"We could if we weren't already soaking wet," Brady replied. "I don't know about you men, but I would like to get clean and dry. That old trading post won't offer much protection."

Jim said, "I agree with Brady. We all probably smell like wet horse blankets or worse. We need to find a place where we can sleep inside and have a chance to clean ourselves and our clothes."

"That sounds okay with me," said Frank. The men remounted their horses and made their way back toward town. They found a boarding house with three beds available and a room with a tub, soap, and towels they could use for an additional small fee. The discouraged scouts settled in for the night.

The men awoke about sunup. The sky was partly cloudy, but the rain had subsided. They were anxious to be on their way home as soon as possible. The boarding house offered a man-sized breakfast, which the scouts ate voraciously. They gathered up their belongings and went out to retrieve their horses from the small stable the boarding house provided for their boarders. They fed the horses and curried them, something that they had neglected over the past few days. Each man saddled his horses and checked his mount's hooves. They rode back down toward the river's edge. The rainwater had filled every horse and wagon track left by yesterday's travel along the street. Muddy water splashed on the men's legs as the horses made their way toward the river. When they arrived, they could see right away that the rains had swollen the size of the river, and the water was rushing and churning as it made its way past them. The ferry was docked securely, although the turbulent waters caused it to roll about when large waves came against it. It was an hour before departure time, and the scouts hadn't noticed that more rain clouds were filling the skies. They were the only people hoping to make the crossing at this time. Once again they tied their horses and proceeded down to the ferryman's shed. While they were visiting with the ferryman, two more men came to check on the possibility of crossing the river.

★ ★ ★ ★ ★ ★ ★ ★ ★ ★ ★ ★ ★ ★ ★ ★ ★ ★ ★

Meanwhile, the Shawnee warriors were approaching the area of the boat dock. They were intent upon fighting and killing their enemies, the white people. They had crept up as close as they could without being seen, and were hiding in the trees and brush of the riverbank. They talked among themselves as they planned their attack.

★ ★ ★ ★ ★ ★ ★ ★ ★ ★ ★ ★ ★ ★ ★ ★ ★ ★ ★

Half an hour passed. The ferryman decided it would be safe to run the ferry. "The river is rough, but not dangerous," he told them. The men came out of the shed and went to get their horses. They led their horses down the riverbank and put them aboard the ferry. Lightning flashed, thunder roared, and the heavens poured down rain.

"Oh, no! Not rain again!" Jim said loudly. He looked skyward and raised his fisted arm. "I would like to stay dry for one day," he yelled toward the heavens.

Just as they secured the horses the Indians charged out of hiding. The scouts tried to grab their rifles, but they didn't have time. Three Indians had jumped onto the ferry, wildly swinging their tomahawks in hand-to-hand combat with the scouts. Frank hit one Indian hard and knocked him into the water. The ferryman ran into the shed for his gun, came out, and fired toward the Indians who were attacking the two men still on shore. One of the attackers fell down and lay still, and the other one was shot in the leg. He tried to get up and run away, but he wasn't able. Another Indian, who had stayed back in the brush, ran to the ferryman and hit him with his tomahawk, knocking him down. He lay still on the ground, his head bleeding.

The Indian in the water swam toward shore. While the fighting was going on, he crawled onto the bank, took a large knife from his waistband, and started sawing the heavy rope that held the ferry to the dock. The Indian who had knocked the ferryman down now attacked the two men on shore. No one noticed the Indian who was cutting the ferry loose. At the moment they did notice, the last rope broke loose and the ferry swung out into the current, held only by the single rope from the opposite side of the river. The ferry—and Brady, Jim, Frank, their horses, and two of the attackers—were at the mercy of the river current. The horses struggled to maintain their footing. One Indian knocked Jim down hard onto the ferry deck. Jim landed on his injured side, a groan of agony escaping his lips. The Indian jumped on him and was ready to crack his skull with his tomahawk, but Brady had managed to retrieve his gun and fired. The injured warrior lay quiet as he bled from a shot to the gut. Frank struggled with the last remaining Shawnee, and they both nearly went into the river together. Brady grabbed the Indian from behind and slung him away from Frank. Frank quickly threw a hard punch at the warrior and knocked him out cold.

Still fastened to the opposite bank, the ferry flopped and jerked wildly at the mercy of the churning water. It careened down the river and swerved toward the opposite riverbank until it was held fast by the rope. The ferry banged against large rocks and tree roots, jolting the men and the horses, making it difficult to maintain their balance. Frank grabbed a rope from his saddle, intending to use it to tie the loose end of the ferry to a tree on the bank. Recognizing his friend's plan, Frank spoke, "Brady, you tie the rope here and I'll jump onto the river bank and secure the other end to a tree." Their plan worked. The ferry ceased its floundering. Jim rose from the deck. His injury hurt him, but he would be all right. The three men led their horses onto the riverbank and found a place to tether them. They had no more than secured the safety of their horses when the Indian lying on the ferry deck began to gain consciousness.

Jim called out, "Frank, Brady, the Indian is waking up!" The two ran back onto the ferry, grabbed the Indian, removed his knife, and quickly tied his hands. The warrior spat at Frank and Brady and talked hatefully in his own language, all the while trying to wrestle himself free.

Jim said, "Bring him over here and we'll tie him to a tree. We can go to the ferry landing and have someone come take him."

"I'll go with that," Frank agreed. The rain continued to fall as the men dragged the warrior up the riverbank and tied him securely to a tree. The Shawnee warrior strained against the ropes as he cursed and yelled when the men got on their horses and rode off.

The thunderstorm continued pouring down rain. The scouts found a trail that led them from the riverbank eastward toward the ferry dock on the Kentucky side of the river. After about five minutes they arrived at the dock. The men were thankful to be alive and to have survived the attack of the rogue Indian warriors. It made getting soaking wet a minor matter in their lives. They even managed to laugh among themselves as they talked about leaving the furious Indian tied to the tree.

CHAPTER TWENTY-THREE
WHERE IS HE?

When Anna Marie arose on Thursday morning she looked outside. It was a grey, cloudy day that matched her spirits perfectly. She strained expectantly to see if it was possible that Brady could be riding up the pathway to their home, but he wasn't there. Dejected, she hung her head. She was tired—tired of living alone with the total responsibility of Pat; tired of cooking and cleaning, just to have to do it all over again; tired of pretending to her friends that everything was just fine; tired of not having a reason to brush her hair. She was *so* tired! She went into her living room and sat down in her rocker. She looked down at her ever-enlarging belly and rubbed it as if loving the little one growing inside her. Pat walked over to her. She took one of his hands and put it on her swollen stomach and said, "Can you feel the baby moving inside?" He nodded his head and hugged her legs. She stroked his hair lovingly. He looked at his mother and smiled, then he went about his play.

She sat there in the rocker, lost in thought. *Where is he? Is he on his way home or is he even going to come home? I can't stand this much longer.* She heard raindrops hitting the windows and roof. As if a switch had been turned on, her eyes also clouded up and rained. Tears spilled down her cheeks. The tears rolled down in uncontrollable streams. She picked up her kerchief, and in minutes it was soaked. Her eyes shed their tears until there were no more. Feeling as if she were completely spent, she closed her swollen eyes and took a long, deep breath. She suddenly shuddered as if she could feel that something was happening to Brady. She could almost feel the danger. *Was that a scream?* She jerked, and her eyes popped open.

"Anna Marie, are you there?" a voice called.

She took a quick breath and realized that someone was calling her from the front porch. She heard it again, "Anna Marie, are you okay?" Anna rose from the rocking chair and struggled to the door and opened it. She was surprised and happy to see Pricilla standing on the porch. In one hand she was holding a bouquet of wildflowers tied with a yellow ribbon; in the other she was holding a loaf of sweet bread. Anna Marie was so glad to see her that she gave her a big hug.

"I am so happy to see you. Please, come inside out of the rain. Tell me, why are you here?"

"Jeremiah went to Richmond to get supplies, and I stayed home. He'll be gone two or three days and I thought about you being alone for such a long time so I decided to come and visit. Anna, have you been crying? Your eyes look red and swollen."

"I've been feeling sorry for myself. I sat in my rocking chair and had a long cry. A strange feeling came over me that something bad was happening to Brady. It probably didn't mean anything," Anna said as she tried to brush it aside.

"Brady should be coming home any day now. I'm sure of it," Pricilla consoled. "He loves you and he *will* return to his family."

After the women took care of Pricilla's horse and carriage, Anna made a fresh pot of tea and served a dish of pudding that she had made that morning. The women sat and talked for over an hour. After a while, Anna took Pat into the bedroom and laid him down for a nap.

"Do you know when Brady will come home?" Pricilla asked.

"No. He planned to be gone for four weeks and it's been six. If he doesn't come home soon, I'll have to do something different. It's just too hard to be here alone."

"Give it a little more time—say two weeks," suggested Pricilla, "and if he doesn't come back, you can come stay with Jeremiah and me. I don't think he'll be gone much longer." she consoled. "I believe he's on his way home right now. That's probably what you're sensing."

"I want to believe you're right. Pricilla, could you stay the night? It would be so nice to have you here."

"Well, I did bring a bag along with me with that in mind—and

I brought some quilt pieces with me. Maybe we can work on them together. How does that sound?"

"Perfect. Pricilla, you are a lifesaver! I can't begin to tell you how pleased I am that you came to see me."

★ ★ ★ ★ ★ ★ ★ ★ ★ ★ ★ ★ ★ ★ ★ ★ ★ ★ ★

After Brady, Frank, and Jim checked their horses over for injuries and found them sound, they continued toward the ferry site. They came upon the ferrymen, who were making their way downstream toward the ferry, and explained what had happened and where the ferry was now. "You men survived an Indian attack?" said one of the ferrymen. "We'd heard that a band of Shawnee had been spotted. Glad to see that you men came through it alive!"

"Yeah, they jumped us just as we were loading our horses onto the ferry. They tried their best to kill us," Frank stated.

"We left a very angry Indian tied to a tree. He was spittin' mad!"

"We'll be glad to deal with him! We're sure glad you men are all right. We owe you thanks for taking care of our ferry."

The men shook hands and bid each other a safe journey. The scouts were relieved that that part of their trip was behind them. The rainstorm had finally let up some, and the rain was now only a faint drizzle. The scouts knew that they had lost valuable time. They also knew they could have lost their horses or their lives during the surprise Indian attack. They came through the incident with bruises and lumps, but no serious injuries. Neither Shawnee warriors nor anything else would lessen their drive to continue their trip homeward. It was still before noon, and the scouts decided that they would ride on—and ride they did. They pushed their horses for a solid two hours before stopping to rest. They had probably covered at least fifteen miles. They continued the pattern of riding two hours between rests. They rode through a town called Owenton at about three in the afternoon. They found a boarding house and ate a tasty meal of meat, mashed potatoes and gravy. By the end of the day, the men had covered close to fifty miles, and they began looking for a place to spend the night. The skies had cleared the clouds away, and it had become calm. The temperature warmed, and the scouts' clothing was beginning to dry. They were probably twenty miles north of Frankfort when they found shelter and stopped riding.

★ ★ ★ ★ ★ ★ ★ ★ ★ ★ ★ ★ ★ ★ ★ ★ ★ ★ ★

The sun shone brightly on Friday morning signaling that the rain had ended. Anna Marie arose shortly after dawn and finished her chores early. Pricilla played with Pat as Anna Marie prepared breakfast. Anna Marie hummed a little tune as she stirred the flapjack batter. She hadn't felt this lighthearted since Brady had left with the scouts. She quickly brewed a fresh pot of tea and set a bowl of honey on the kitchen table. As she fixed the tea, she remembered with fondness that Brady had surprised her with the teapot. She carefully placed the matching teacups beside the teapot.

"Come on in for breakfast," Anna called out. Pricilla and Pat took their places at the kitchen table. "Oh, what beautiful teacups and teapot!" Pricilla said. "Where did you get them?"

"Brady got these for me last Christmas. He picked them out because I love the wildflowers so much."

"They are truly special. I'll be sure to hold them daintily, with my pinkie finger curled up high," she said as she laughed. Anna joined her in the joke.

After breakfast the three planned their day. They decided to take a buggy ride and enjoy the sunshine. They would look for wild flowers alongside the road and then maybe go into Reeds Crossing.

Pricilla said to Pat, "If we go to pick wild flowers you need to find a basket to put them in, right?"

Pat ran quickly to the shelf where the garden basket sat. He brought it back and said to Anna Marie, "Momma, go with 'Cilla."

"Yes, Pat, you and Pricilla can put your flowers in the basket. Are you ready to go for a buggy ride?"

"Go, Momma. Go ride," Pat replied.

Anna Marie hitched Mandy to the buggy as the three anticipated what the day would bring. They had donned coats as the early hours of the day were chilly. The warm sunshine would dry the roadbeds making for good travel. A sunny day would lighten Anna Marie's mood and push back the sadness that the clouds had brought to her only the day before.

★ ★ ★ ★ ★ ★ ★ ★ ★ ★ ★ ★ ★ ★ ★ ★ ★ ★

On Friday morning the scouts rolled out of their blankets when the first rays of sun crested the horizon. The ground was damp, and a chill filled the air. Frank quickly stirred the campfire and added branches to encourage the flames that would boil the water for their morning coffee.

"I'll sure be glad to get home to have my side checked by a doctor. It pained me most of the night," Jim told his friends.

"Do you think you can ride at the same pace today as we rode yesterday?" Brady asked him.

"I'm pretty sure I can if I my horse don't throw me off," he replied half jokingly.

"I'm glad to hear that. We'll have our coffee and bread and head out," Frank said.

"Look over there. Is that an apple tree?" Brady stated.

"By darn, I think it is. I'll go see if any apples are ready to eat," Frank said. He went to the tree and picked an armful and walked back to the camp. "Mother Nature has generously provided fruit to go with our breakfast," he said with a chuckle. "She knows a man can't ride far on a crust of dry bread!"

Jim raised his mug of coffee and made a toast, "Here's to the man who planted the apple trees."

Both Frank and Brady raised their mugs and repeated, "Here, here."

The men, full of good spirit, ate heartily of the newly found fruit, then as soon as they broke camp, they and headed south toward Frankfurt. They tried to pace their horses as they had the day before. If they could make another fifty miles today, that would be a good day's ride.

The men arrived in Frankfurt just before lunchtime. They rode through the main street and gazed at the businesses and the new buildings. "Frankfurt sure is growing," Jim remarked as they trotted along. "Too bad Charlie and Joker aren't here to see this." The scouts were astonished at the size of the new buildings and the architecture. As they made their way along the cobblestone street, they drank in the modern look of the city.

"Fellows, I'm gonna' have to find a blacksmith. My horse is limping," Frank stated. "I need to check what's wrong."

It didn't take long to locate the blacksmith, who immediately discovered the problem—a small, sharp stone lodged in a back hoof next to the frog. When the smithy removed the stone, he saw that the stone had caused a cut the sole, which was bleeding. "This horse needs rest so he can heal," the smithy announced.

"Listen," Frank said with great concern, "I can't stay around. My buddies and I are on our way home and we have about two more days of riding ahead of us. Can you do something for my horse so I can still ride him?"

"I have some ointment I could put on his wound. Maybe I can find a way to wrap his hoof to help keep it clean."

"Whatever you can figure out to help him, I will be grateful. We'll go have a hot meal and come back for him."

This was just one more delay in the long list of delays the scouts had dealt with. They would never have guessed how a three- or four-week trip would turn into one twice as long. The arduous trip was now feeling like torture to Brady. He was aching to see his Anna and to hold her lovingly. *I wonder what she is doing at this minute. Are she and Pat all right? I'm so close to being home. I promise that I will never leave you for this long again,* Brady thought.

The men ate a big noon meal and went directly back to the blacksmith's. Frank walked his horse around by the reins to see if his foot was better. Satisfied that the horse would be all right, he paid the smithy for his services, and the scouts left Frankfurt with the hope of reaching Lexington by evening.

★ ★ ★ ★ ★ ★ ★ ★ ★ ★ ★ ★ ★ ★ ★ ★ ★ ★ ★

Anna Marie drove along the road to a meadow where she knew the wildflowers grew. She halted the buggy beside a birch tree and tied

Mandy where she could graze on the clean, cool grass. Anna Marie walked with Pricilla and Pat for a while, but soon she became tired and went back to the buggy. She spread a coverlet on the ground and sat with joy as she watched the interaction between her friend and her son. Pricilla took Pat by the hand as they walked from one patch of flowers to another. Pat picked handfuls of flowers and put them in the basket, jabbering with Pricilla the whole time. He squealed when a couple of yellow butterflies landed on his basket and flitted from flower to flower. He was totally thrilled watching these small creatures of nature.

All the factors of the day soothed Anna's spirit—the sunshine and warm air, Pat's happiness in the out-of-doors, the peace and quiet of nature that she so loved. *I know Brady is thinking of me and is on his way home,* she thought. She watched a pair of squirrels run around a tree trunk then suddenly scurry up into its leafy sanctuary. A woodpecker began hammering high on another tree. A butterfly floated nearby and actually sat on a flower printed on the coverlet right beside her. Anna Marie smiled as she watched the butterfly, free and beautiful, doing what it was created to do. *Brady is a product of nature,* she thought, *feeling free and doing what he was meant to do.*

Pat and Pricilla returned to the birch tree. Pat wore a grin as he struggled to carry the basket of flowers to his mother's side. Anna Marie took a wet cloth that she had brought along, and wrapped it around the flower stems to help keep them fresh. She handed the bouquet to Pat, and he put them into a large tin can. He was so proud of those flowers.

They had spent about an hour in the meadow when they decided to get back into the buggy and continue on their outing. As they trotted along the road toward town, they approached the home of Preacher Martin and his wife, just at the edge of Reed's Crossing. Preacher Martin and Naomi waved hello and beckoned for them to stop. Anna Marie guided Mandy up to their house.

"Where are you lovely ladies going on this beautiful day?" Preacher Martin asked.

Pricilla answered, "I'm spending some time with Anna Marie and Pat. Today we decided to go for an outing."

Naomi said to them, "We were ready to go inside and have a bite of lunch. Would you care to join us?"

The young women looked at each other and nodded yes. Anna Marie replied, "It would be a pleasure to eat with you."

"Well, just come inside with me," Naomi told them. Preacher Martin held the buggy steady as the three climbed out and headed for the house. He led the horse over to his hitching post and gave her a bucket of water then went to join the women and Pat.

The three spent stayed most of the afternoon visiting with the Martins. They laughed and visited until Anna Marie looked at the clock on the fireplace mantle and realized how long they had been there. "Oh, dear me," she exclaimed as she stood up, "it'll be chore time soon. It's been so nice to visit with you, but I think that we had better go back home. Thank you for lunch and the enjoyable afternoon."

Pricilla also rose out of her chair and said, "Naomi, we have had a wonderful visit here today. Thank you for everything." The three women all hugged each other and Naomi picked up Pat and hugged him. "I want you to be a good boy for your momma, okay?"

Pat said, "Good boy." They all walked outside, and Anna Marie, Pricilla, and Pat got into the buggy and started down the lane.

Anna Marie said to Pricilla, "I would like to go on into town and check to see if there might be some mail if you don't mind."

"I don't mind at all. You get your mail and I'll take Pat with me to the general store to get a couple things. It won't take me long."

They drove the buggy to the post office and hitched the horse. Pricilla took Pat and headed for the store as Anna Marie made her way into the post office. She was more relaxed going in this time. She had to wait a few minutes before she was able to talk to the postmaster. When he came to the window, she gave her name and asked for her mail. He handed her a letter from her mother and said, "That's all you have, ma'am."

"Thank you," she replied and walked back to the buggy. She felt a lump in her throat as she read the letter from her mother. Feelings of emptiness entered her body and soul. *I should lock up the house and go live with my mother until Brady returns*, she thought. *I need someone with me*

177

until I deliver my baby. She realized that she was, indeed, homesick for her family. She decided that if Brady hadn't come home by Monday, she would talk to Lucy and Big Al and make arrangements to go visit her parents.

Pat and Pricilla walked out of the store and went over to the buggy. "Did you get any mail?" she asked Anna Marie.

"Only a letter from my mother," she replied with a raspy voice.

"Are you all right?"

Anna Marie cleared her throat and said, "I was just thinking about visiting my mother and father, that's all."

"I think that would be good for you, and Pat would get to see his grandparents."

"We'll see," Anna Marie replied. "First things first. We need to go back to my place now."

As soon as they arrived at the Patterson farm, the two women took care of the chickens. Anna Marie fixed the evening meal, and Pricilla played some with Pat. He was tired from all the activities of the day, and he became sleepy early that evening. As Anna Marie put him to bed he asked her, "Momma, daddy home?"

"Very soon I hope. Let's say a prayer for daddy. Fold your hands and close your eyes," she told him. "Jesus, we asked you to bring Pat's daddy home soon, safe and sound. Bless our home and our family. Keep us safe through the night. Amen," she prayed.

All through the evening hours Pricilla and Anna Marie enjoyed quiet conversation as they deepened their friendship by sharing their lives as they stitched away on the quilt pieces.

★ ★ ★ ★ ★ ★ ★ ★ ★ ★ ★ ★ ★ ★ ★ ★ ★ ★

Frank could tell that his horse was not keeping up with the other two horses as he had before. After they had ridden about an hour and a half Frank called to Brady and Jim to stop. He dismounted and carefully checked his horse's sore foot.

"Is there a problem?" Brady asked him.

"The wrap seems to be holding, but he is still favoring this leg."

"Can you make it to Lexington? We're not quite halfway, I'd guess."

"I'll try to. I'll guide him to trot on the grass beside the road."

Frank remounted, and the scouts continued on their journey. They took one more break after that, and finally rode into Lexington at the supper hour. They rode slowly down the main street and found a place to rest and eat. Frank checked his horses' foot once more. He decided that he would have to clean the hoof again and put on a new wrap before he would allow his horse to carry him any further.

Brady asked the other two scouts, "Do you want to ride on another hour or two or do you want to stay here for the night?"

Frank replied, "I don't want to push my horse any further today. He needs to rest and heal."

Jim said, "I can go either way. We still have daylight to ride, but I don't know where we'll bunk for the night if we go on."

Frank spoke up, "Fellas, if you want to move on tonight it's all right with me. I'll rest a day then I'll ride on home."

"Let's not take any chances sleeping outdoors," suggested Brady. "We'll stay here for the night and head home as soon as we can in the morning. Frank can wait till then to decide if he should rest his horse another day. What do you say?"

Jim and Frank both agreed with Brady. The men found an inn where they could all stay for the night. Frank took his horse to the livery stable to care for his sore foot. Shortly after dark, all three men were cleaned up and in bed.

CHAPTER TWENTY-FOUR

THE LAST THIRTY MILES

Saturday morning. The scouts rose early as usual and ate a hot breakfast at the inn where they had slept. As they went outside to get their horses from the stables, they noticed a cloudbank in the north. Some of the clouds were swirling, and others were stretched out like long strands of hair waving in the wind. Each man wondered what kind of day it was going to be. Suddenly, a gust of wind blew Jim's hat off and sent it rolling down the street.

The stable keeper had fed and brushed their horses down. The scouts were pleased with their condition.

"How's my horse this morning?" Frank asked as he stroked his horse's neck. He lifted the injured hoof and checked its tenderness.

"His hoof seems to be healing," the stable man replied. "If you don't push him too hard, he should be all right."

The men settled their bill and thanked the stable keeper for taking good care of their horses. They then filled their canteens with fresh water, saddled their horses, and rode out of town. Jim remarked that his horse didn't seem to be limping at all this morning. The wind began to blow steadily from the north. The men pulled their hats down tightly on their heads, put their heads down, and continued forward with determination. The wind steadily increased in velocity, whipping up dust, sticks, and leaves that pelted the men and their horses. After an hour and a half of riding, the men guided their horses into a grove of trees, which offered some protection, and dismounted. They had covered about twelve miles of the last thirty of their journey.

"Holy cow. That wind could blow me right out of the saddle!" Jim exclaimed. "What should we do now, keep riding or hold up for a while?"

Brady couldn't stand another delay that would keep him from seeing his wife. He spoke up, "Men, we can't afford to stop yet. I suggest we keep going at a steady pace. Maybe the wind will blow itself out in a few hours."

Frank agreed, "Let's keep going. If the weather gets worse, we'll make another decision." With that being said, the men got back up on their horses and headed on their way. The wind continued whipping dirt and debris upon the scouts and their horses, but they rode on with determination.

★ ★ ★ ★ ★ ★ ★ ★ ★ ★ ★ ★ ★ ★ ★ ★ ★ ★ ★

It was Saturday morning at the farm. Anna Marie, Pat, and Pricilla were sitting at the table enjoying fried eggs with fresh-made biscuits. They sat and visited, unaware of the time. Pat had been playing on the floor, but had become distracted and was standing by the kitchen window. He turned to his mother. "Look, Momma, look!" he hollered.

What could it be now? Anna Marie thought. She got up and went to the window. She could see that the trees were swaying back and forth and her chickens were running around, wings spread out as if they wanted to fly. "Good grief!" she exclaimed. "Look how hard the wind is blowing. I had better get the chickens in the chicken house and make sure the barn doors are shut tight."

"I'll help you," Pricilla told her. "Let's hurry!"

Anna Marie said to Pat, "Momma's going outside, but you stay inside. I won't be out very long. You can look out of the window and watch us with the chickens, okay?" Pat nodded his head and went back to the kitchen window. He put his index finger on the windowpane and moved it back and forth as he followed the chickens' awkward movements in the chicken yard.

Anna Marie and Pricilla quickly put on their shawls and wrapped scarves around their heads before they dashed outside. Pat stood at the window and watched until he saw the two women. He smiled and patted on the windowpane, but they didn't see him as they were busy corralling the chickens. It wasn't an easy job with the frightened birds scattered all over the pen, but they finally succeeded and shut the door firmly. Finally they secured the barn door and headed for the house. With their heads bowed against the wind Pricilla said, "You know, I think I had better gather up my things and go back home. I need to look after my place. You understand, don't you?"

"Yes, I do understand. I'd do the same thing. Come on inside and I'll help you."

Pricilla held the door for Anna Marie to keep the door from slamming against her. The two ladies made it safely inside and Pat came running to greet them. "I saw chicks, Momma," Pat said. Anna Marie and Pricilla stopped and stared at Pat. Pricilla said, "He talked in a full sentence. I can't believe it! Come over here and let me give you a big hug." He came to Pricilla, and she bent over and wrapped her arms around him and gave him a squeeze.

Anna Marie sat in her rocking chair and removed her scarf and shawl. Pat went over to his momma and crawled up on her lap. "You're getting to be such a big boy," she told him. Pricilla gathered her belongings and put them in her satchel. There was rapping on the front door that startled the two women. They were quiet and listened, and again there was rapping. A voice hollered out, "Anna Marie, it's Al. Are you okay?"

"Just a minute, I'm coming." Anna struggled to get up from the rocking chair and went to open the door. "Hello Al. Please, come in."

"Is everybody all right? I haven't seen you for a few days. Since the darned wind has come up, I thought I should come over and check up on you and Pat. Hello Pricilla. I didn't realize you were here."

"Thanks, Al. We're fine." Anna Marie smoothed her hair and looked at Pricilla. "Pricilla came over Thursday and has stayed two days with us. When the wind started blowing so hard, she helped me with the chickens, but now she's decided she should leave for home."

"Do you need help, Pricilla? I could hitch your buggy for you."

"Thank you, Al. That would be nice of you."

Al went back out to the barn, hitched Pricilla's horse up to her buggy and brought it to the front of the house. She and Anna Marie were saying their good-byes and hugging one another.

"It was so nice of you to come and visit Pat and me. Thank you for being such a good friend. Please be careful as you go home."

"Don't worry about me. I'll be just fine. You take care of Pat, and I'll plan to see you in church tomorrow," Pricilla told her. Pricilla got into her buggy, snapped the reins, and started off toward her home.

Big Al went back inside the cabin with Anna Marie. He said, "I brought some milk over for you and Pat. Is there anything I can help you with?"

"I guess not. I have decided that if Brady isn't home by Monday, I'm going to pack bags for Pat and myself and go visit with my mother. I need to be with family."

"I can understand that," Big Al replied. "You know you are always welcome to come and stay with Lucy and me."

"Yes, thank you, I know. I guess I'm just homesick for my own family." Anna choked back tears. Big Al stepped toward her and pulled her close to his side.

"It's been hard for you these past few weeks, but I just know Brady will be home soon and he'll have good news for you. You must be strong. If you change your mind about staying here alone, come stay with us for a few days. We have enough going on with our big family to keep you from being lonely." He eased his hold on Anna, and she stepped back slightly.

"Al, you and Lucy are so good to me. I'll see how I'm feeling later before I decide to come to your place."

"All right, we'll leave it like that for now. I'll go on back home. If I don't see you later today, I'll plan on seeing you tomorrow. Come over here, Pat, and give Al a good-bye hug." Pat ran to him and squeezed Al's big neck. "You need to be good for your momma, you hear?" Pat nodded his head affirmatively, turned and smiled widely at his mama.

Anna Marie walked to the door with Al and stood there as she watched him ride off. She could see that the strong winds were still whipping through the trees and sending leaves and dust everywhere.

★ ★ ★ ★ ★ ★ ★ ★ ★ ★ ★ ★ ★ ★ ★ ★ ★ ★ ★

The scouts rode on, the wind persistently beating at them and their horses. By the time they had ridden another two hours, their eyes and ears were full of dirt and their lips were chapped. They hadn't made good travel time. The horses had started shaking their heads and whinnying while sidestepping at times against the strong gusts that blew upon them. The scouts were approaching a rather large farm.

"Let's see if we can stop and rest the horses here and take a break from the weather," Frank suggested.

"I agree," Jim stated. "Would that suit you, Brady?" Brady nodded in agreement.

As they rode along toward the farmer's barn, they saw the farmer and a couple of his boys out chasing pigs. When they got closer, they realized that the gate to the pigpen had been knocked down. Five sows and all their little piglets were running loose in the front of the house, on the road, and everywhere else in the barnyard. The scouts jumped off of their horses and quickly tied them to the barnyard fence.

"Could you use some help?" Brady asked the farmer.

"I sure could," he responded.

The scouts weren't too sure how best to corral pigs, but they tried. If they picked up a piglet, the sow, in an attempt to protect her brood, became angry and mean. The scouts knew that an angry pig, boar, or sow, could be very dangerous. It was nothing short of chaotic with the pigs and the men zigzagging back and forth with not much being accomplished.

Frank went over to the downed gate, picked it up, and held it across the opening to the pigpen. "Have one of your boys put some feed into the feed trough. The food should interest the sows. Drive the sows in here first," he suggested, "and I'll open the gate until they are inside, then I'll hold the gate shut on them. You can gather up the piglets and put them inside. Let's see if that will work." The farmer and the scouts agreed.

The two boys were faster at chasing the piglets but weren't having any more success at catching them than the men. Finally, though, one by one, each quick little rascal was caught and put inside the pen. By the time the last piglet was caught, everyone was panting with exhaustion. The farmer wired the gate shut, certain that the pigs were in to stay.

"Fellas, let me shake your hands. I don't know if my boys and I could'a got all those pigs in by dark by ourselves. Is there anything that I can do for you?"

Brady spoke up, "We've been riding in this wind for several hours. We would like to rest our horses if you don't mind."

"Sure thing. Follow me to the barn and I'll make a place for them." The farmer led the scouts to the barn. He held the door open against the gusty wind until the three scouts had led their horses inside to an open stall with a feed trough. "Take some buckets so you can fetch water from the water trough outside," he suggested. "I'll wait until you finish then you can come to the house and we'll visit a while."

The scouts removed the saddles from their horses and gave each horse a bucket of water. Satisfied that their horses were taken care of, they went with the farmer to his home. They tried brushing some of the dirt off of their hats and clothes before entering. They could feel the grit on their hands and faces.

"Come on inside, fellas. You know we never told each other our names. I'm Joshua and this is my wife, Clara." The scouts each gave their name and greeted Clara. "Come on in to the kitchen table. Have you men had something to eat?" Joshua asked.

Frank replied, "We had breakfast early this morning before we started out."

"You can join us for our meal," Clara said. "It's been ready for two hours. We didn't count on the pigpen gate getting knocked down and letting all the sows and their little pigs run loose. It sure was a good thing you came along and helped."

Joshua, Clara, their four children, and the scouts gathered around the kitchen table. They ate their meat, potatoes, and gravy meal with great pleasure. Clara had made two berry pies that morning and carried one of them to the table. She asked, "Would anyone have room for a piece of pie?" Everyone quickly answered yes. "All right, I'll brew some coffee to go with it. Children, you can have milk with yours."

The respite from the wind, and the delicious, nourishing food revived the scouts. When the kitchen was tidied, Clara picked up her crochet needle and yarn and worked on a doily while the men talked.

Brady watched her work. He looked around the kitchen and saw several doilies that Clara had placed under vases and glassware. He began to think that one of her doilies would make a nice gift for Anna Marie. "I'd sure like to buy one of your doilies for my wife. Would you sell me one?"

"What color would you like?" she asked him.

"Any color would be all right. You pick one out and I'll pay you for it."

She went to box in the corner of the bedroom and brought out a light blue one trimmed with dark blue. It was about the size of a dinner plate. "Would this one work?" she asked him.

"That's perfect. How much do I owe you?"

"You don't owe me a thing. You helped Joshua with his farm work, and that was worth a lot to both of us. You take it and give it to your wife along with a hug from me. I'm sure she's a very special lady."

"That she is," he replied. Clara put the doily in a small, cotton drawstring bag that she had also sewn.

It was now about three o'clock in the afternoon. The men thanked Joshua and Clara for the hearty meal. They walked out of the house and realized that the unrelenting wind they had fought against earlier had ceased and had been replaced with a gentle breeze. Gone were the dark, threatening clouds of the first part of the day. Scattered rays of sunshine beamed through the broken clouds that were left in the sky. The men made their way to the barn, saddled their horses, and brought them out.

Jim spoke up, "It was very neighborly of you to allow us to rest here, not to mention the good meal that your wife gave us."

"It was a pleasure for us to visit with you."

Once again the scouts mounted up and rode down the road. They had about ten miles left to reach Reeds Crossing.

★ ★ ★ ★ ★ ★ ★ ★ ★ ★ ★ ★ ★ ★ ★ ★ ★ ★ ★

At three o'clock in the afternoon, Anna Marie sat in the rocking chair, daydreaming. She had closed out the rest of the world, and sat enveloped in sadness. She wasn't sure what she should do. She was roused when she heard Pat calling out "Momma! Momma!" as he awoke from his afternoon nap. She heard the pitter-patter of his feet as he ran from the bedroom toward her.

"Hello. How's my little boy?" she said. "Did you have a good rest?" Pat nodded yes. "What should we do now?" Pat went to the front room window and looked outside. He patted the window and squealed as he said, "I see birds." Anna Marie went and joined him. She knelt down and looked outside with Pat. She realized that the wind had subsided. "Do you want to go outside?"

Pat pointed and said, "Outside."

"Okay," said Anna. "Let's put on our shoes and we'll go outside for a little while.

Mother and son walked around in the yard. Pat picked a few flowers along with some blooming weeds. Each flower he picked he smelled and wrinkled his nose. *He's just like his father,* Anna Marie thought, *enjoying being in the out-of-doors.* The skies were partly sunny, the day was pleasant, and Anna Marie's heart had become lighter. Pat busied himself walking around in the yard, picking up leaves and rocks and placing them on a tree stump. They had been outside for a while when Anna Marie said to Pat, "Would you like to take a buggy ride and go see Big Al and Lucy?"

Pat clapped his hands and said, "See Lucy."

"All right, then, we'll go inside, have some milk and a cookies, and I'll pack a bag for us."

Anna had Mandy hitched to the buggy. She lifted Pat into his seat and they trotted up the lane to the road that led to the Bennings' farm. Mandy spirited up the road, raising her knees high with each step, her very manner expressing the joy of freedom away from the fenced barn lot. The buggy and its travelers approached Muddy River. Anna carefully guided Mandy and the buggy across the river and continued up the riverbank on the other side. They traveled up to a curve in the road when she discovered that the strong wind that had blown most of the day had uprooted several trees, and they had fallen across the road. The one closest to them was a tall evergreen. Anna Marie pulled on the reins and drew the buggy to a halt. She couldn't believe what she saw.

What was she to do now? She got out of the buggy and walked around looking to see if she could get past the blocked road. It seemed that there was no easy pathway. She decided that she would unhitch Mandy and leave the buggy there on the road. She would walk and Pat would ride Mandy on up to the Bennings' home. Tomorrow she would come back to the buggy and go back home.

★ ★ ★ ★ ★ ★ ★ ★ ★ ★ ★ ★ ★ ★ ★ ★ ★ ★ ★ ★

Frank, Jim, and Brady were getting close to Reeds Crossing. They had held their horses at a steady gait since they left Joshua and Clara's place. Their conversation had been light and filled with reminiscences of the past few weeks.

Brady asked Jim, "What are your plans now that we're nearly home?"

"I need to clean and fix up my cabin, maybe add on another room. I need a newer kitchen table and chairs," he replied.

"Why do you need to fix up your cabin?"

"I plan to go back to Little White Feather and ask her to marry me and come live in my home. I'll need a room for her son."

"How about you, Frank, do you have plans?"

"I'm going to work hard and save my money so I can move to Indiana when you go next spring. I'm going to look around for a sweet lady to take for my wife, so she can go with me."

"That sounds like a good plan. After all, you're not getting any younger, you know," he told Frank jokingly.

They reached the road where Brady would turn toward his farm. The men shook hands and wished each other well, then parted. Brady could hardly contain his eagerness to reach home and his family. The men waved good-bye to each other as they rode their separate ways. Brady rode a short while and spotted a small water pool. He decided to stop there and let his horse drink and rest a few minutes. Truthfully, Brady was saddle sore from the past few days of riding and he needed some rest. After a ten-minute rest, Brady remounted his horse and they continued on the final lap of the journey.

★ ★ ★ ★ ★ ★ ★ ★ ★ ★ ★ ★ ★ ★ ★ ★ ★ ★ ★ ★

Anna Marie and Pat arrived safely at Big Al and Lucy's home. "Hello, Lucy, I came to visit and stay the night if it's all right. I need to be with friends." The two women hugged each other. Anna Marie and Al greeted each other. "It's good to see you," he said. "Glad you came."

"You're welcome here anytime," Lucy told her. "Al, would you take Anna Marie's horse to the barn? Now tell me, why are you here without your buggy?"

"Pat and I were on our way to visit you and were getting right along. I guided our buggy carefully across the river. We went up the hill and when we approached the curve in the road I found that trees had been blown down on the road from the strong winds earlier today. I couldn't figure out how to get the buggy around them—there were limbs down and brush everywhere—so I unhitched Mandy and came on foot with Pat riding Mandy."

"You can definitely take care of yourself when you decide to do something, can't you?" said Lucy.

Anna Marie looked at Lucy, smiled, and said, "I guess we farm women learn to be self-sufficient, wouldn't you agree?"

"Yes, we do what we have to do when we have to do it. Come on inside with me. I'm happy to have you here." Lucy's younger children took Pat's hand and led him inside to play as Lucy and Anna Marie followed. The older children were out behind the house shelling corn for the chickens. After that job was finished, they were to go to the barn, throw in some fresh hay for the horses, and brush them down. By the time all those chores were finished, it would be suppertime.

Lucy got busy making a big pan of cornbread for supper. Then she cut up some ham and sliced some fresh ripe tomatoes, green peppers, and onions. She planned to fry the ham in some grease and then stir up a big skillet of gravy. Lucy knew that it took a lot of food to fill up her big family. Anna Marie sat at the kitchen table, watched all the activity around her and enjoyed being with them. Al came into the kitchen through the back door. He walked over close to Lucy and tried nuzzling her on the neck. She flinched and said, "Now cut that out! Can't you see I'm working?" She turned her head and smiled at him and he gave her a peck on the cheek. He laughed and gave her a little pat on the backside and went over to the kitchen table and sat down.

An hour later all of the family had come into the kitchen, ready for their evening meal. The home was filled with talking and laughter. The day was drawing to a close as the sun sat low on the horizon. Anna Marie felt safe and cared for.

★ ★ ★ ★ ★ ★ ★ ★ ★ ★ ★ ★ ★ ★ ★ ★ ★ ★ ★ ★

Brady and his horse were somewhat refreshed after their brief rest. The closer he got to home, the faster he urged his horse to trot. He rode past the Bennings' home and didn't see anyone outside moving about, so he pressed onward. He came to the place in the road where the trees had fallen. He didn't give it much thought at the time. He took his horse around all the limbs as best he could, and when he reached the other side, he saw the buggy sitting there. He knew immediately that it belonged to Anna Marie and him. His heart leapt and began to pound like a sledgehammer inside. He was confused. *What happened? Why would the buggy be sitting here without the horse?* He dismounted and examined the buggy. *Nothing seems to be broken. I better go home and to see if Anna Marie is all right.* Brady kicked his horse up into a full gallop. Down the hill and across the river he sped. When he drew his horse up in front of his house, his horse was lathered up and winded. Brady jumped down out of the saddle and quickly went into his house. He called out, "Anna Marie, are you here?" No answer came back. The only sounds he heard were the ticking of the clock and the chirping of the birds coming into the house from the outside, but nothing more. He walked all through the house and saw all was in order. The pounding that he felt in his heart had moved to his head and then spread throughout his whole body. He checked the barn and chicken lot and found no one. He was near panic. He led his horse to the water trough and allowed him a few swallows of water then he remounted and headed back up the road. He would stop and see if Big Al and Lucy knew of Anna's whereabouts.

Brady's imagination was running wild. *I should never have left her. What was I thinking, going off with my friends to explore the land?* Brady scolded himself. He again arrived at the point in the road where he had to detour around the fallen trees. Brady's horse stumbled once as he picked his way through the debris. Once they were back on the road, Brady urged his horse once again to a full gallop. He turned quickly onto the Bennings' lane and came to a sudden halt at their hitching post. He literally leapt off of his horse and bounded on to the front porch and pounded on the door.

★ ★ ★ ★ ★ ★ ★ ★ ★ ★ ★ ★ ★ ★ ★ ★ ★ ★ ★

The loud knocking on the front door startled everyone sitting at the kitchen table. The small children looked at their parents, wide-eyed, and two or three of them actually hollered, "What's that?" Lucy said, "Mercy sakes, who might that be?"

Big Al and his oldest boy got up from the table and headed toward the door. Before they got there Brady had opened the door and stepped inside the house.

Brady had a frantic look on his face and it reflected in his voice. He talked quickly, "Al, I can't find Anna Marie and Pat. I went home and she was gone. I looked everywhere. Do you know where she is?"

His voice had carried into the kitchen—Anna Marie and all the others had heard his frantic voice. Before Al had time to answer Brady's question, Anna immediately got up out of her chair and ran for the front door. Brady looked up and saw Anna Marie coming toward him.

"Brady, you're back. Thank God!" she said as she ran toward him.

He quickly moved toward her and pulled her close. "Thank God I found you safe and sound. I was so worried about you. When I found the empty buggy, my whole body trembled with fear."

Tears of joy streamed down Anna Marie's face. "Just hold me," she told him.

By this time everybody had left the kitchen and had come into the living room. The older children were telling Brady, "Welcome back." Brady saw Pat toddling along with the others. He released Anna Marie and squatted down beside Pat. He swooped Pat up into his arms and gave him a little squeeze. "You've grown. How's my boy?" he said. Pat wrapped his arms around his daddy's neck and hugged him. "Daddy home!" he said.

"Yes, Daddy's home to stay," Brady replied. The next fifteen minutes were filled with happy conversation, hugs, and handshakes. Lucy said to everyone, "Let's go back and finish our meal and let Brady and Anna Marie have some time to together."

Brady wrapped his arm around Anna Marie's waist and guided her out to the porch. He kissed her fully and passionately. When he released her lips, he held her close by his side. As they stood there, lost in the moment, they looked toward the western sky. The setting sun was poised above the horizon, its golden glow shining brightly on the countryside. Anna Marie turned to face Brady and said, "Every setting sun these past weeks reminded me that we would soon be together."

"You were on my mind every morning sunrise and every evening sunset. I'll never leave you alone again," Brady told her. He kissed her once more with longing then they went back inside the house.

Lucy had prepared a place for him at the supper table. It was a joyful time for both families.

When the meal was finished and the table was cleaned up, Lucy asked Brady, "Do you want to spend the night here and go home in the morning?"

"Thank you, but I want to take my family home," said Brady.

Al sent his oldest boy, Matthew, to the barn to bring Lucy's horse out and up to the porch. Then he turned to Brady. "Why don't I hitch up my horse and buggy and give Anna Marie and Pat a ride to your buggy? We'll tie Mandy behind. When we get there, you can hitch up Mandy and go safely home."

The last few moments of twilight gave away to night as the four of them arrived at the blocked road and the men helped Anna Marie and Pat to their own buggy. Al told them good night and returned home.

Brady and his family traveled toward their home under a clear, moonlight sky. After they arrived home, Brady put the horses and buggy in the barn as Anna Marie put Pat to bed. Brady returned to their home and immediately took Anna Marie into his strong arms and pulled her tightly to his body. He began kissing her fervently and she responded to his passion. The past few weeks of loneliness melted away as he kissed her face and neck, then he led her into the bedroom. He removed the combs from her hair and gently ran his fingers through her long, auburn hair while gazing into her beautiful green eyes. The light from the nearly full moon shone softly through the window and created an almost heavenly glow throughout the room. They held and caressed each other with such passion that their bodies burned hot with desire. She ran her hands over his muscular back and arms, causing him to shiver with anticipation. They quickly removed their clothing and went to the bed, yearning for each other as if they were making love for the first time. Their lovemaking climaxed soon after they lay on the bed. They lay quietly, holding each other, as they calmed from their fervent passion.

Brady laid his hands on her swollen belly and said, "Our baby has grown while I've been away. Are you feeling all right?"

"Yes, I'm doing fine—except that I'm clumsy." She chuckled.

Brady and Anna Marie lay together and talked. Each one told of the events of the past weeks. Brady told her all about the land that he found in Indiana and the people who had helped him claim it.

Brady enveloped Anna Marie into his arms. "Sweetheart, I can't tell you how much I've missed you. You've been so strong while I've been gone, caring for Pat and the farm. I promise that we'll be together for the rest of our lives. You're a wonderful wife and I love you."

"I love you, too. We'll be together whether here on this farm or somewhere else. I will never let you go without me ever again."

Brady and Anna Marie knew that their love for each other would hold them together for the rest of their lives. Their future held before them another child and a new home.

AUTHOR BIOGRAPHY

Carol Walls Howell and her husband, Carl, are retired and live on a small farm in Macon, Missouri. They have two children and three grandchildren. Carol was a music teacher and librarian for twenty-two years. Her genealogy research and love for writing inspired this historical novel, her first book.

CPSIA information can be obtained at www.ICGtesting.com
Printed in the USA
LVOW120336020812

292505LV00003B/5/P

9 781458 203229